THE CARE
and
FEEDING
of HARRY

THE CARE

and

FEEDING *of* HARRY

RAY FINDLAY

ARPress
45 Dan Road Suite 36
Canton MA 02021

Hotline: 1(800) 220-7660
Fax: 1(855) 752-6001

Ordering Information:
Quantity sales. Special discounts are available on quantity purchases by corporations, associations, and others. For details, contact the publisher at the address above.

Printed in the United States of America.

ISBN-13:   Paperback   979-8-89389-825-5
                 eBook   979-8-89389-826-2

Library of Congress Control Number: 2024923241

CONTENTS

CHAPTER 1

Genes Will Out

Grandpa Flapper, Harry's paternal grandfather, was a bachelor for some years before taking a wife. He occupied his long lonely bachelor evenings by building a house for himself. He started by buying a lot on the "edge of town" at a tax sale, sight unseen. The property was described as "a desirable property close to all amenities, on rich farmland, complete with a natural pond." It wasn't until he had the deeds in hand that he got to see the property. It was a mile outside town, nestled between a swamp and a bog. Since the swamp extended for a mile in either direction clear back into the bush, the pond referred to in the literature must have been the bog, a mud slough that never dried out, winter or summer.

Grandpa decided to make the best of the matter. He became dedicated to the great outdoors. "Wonderful opportunity to observe nature!" he would say. There were some disadvantages to his situation, though. Winged insects, the stinging, biting and blood-sucking kinds, seemed to enjoy Grandpa's presence. Crawling insects took root in his clothes or on his person, while other types of beasties made his life miserable in other ways. The porcupines took special interest in the lumber Grandpa had delivered for his house. Groundhogs and other tunnellers undermined the ground he walked on. And the bears soon realized that Grandpa kept food around and devised ways to relieve him of it.

Grandpa dug the basement in the fall when the swamp had receded to manageable proportions. He got carried away with his enthusiasm for the project, resulting in a rather exotic pattern that was not even remotely rectangular, taking on the shape of a somewhat complex jigsaw puzzle piece instead. It was only after Grandpa had the stone walls for the basement in place that he thought about what might go on top. He opted for a massive living room for the first floor. He thought that would be easy to execute. As an afterthought, he added a second floor for the bedrooms.

It was shortly after a somewhat heavier than usual rainfall that Grandpa discovered another one of nature's mysteries when the swamp overflowed, travelling through the basement to join the bog on the other side. He stood around in the wet, perfecting his vocabulary for awhile before he actually got around to doing something about the problem. Then he took his old bicycle apart, connected the rear axle to a mechanical pump, and spent the next three days cycling but going nowhere, all the while trying out new swear words in a rich baritone, as the basement slowly emptied of the muddy water.

No one ever questioned Grandpa's ingenuity. It was somewhere between the drawing board and the execution that things usually went wrong. So, although he could design a house that looked wonderful on paper, his ambitions far exceeded his skills. He couldn't make sense out of a carpenter's level resulting in a floor that tended to meander up and down hill. The walls, too, leaned a bit. The uprights could hardly be called that. Grandpa would stand with the level in his hand against the upright. As long as he could see the bubble, he figured it must be about right. Even when the level was the wrong way to, he could see the bubble, perhaps a little off centre, but if he looked hard enough, the bubble was there, somewhere. He would happily declare it satisfactory, totally oblivious to the obvious slant. Grandpa often remarked that the level was the one instrument that he felt at home with. "And," he said, "you simply can't go wrong with a level."

Not once, in all the years he had one did Grandpa hammer his thumb with his level, nor saw halfway through his hand with it. He liked it so well he hung it up over the mantle, along with his rifle and his shotgun. He said they were much the same sort of thing, one got him his game, the other his house. A visitor, on hearing this, could never tell whether Grandpa was pulling his leg or not.

Grandpa had difficulty with the mechanics of sawing. He would carefully measure the board to be sawed, mark it, use a square to scribe the cut line, then begin sawing. The board would be too short. So he would try again. This time he marked it a little long, carefully followed the cut line and wound up with a board that was crooked by a quarter inch in four. Jamming the board into its designated spot he would pound nails in to hold it, ignoring the spaces between the butt ends of the boards and the knot holes that somehow got pushed through. It rapidly became apparent that his favourite task was hammering. It gave him great satisfaction to hear the bang of the hammer on the boards, and occasionally on the nails as well. There was a trail of little hoof marks from the hammer head around each nail. Each board was held in place by hundreds of nails. The weight of iron alone in the building was enough to keep it anchored throughout any gale.

All through the years following, hunters and hikers would turn up on the doorstep, drawn by their compasses, all pointing "North," but actually pointing to the masses of iron in Grandpa's house. They would travel through the swamp, avoiding the bog, and eventually they would wind up on Grandpa's back stoop, wet, muddied, wearing a bewildered expression. Enquiring directions they would find themselves wildly off course.

There was quite a collection of discarded compasses littering the countryside around Grandpa's house. He would find one and puzzle for days over how it got there. They all seemed to operate quite well. Whenever Grandpa was lost they would unfailingly point the way home.

On occasion, the odd aircraft would get itself locked on to the beam and search for an airport around the house, the pilot finally retiring in confusion to Farmer Garter's field to land when his fuel ran out. The odd jet aircraft would sally through, but mostly they were going so fast that they got themselves out of range before trouble occurred. All, that is, except one that was forced to crash land into Farmer Garter's field with all 286 passengers on board. They were all put up in Farmer Garter's barn to await rescue.

Most of the passengers thought it was a great lark, all, that is, except the stock brokers and civil servants on board. The former wandered around like lost souls searching for ticker boards and coffee and comparing notes on the latest stock market trends. The civil servants, on the other hand, all discussed ways to increase taxes and their salaries, in no priority order.

Eventually all were rescued by airlifting "back to civilization" in a helicopter commissioned especially for the purpose. The civil servants volunteered to be rescued first to get to their appointments the quicker and to try out a few of their ideas on increasing taxes or salaries, it didn't really matter which. Both exercises were fun and had the same result. The stock brokers braved the dangers next, followed by the women and children. Lesser beings like brick layers and professors sat about smoking their cigars and pipes, respectively, patiently awaiting rescue from the dangers of the countryside, while discussing erudite topics like the temperature scale, whether 86 degrees Fahrenheit was warmer or colder than 30 degrees Celsius. And if it was warmer, whether the fish would bite anyway.

Although he might not have agreed, stairs were not among Grandpa's strong points. But he was a little cautious about volunteering assistance for anyone who might need his expertise on the matter. "I don't do stairs anymore," he remarked in later life. He first tried to build a circular stairway. He had a beautifully cut pole of white pine stuck right through the basement and up to the attic, sawing a wide circular hole through both the first and second floors to accommodate it. He next tried to build steps. On his first effort he glued boards all around the pole leading from the first floor to the second, to act as the steps. He went so far as to inset the boards by a quarter inch into the pole, a feat that cost him dearly in both time and language. When he was finally through, he proudly surveyed his handiwork then climbed labouriously up a ladder to the second floor and so to bed, letting the glue dry over night.

Next morning, still scratching himself under his arm, not really paying attention to where he was going, he descended the stairs. That is a perfectly accurate description of what happened. He descended the stairs, except they descended with him. Stairs, Grandpa, and all kept right on going clear through to the basement where they met the annual influx from the swamp. As Grandpa had long since assumed that the swamp problem had been solved, it came as something of a shock. Although rather groggy at the top of the stairs, he was wide awake at the bottom. In fact, had he not been, he would have drowned.

He found himself swimming around in the basement, trying to find some hand-holds to pull himself out. He was also swearing at the top of his lungs. At least that is what Mrs. Williams, the minister's wife said, when she came to rescue him. She was a little bird-like woman, with a beaked nose and glasses that perennially twitched on the very end of her nose. Her parents, with great percipience had called her Robin. It was because, they said, when she was born, she had a red breast. It turned out to be a rash that she never quite outgrew.

The Reverend Mr. Williams, thinking her very prim and demure because of the high-necked blouses she always wore, was quick to invite her to share his life. As she lacked better prospects, she agreed, with some reluctance, which he took for shyness. To Robin's great joy Mr. Williams was not without a certain expertise in more earthly matters. To her own surprise, after their marriage she fell in love with him, sharing the minister's circumspect lifestyle in public, while indulging in abandoned passion in private.

With the excuse that she had heard someone crying for help from outside, Robin came into Grandpa's house to allay her curiosity. Every gossip in town, except for Robin, had a tale to tell about Grandpa's house. She decided to rectify the matter at the first opportunity. She had time while helping Grandpa to confirm every tale told. Grandpa was so glad to find the rope dangling down for him to catch that he didn't think to inform Robin that he was entirely naked. He lunged for the rope with relief. Robin, seeing his all-together was momentarily taken aback. She had not yet had time to fasten the rope to anything stationary, so in double quick time she soon found herself and the rope swimming around in the basement with the still naked form of Grandpa. His roars of wrath at the unfortunate woman were not in the least tempered by the knowledge that she was the minister's wife.

Someone thought to call out the volunteer fire brigade to respond to the alarm set up by Grandpa's roars and Robin's now hysterical pleas that he should cover himself. On hearing the latter, thinking that a whole bevy of damsels were in the process of being assaulted, one hardy soul bravely set out to call in the town police force. Another thought to call in a fleet of ambulances from the other side of town. They all arrived within a few moments of each other.

The police all dashed inside the house with guns drawn and night sticks at the ready. The firemen followed with hatchets drawn and fire hoses at the ready. They were followed shortly by the ambulance attendants with bandages drawn and stretchers at the ready. Children, wives, husbands, passing hippies and the town drunk all decided to join them to see what the ruckus was all about. What with all the pushing and shoving in the cramped quarters, it wasn't long before half the town had joined Grandpa and Robin in the basement, Grandpa still roaring and Robin still squealing. Eventually all were rescued. Grandpa was packed off to the hospital, thus satisfying the honour of the ambulance men. The policemen went off with sirens at the wail to accompany them. Then the police stayed around the hospital to dry off and chat up the nurses. Robin was taken home in a faint by the firemen. At this point she had decided it was better to faint than to attempt to explain to Mr. Williams why she was swimming around with a nude man in a basement.

The whole matter was assiduously reported in a special edition of the town newspaper, The Newnham Tattler, complete with pictures of Grandpa, his house, and the "basement swimming pool" into which poor Mrs. Williams had fallen when she came on a mission of mercy to the ailing Mr. Flapper, so the story went. Hearing her cries, he had got off his death bed and, unmindful of the threat to his own health, had leapt in to save her. The townsfolk, on reading what had "actually happened," decided to nominate Grandpa for the Governor General's Gold Medal for bravery, which, in due course was awarded to a thoroughly confused Mr. Flapper. And so the legend of Grandpa Flapper got off to a flying start.

Some folks thought Grandpa Flapper was a bit eccentric. Others, including his wife, figured he was just crazy. It wasn't until some time after they were married that Grandma realized her spouse was more than a bit eccentric. By then it was too late. She was pregnant, so she decided to stick it out. Grandpa might be crazy but he was still lovable. She took to drink instead.

Grandma, brought as a bride to the house, immediately found fault with it. "There's no kitchen," she complained. "And where in thunderation did you put the bathroom?" "No cupboards or closets," she went on, until Grandpa began to wonder why he had married her. "How is it heated?" she asked. Grandpa rather wished she hadn't. "How do we get water?" "What's this pole running from the basement to the roof?" she asked. And most important of all, from Grandma's standpoint, "How do you get to the bedroom?" in a puzzled tone.

By this time Grandpa was out of sorts too. "I know there are a few small details to look after," he said, feeling injured. "Think of it as a work of art." Grandma snorted and went back home to her mother to await events. Grandpa looked after the renovations. A friend got him an old wood-burning furnace out of a hotel, very cheap. The furnace took up most of the basement, but kept the house wonderfully warm and without ducts or radiators either, except during spring swamp days when the fire was extinguished by natural phenomena. In winter Grandpa would put on his silvery asbestos fire shield to stoke up the fire. Opening the great maw that served as a door to the furnace, he would pitch in half a cord of hard wood, then shut the door to draw breath. With the fire damped down, the fuel would last most of a week. After the furnace had been installed, Grandma, wary of gossip and beginning to show, allowed Grandpa to sweet talk her into returning to the house.

Next Grandpa put a huge water tank in the attic for hot water. There was no room in the basement for it. The hot water drifted up to the tank from the furnace by convection and returned through the forces of gravity. Occasionally steam would develop in the water pipes. Grandpa installed a relief valve on the roof to let off the excess steam when the pressure got too great. The relief valve was from an old steam locomotive engine. When it let go it was accompanied by a piercing wail, notifying the entire town and the country around that something drastic had happened. The excess steam rising in great billows towards the sky would sometimes be mistaken for a thundercloud. Usually it was mistaken for smoke. The first time it happened everyone for fifty miles around came to help put out the fire. Grandpa came home to find them pouring water on the roof.

The ensuing party cost Grandma most of her reserves of scotch which she added to the great vat of coffee she made for all the would-be helpers. She did manage to hold on to her hidden supply of vodka. The spiked coffee lulled the helpers into a state of well-being. Grandpa, never one to miss a trick, invited them all to help put up the barn, as they were there anyway. Grandma was a trifle glum about that, figuring, quite rightly, that it would eat into her vodka reserves as well. Her reputation as a cook was founded that day on her ability to make coffee.

C H A P T E R   2

Bathrooms and Other Irrelevant Details

There was no room on the second floor for the bathroom. So Grandpa built it out the side of the house on a little balcony of its own. It had lots of light, with windows on three sides. Grandpa said he could put windows in the floor and the ceiling as well if Grandma wished. But she declined. From the vantage point of the bathtub one could look out over three directions for miles around. Grandpa loved the view. He could sit in the tub with his binoculars and admire the Misses Trilby, as they sunned in their back yard some four hundred yards down the road. For their part, the Misses Trilby were entirely aware of their effect on Grandpa. They even found a way to do it in winter. On sunny days, they erected a clear plastic tent and lay about in their bikinis, waiting for Grandpa's bathroom to start vibrating.

When Grandma found the binoculars in the bathroom, and trained them on the nearly nude forms of the Misses Trilby she decided on some renovations of her own. She blocked off the windows, painting over them with whitewash and adding curtains. It looked much more cosy that way, she said. Grandpa went off to try building a platform on the side of the barn, but it didn't have quite the same appeal. His first effort fell off into the pig pen during a windstorm. Grandpa wouldn't have minded had he not been on the platform at the time. The old sow took quite a bit of exception to Grandpa's surprise visit. His pants were in tatters before he managed to convince her that he meant no harm. It didn't much matter, though, as Grandma made him strip on the doorstep before allowing admittance to their home. As she said, "It's all right for you to play in the pigsty with the pigs, but you aren't coming in here coated with that muck. You can just remove your clothes before you come in and leave them outside. Just you wait here until I get the hose." Having looked after that little matter, she shoved his clothes into a bag with a stick to be ready for burning later.

The controls for hot and cold water in the shower were non existent. The water came out either boiling, straight from the water heater, or freezing, straight up from the well. Grandma and Grandpa both decided they preferred a bath rather than a shower anyway, so avoided the problem. Their guests rarely found out about that little difficulty until it was too late, by which time they were in the shower and either cooked or frozen, depending on the starting point. The other apparent disadvantage to the balcony bathroom was that it was frigid in winter. Trips in and out at that time of year tended to be very short, limited to the bare necessities.

Some renovations were needed in the rest of the house too, although it wasn't until Grandma's pregnancy became obvious that Grandpa decided to replace the ladder with stairs. Meanwhile, he preserved the pine pole as a quick route downstairs when speed was necessary. He forgot about it after the stairs were built, so it remained an integral part of the house. From the first floor looking up, the pine pole was a topic of discussion of a winter evening for guests. Those unfortunate enough to stay the night discovered the hard way that it was in a direct line from the bedroom to the bathroom. If the visitor were lucky he would be found in the morning, clinging to the pole, the less fortunate, caught on the way to the bathroom, the others on the way back to the bedroom. Some were found the next morning wandering around the basement, vainly trying to find the bedroom, with no conscious memory of the terrifying slide down the pole in the middle of the night.

The kitchen stuck out as an afterthought on the back. It was graced with a sunny southern exposure looking out over the bog. Grandpa built a deck off the kitchen so Grandma could sit out on sunny days to admire nature in the raw.

Grandpa tried to lure the song birds and swallows into the yard by strategically placing feeders all around. He added bird houses on tall poles. With Grandpa's usual skill, the bird houses did not turn out exactly as designed. When he got through correcting all his errors, the houses were massive apartments, more eagle size than for swallows.

When Grandpa set out seed, nuts, suet and even meat in the feeders, it wasn't long before the eagles and hawks took up residence. The squirrels loved the feeders. So did the eagles and other birds of prey. Soon the backyard was a war zone. The eagles dive-bombed anything that moved. No one except Grandma dared venture out. The eagles left her strictly alone, perhaps recognizing the voice of authority. They did not accord Grandpa the same degree of respect.

When Grandma first became aware of the interpretation the eagles put on her "bird-feeder," she declared she was ill and went to bed. Grandpa thought the matter over for a while and decided to get ill, too. He joined Grandma in bed.

The result of the union of Grandpa and Grandma was two sons, the younger one who was our hero's father This second son was christened Crawford, but everyone called him Bull, not after the four legged creatures that trot around the fields in search of cows, but after the bullfrogs in the swamp, either because he resembled them or because he sounded like them. It was never established which. Gronk, Bull's brother, was six years older. Gronk was actually named Anthony Thomas Flapper. His first word was "Gronk!" So were his second and third. Naturally, he was nicknamed Gronk.

Bull spent most of his childhood collecting wildlife in the swamp to liven up the house. His mother's nerves were soon shot. It wasn't the tadpoles that somehow managed to find their way into her orange and cherry jelly surprise. It wasn't the snakes that took over the kitchen: as she remarked, they did keep the mice down. The eagles, avidly awaiting their prey in the back yard, didn't help. The raccoons that came to the back door for handouts might have affected her adversely, as they normally appeared about four in the morning. If Grandma, perchance, forgot to leave something out for them, they would pound on the door. And if there was something, they fought over it, snarling and screaming and spitting, the whole while. When the beavers started coming around to cart off the back stoop for dessert every night, it was a bit too much. She didn't mind the cute little animals smacking about in the swamp. She frowned, however, at their approach to her wooden ware.

Somewhere around his sixteenth birthday Bull discovered girls. To be sure, he had always known about them, in a vague dissembling way. He knew, for example, that they usually had long, soft hair and had trouble growing beards. On the occasion in question, he was caught in the act of pulling a girl's hair. Something went wrong. Bull and the girl wound up in a heap on the ground. He discovered her soft, unmuscled thigh next to his. Her breasts accidentally found themselves beneath his hands. For her part, the girl discovered Bull's soft unmuscled thigh next to hers. His hands might have been doing pleasurable things to her if they had belonged to a six-foot tall, football line-backer. As they didn't, she proceeded to beat Bull about the head with her physics text. Bull retired from the field in confusion. The confusion plagued him for the next few years. Having discovered girls, and that he liked them, he didn't quite know what to do about it.

Almost useless in every other respect, it turned out that Bull had a talent for pulling fish out of the swamp. His only problem was getting out to where the fish were. He eventually decided, after giving the matter great thought, that a boat would do the job adequately. He turned to his father for advice, but he discovered that his father had a certain aversion to boats. Ever since his experience in the basement, Grandpa admired the water, but only from a distance. If he had to take a bath in the tub, that was one thing, and to be avoided for as long as possible, or until

Grandma exerted some influence. But getting into a large body of water on your own accord was not something Grandpa would any longer willingly do. It was something of a mystery to him why his younger son would want to be bothered. There were so many more interesting things to occupy one's time. One could be running the tractor with attached ploughshare down the furrows, or chopping up wood for the coming winter. He loved to see his sons mucking out the barn. Shovelling snow ranked high on his list of winter chores to be fobbed off on the two boys. But swimming or angling about in a boat seemed to go against all his scruples. The result was that if Bull wanted a boat, he first had to build one. If he wanted to keep the boat, it had better be kept out of sight of Grandpa.

Bull built a boat. His skills with a saw were not as widely acclaimed as those of his father. His father was only marginally inept, whereas Bull was totally inept. Bull designed a little flat-bottomed canoe, pointed at either end. The bottom was cut out of a piece of plywood. The sides, which went straight up, consisted of single boards stretched around either side. At the middle there was a thwart which acted as a spacer to keep the sides apart, and doubled as a seat. It was the width of a skinny person's bottom.

It required perfect balance to sit in the boat. Paddling it without tipping was difficult in the extreme. But, Bull mastered the art of paddling it and even fishing from it. His mother appreciated the variation in diet, provided Bull cleaned the catch. Bull's father began to suspect something the second year Bull had the boat. Grandpa decided to take Bull in hand. He insisted that Bull show him the boat. When Grandpa saw the craft, all his old love of angling and hunting surfaced in a rush. Grandpa decided to try it out, even though Bull tried to dissuade him. Grandpa was adamant.

Bull decided Grandpa could try it out by himself, so he retired to the sidelines to watch while Grandpa loaded in all the fishing gear. In got Grandpa. That isn't quite the way to put it. Grandpa stepped into the boat and continued on over the other side, as the boat turned turtle. Grandpa sat in the muck on the bottom and swore, while Bull pretended not to notice. Grandpa's fishing box floated out a way then sank. His fishing pole was lost in the muck on the bottom of the swamp. Bull was required to feel around in the muck to retrieve it. Eventually everything was found and laid out on shore to dry. After a reviving cup of tea, Grandpa was ready to give it another try.

On his next effort, Grandpa instructed Bull to hold the boat. When Grandpa was safely seated, Bull let go. The boat turned upside down, depositing Grandpa head first in the muck on the bottom of the swamp. Bull left at a run. On coming up for air, Grandpa had a discussion with God, at least that was what he said he was doing when questioned later. He gave Bull some advice on boat building, which, unfortunately, was not recorded. Most of it Bull didn't understand anyway, and the rest was irrelevant.

CHAPTER 3

One Tooth Jack and the Dune Buggy

Over the years Grandma had graduated from the wine spritzers served at her wedding as cheap champagne, to something a little more potent, 151 proof rum, straight from the bottle. She hid little caches of flasks all over the house in case she "all of a sudden came over queer" and needed a fix. Grandpa, a teetotaller, never realized his wife was overly fond of strong drink. Occasionally he complained that her mouthwash was a little pungent. Gronk and Bull had great fun playing hide and seek, mainly seek. They learned how to find a flask in the most unlikely places: in the linen closet, hidden in the reservoir of the toilet, in the post of the wringer for the washer, or hidden in the bookcase behind the big family Bible. They didn't have the opportunity to put their knowledge to any good purpose for a few years.

Eventually, as is the wont of young men from to time to time, they got around to building a little shack in the woods, more through Gronk's carpentry skills than Bull's. Then they began to invite their friends over "for a little party." They had to resolve the problem of sneaking their mother's booze without her knowledge. The usual trick was to pour some out then fill the bottle up again with something more or less the same colour. Grandma's rum was pretty tough to disguise. Her whisky could be safely diluted by half with tea, they found. Her vodka could be diluted any amount, with water, and it didn't even appear to affect the taste, at least not too much.

On one occasion, a large party was in the offing, with girls, or so they thought. After half emptying the vodka bottle into a flask, they decided they might as well go the whole way. The entire bottle, except the single fix Grandma had already taken, was replaced with water. Grandma came in after a particularly trying day shopping for frillies. She desperately needed a fix. She cuddled up to her bottle around the kitchen table. Several shots later she tried to feel muzzy, but it just wouldn't come. I'm so drunk, she thought, that I feel sober. Then with a new jaunty outlook on life, and at how well she could hold her liquor, she was ready once again to face the world.

At some time in the next few years, Grandma discovered the boys' hideaway on the other side of the swamp. Sworn to secrecy, she soon made regular use of it, joining the boys' parties, and even on occasion had parties of her own there, all by herself, when she felt herself come over queer. The odd stray tramp would be directed up to the facility. They came in all shapes and sizes. One of these hangers-on, One Tooth Jack, became something like a permanent fixture. One Tooth had one very large front tooth from among his upper set, but all the rest of his teeth had long since departed. One Tooth could manage steak, he said, but only if it were tender. For the most part he preferred a liquid diet.

One fall, just after the leaves had turned, between duck season and deer season, the two boys went up to the shack.

It was a chill day. To ward off the chill, they fixed up a snort by emptying half a bottle of coke, then refilling the bottle with their mother's 151-proof rum. Lost in discussion about various aspects of making a fortune, they were surprised to arrive back at the shack without having taken even a sip of their "coke." Their mother arrived shortly thereafter, with One Tooth Jack in tow.

One Tooth had driven Grandma and her bottle up in a dune buggy. In they came, old One Tooth just perishing with cold. Spying the coke, he immediately insisted the boys pour him a drink. Cadging their mother's bottle, they obliged. A generous shot of rum, followed by the doctored coke was poured out in front of him. One Tooth's estimation of that particular brand of rum went up by several notches. Sometime thereafter, he decided he should be elsewhere at that particular moment. Where, he didn't know, but it was imperative that he get there.

Testimony at the inquest later showed that One Tooth had circled three times around the swamp on the way out, failing to find the path each time. He hit four trees, drove over a very large snapping turtle, which took extreme exception to that sort of handling, then on the fourth try around the swamp he met an enraged moose, which gored the dune buggy to death.

One Tooth was found three days later behind the swamp still grimly holding on to the steering wheel and waiting for the world to come to rights. All the while he was muttering about the great coke. His rescuers thought he was talking about coal to warm himself. Neither Grandma nor the boys were prepared to put them to rights. Still, Gronk was so taken with the enormity of events that he decided there and then to found a whole new dynasty of teetotallers.

CHAPTER 4

Enter Victoria

Bull made provision to build a larger boat. He designed a shallow, V-bottom craft tapering upwards towards the bow, complete with a dainty deck and a windshield. A steering wheel was coupled with ropes and pulleys to a tiny outboard motor on the rear. There was a cabin of sorts: it had a pole running overhead down the length from windshield to stern. There were two poles on either side, cross braced and attached to uprights fore and aft. During inclement weather a canvas cover could be pulled over the cockpit forming the cabin. When the sun shone the canvas was rolled back.

Bull's next problem was to get it built with a minimum of effort on his own part. He contrived to start a club devoted to the discussion and philosophy of women in general, and girls of their acquaintance in particular. The club met on Saturdays at the edge of the swamp under an old willow tree, where it could meet in relative secrecy. When the meeting was well under way, Bull suggested that they build a steamer and launch it on the swamp. After some discussion, a compromise was reached whereby it was agreed that they build a small boat similar to Bull's design. His main contribution to the building was to keep up a string of commentary, and to provide purloined sweets and liquid refreshment to his friends who actually built the boat. In the process, Bull's education on female anatomy was vastly improved.

The maiden cruise was taken with Bull at the controls, and all seventeen of his helpers crowded into the cockpit in the space meant for three. All went well for the first fifteen seconds or so. Then the weight of the passengers resulted in the boat sinking to the muddy bottom until the mud began to ooze out from underneath. The boat began to sink through the swamp with all hands on board. They all climbed out except Bull, who had some knowledge of the bottom of the swamp. All seventeen stalwarts stood upright for a few moments until it became apparent that if they didn't take precautions, they would find themselves planted in the swamp. They elected to swim for it.

Seventeen helpers headed for their respective homes, not relishing the task of explaining to sceptical parents how it might be that their clothes were no longer serviceable. Bull waited until they had all left the swamp, then he pushed off. The wind was with him so he was soon clear of the shore. It was at this juncture that he realized there was no fuel in the motor. Furthermore, there was no paddle. Swishing his hands through the water did not bring him any closer to the bank. It soon appeared that the wind would carry him deeper into the swamp. So he hopped out of the boat, grabbed the bow ropes and made for shore.

When he finally crawled out on to the bank, the boat in tow, two things became apparent. Bull had the most offensive muck all over his clothes, far worse than that of his friends. Secondly, he was coated with leeches. The latter he looked upon with great interest. To his way of thinking, leeches were the best fishing bait to be found anywhere. He painstakingly picked off the leeches and stored them in a ten gallon drum of water, firmly resolving to repeat the exercise until he had enough bait to do the season.

The following day, armed with fuel and a paddle he set out to explore the outer fringes of the swamp. With the controls fully open he made the amazing speed of 3 kilometres an hour, frightening the wildlife for metres around. The joy was too much for him to keep to himself. He had to share with someone else.

As luck would have it, a girl from up the road happened to be passing. He dashed up to her, showing a good deal more panache than ever before in his life, and carried her off to share the adventure with him. It was only after the great explosion that he realized his partner was female. She was quite docile while he stowed her in the passenger seat. She didn't flinch when he started the motor. She appeared to listen intently while he explained the fine workings of the steering mechanism. As they set off towards the far reaches of the swamp at great speed, she didn't even hang on.

Bull mistook her silence for interest. He began to regale her with details of the building of the boat, not strictly accurate. She was still in a state of shock from her abrupt abduction, not wholly sure whether the madman at the controls meant her any harm. Gradually it penetrated that he only wanted an audience; he didn't even know that she was female. With this realization came an inner rage. She wanted to be noticed for herself, so she picked up the gas can and belted Bull over the head. Bull's head snapped forward then back as he fell off the seat. The steering mechanism, sadly strained, gave way altogether. The boat hurtled back to the rock in the middle of the swamp where it impaled itself. The motor broke its shear pin on the rock, but continued spinning noisily and uselessly as water gushed in, finally overwhelming the motor and drowning it. Bull recovered himself just as his boat slowly settled into the mud on the bottom once again. As the water slowly crept up over the gunwales, only then did he remember that his partner was a girl.

Victoria gazed at Bull in awe. No one, she figured, could be quite as stupid as he appeared to be. She reasoned that if he wasn't stupid, he must be brilliant. On that premise, she immediately fell in love with him. Bull, by now up to his waist in water, gallantly hoisted Victoria to his shoulder to save her from the ravages of the swamp. With each step he took towards shore, he slipped further into the grime, until only his nose, and Victoria, were above water. On his next step, he all but drowned himself.

Victoria, who didn't fancy being rescued, became the rescuer instead. She dragged Bull's now lifeless form out of the swamp, thwacked him over a log, gave a few pumps for good measure, then applied mouth to mouth asphyxiation. Some time later, they came up for air and decided they had better get married. Due reflection on the matter suggested that their respective parents wouldn't countenance the union at this particular time, and on so brief an acquaintance. They reluctantly decided to keep their engagement secret for a few years, or as long as their patience held out.

CHAPTER 5

Aunt Myrtle Comes to Visit

Bull and Gronk had early memories of sun-filled days and fun-filled nights. They had the most fun of all when Aunt Myrtle decided to visit. Aunt Myrtle, a distant relative on Grandpa's side, was not Grandma's favourite person. Aunt Myrtle was an active and extremely vocal member of the Temperance Union. Fortunately, Aunt Myrtle didn't recognize the smell of strong drink either. Whenever she appeared, Grandma would "come over queer" quite often, seven times in a single afternoon, once.

Bull and Gronk had to give up their bedroom to Aunt Myrtle. She needed the better part of both beds to sleep her vast bulk, while the two boys would wind up camping out on the floor of the linen closet.

Aunt Myrtle's visit would usually coincide with the pilgrimage the old black bear would make to the neighbourhood. The bear was looking for food. It was widely rumoured that Aunt Myrtle was also looking for food. The bear would forage around the garbage box for food, getting into all kinds of mischief and upsetting Grandpa's equilibrium. Aunt Myrtle would forage around

25

in the icebox, eating the morrow's meal and upsetting Grandma's equilibrium.

Grandpa packed his old shotgun, loaded with buckshot up to his bedroom. Every night the raccoons and squirrels took their lives in their paws if they so much as rattled the garbage box lid. After awhile the lid was punctured by holes, and the night air by Grandpa's imprecations.

Aunt Myrtle was capable of sleeping through the din. She could sleep through anything. The two boys took bets on what time her beds would fall apart at night.

"Betcha she doesn't make it past midnight," opined Gronk "She'll make it to at least three." Was Bull's guess.

The beds had been built by Grandpa and were up to his usual standard, more nails than wood. Aunt Myrtle broke through the beds about 4:37 one morning, winning for Gronk. Grandpa woke up with a start, thinking the old bear had broken in. Still groggy from sleep, he grabbed his shotgun and fired towards the noise and a vague shape looming in the doorway. It was Grandma's woolly nightgown, hung casually over the door frame, taking the brunt of the blast. Fortunately, due to some previous hanky-panky between Grandpa and Grandma, she wasn't in it. On the other side of the door and across the hall, her back to it, slept Aunt Myrtle. A great portion of the buckshot found its mark on her bottom. She woke up unexpectedly. For days afterward she tried to figure out how the swarm of bees had all amassed on her backside in the middle of the night. Grandpa didn't think to enlighten her. In fact, he actively encouraged her in her delusion.

Even today there is speculation that her last visit to the senior Flapper household might not have ended so tragically if only she hadn't become too curious about the ten gallon drum in the bathroom. She wanted to take a shower. So she tipped over the ten gallon drum, emptying Bull's entire collection of leeches into the bath tub. Still groggy from sleep she stepped in, grabbing the water taps to turn the water on. Only then did she notice that the tub was full of leeches. Screaming didn't seem to help much, so she grabbed the taps, completely forgetting their unstable nature. Twisting them back and forth she first suffered under boiling water, then ice water from the well. As neither condition gave much relief, she finally resorted to pulling the taps, trying to climb up the walls of the shower to escape the ravages of the leeches. It was not a wise thing to do. The pipes were not very strong. Plumbing, it turned out, was not one of Grandpa's strong points, either. Down came the entire hot water tank from the attic. It crashed into the bathtub. Bathtub, Aunt Myrtle and all, swept on down to the ground. Aunt Myrtle, blessedly cushioned by leeches, came to no great harm until she noticed what she was laying on and what by now was securely fastened all over her body. She took off screaming straight down the centre of Main Street.

The Reverend Mr. Williams came out to see what the excitement was about. When he saw the vast nude bulk of Aunt Myrtle hurtling straight for him, he tried to turn and run. Aunt Myrtle, though, had built up quite a head of steam. She caught up to him, grabbed him, and carried him along with her. The Reverend Williams fainted. When he came to, he was naked, covered in leeches, and three miles the other side of town. It was widely rumoured that a queer-looking minister had been seen getting onto the bus for the city from a country corner. The strange minister was squeezed into a suit some sizes too small, with a collar that threatened to choke "him." His language wasn't very minister-like either. "He" seemed to be in the middle of a fit, kept muttering dim threats about leeches, some of which could be seen dangling down from the back of his head.

Grandma came over queer several times that day. Reverend Williams swore off the cloth. He had none left anyway. Besides, it offered no protection. Instead he took up a less hazardous occupation, stunt-diving from the cliff into the old quarry for the amusement of visiting tourists. Grandpa sighed and began rebuilding the bathroom. Bull sulked for the rest of the summer over his stolen leeches. Aunt Myrtle never bothered to come back again. Every swamp has its song birds!

CHAPTER 6

Bull Goes A' Courtin'

Bull was ill-equipped to help around the farm. He was clumsy, not particularly practical, and could be relied on to find trouble anywhere. Grandpa, lying on his back under a dismantled pump would send Bull to the house for a wrench. Bull would come back with a screwdriver. Sent back to rectify the error, Bull would get himself waylaid by a butterfly. After several minutes admiring the creature, he would meander off, completely forgetting his mission. Sometime later he might come across his father patiently holding up the pump and waiting for his wrench. Remembering, Bull would swiftly return to the house to fetch the promised hammer.

Improbable though it seemed to his parents, Bull had somehow managed to graduate from high school, and with relatively good marks, too. But all attempts to get Bull to actually do anything useful around the farm, inevitably ended in disaster. Consequently Grandpa Flapper decided that as Bull was not fit for much of anything else, he should be sent to university. Bull discussed the matter with Victoria at length. It took a great deal of time to effect the discussion. Underneath the old willow tree, hidden from the road, they would set out with the best intentions to cover the topic. Other matters kept occupying their attention though. When they came up for air, they would slide a few words in before practising their brand of mouth to mouth resuscitation again. It seemed quite apparent that separation, even during the week, was going to be a hardship neither wanted to bear. As their respective parents were ignorant of the fact they spent most of their time in each other's company, they held out little hope that they would be allowed to marry. At last they came to the conclusion that they had better let it be known they were at least courting. Then, when the time might be ripe, they would try to get their parents to agree to a wedding (with costs).

To start the public courting, they decided to go to a dance. Mother Sharp was not too keen on her daughter attending one of those modern dance affairs. She was not persuaded by her daughter, whose tenacity was very well known in the Sharp household. Victoria, a late arrival, born some ten years after her brother, was the darling of her father and her brother. Her mother and older sister had her measure, though. Mother Sharp decreed there would be no dancing for Victoria. Victoria, sent to her room, had her heart set on the dance. She immediately changed into her finery and escaped through the window, totally forgetting the object of the exercise.

Bull borrowed his father's car for the occasion, neglecting to tell his father. As most of Bull's training in the art of driving revolved around the farm tractor, his ability to conduct a car was not among his stronger accomplishments. However, they arrived safely at their destination. Bull carefully parked the car well off to one side, next to the paddock. As it was dark by now, it was not easy to tell where the drive ended and the verge began. He turned the car about in case a quick departure should be needed. The dance was being held on the second, or straw floor of the Garter family's barn. From down below the aroma of fresh cow flap would occasionally drift up. As it turned out, the barn hadn't been mucked out for a few days. Due to the other preparations for the dance it had been neglected, an oversight that was later to be regretted.

Bull and Victoria discreetly danced in the dim light of a corner, not wishing to be too obvious. The floor was soon crowded. It was said to be the largest dance in the county for some years. The combination of a bright star-lit night and the breath of heather in springtime proved an irresistible combination. Not leaving anything to chance, the promoters had hinted to a few of the town gossips that there were strange goings on at the Garter farm.

People who hadn't attended a dance in years showed up, with no real inclination to dance. They just sat about drinking, waiting for the great revelation, and discussing among themselves all manner of improbable scandals about the farmer, his family and their immediate neighbours. More and more people arrived as the hour rushed on towards midnight. By then the floor was positively creaking under the weight of sweaty, stomping bodies. And the beer was flowing freely.

Gerty Clamper's Band just about had the rafters vibrating when disaster struck. The centre of the floor slowly began to descend towards the lower regions of the barn. A great hole opened up at the bottom of this depression, providing direct access to the cow manure below. The folks on the fringe joined those in the centre, scrabbling to try to gain purchase before they all fell onto the dung heap below. Bull and Victoria, among the first to fall through, were pitched in up to their elbows. Bull hastily extricated himself and Victoria, then began to help the other patrons up and shoo them out through the front entrance, trying to ensure that they didn't hurt each other in their thrashing about. When everything seemed to be in hand, Bull stopped to take stock of Victoria and himself. It wasn't a pretty sight: they were covered in cow dung. Realizing immediately that they might be found out, Bull dragged Victoria out the lower barn door and raced for the car. He started up the car and careened around the barn, heading for the exit, just as the ambulances started to arrive. Next came the fire truck, manned by one single volunteer and his girlfriend who had been looking for an excuse to join the party all night. Bull, already shaking from reaction, twitched a little too far to the right, then watched in horror as the car, with a mind of its own, took him and Victoria straight through into the pigsty and plunked itself down smack in the middle of the pig's muck hole. The pigs all gathered around to admire them for a while, before losing interest and going off to more piggish pursuits. Gradually the pig smell combined with the aroma of fresh cow manure to deprive the warm interior of the car of what little oxygen there might have been.

Victoria and Bull both exited from the vehicle, clambered through the muck and headed for home, taking care to hide themselves well from roads en route. They tried holding their breath to keep out the smell, but found they couldn't do that and run too. Eventually they gave it up, and red-faced, made for the creek that fed the swamp.

There they stopped to immerse themselves, several times. Only then could they draw breath. Afterwards, they spread their clothes on bushes to dry, and set off hand in hand in their underwear, giggling, for home. Bull helped Victoria back in through her window, then set off for his own home to climb up the drainpipe to the bathroom balcony and so gain entrance to his bedroom through that route.

In the morning, Grandpa Flapper was astounded to see a picture of a car identical to his on the front page of The Newnham Tattler. The pigs were all gathered around admiring it. As it turned out, the photographer was unable to get a picture of the inside of the barn, so had made do with the material at hand. As no one was hurt in the barn floor collapse, and there was surprisingly little damage, that part occupied the space of only a few lines. The rest of the article was devoted to speculation on how the car had got where it was, and why the owner had used it for manure storage. There was also speculation, none of it anywhere close to reality, on why the owner might want to deposit the car in the pigsty.

Grandma, listening to Grandpa's chuckles about the poor unfortunate who owned the car, noticed a faint aroma coming from Bull's hair, which had not altogether been purged of the offensive matter in the midnight dip the night before. She quietly extricated Bull from his chair and his breakfast by the simple expedient of grabbing him by his left ear and hoisting him up all the way to the bathroom. Bull's first inclination to holler was cut short when he noticed the expression on his mother's face. That good lady came over queer several times that day, starting immediately after breakfast. Later she needed a little nip when the police officer came around to enquire why Grandpa had stuck his car in Farmer Garter's pigsty.   When Grandpa returned some hours later, brimming with wrath and spouting fire, Grandma quietly reminded him that strong language was not the best image for the town's hero. Before she would let him into the house she had him strip in the foyer, right down to his underwear. As she said, it was all right for him to enjoy himself out in the barn with the manure and other unspeakable things, but he didn't need to think he could bring it inside too. She was having so much fun that, when he would have stopped at his briefs, she insisted he should take them off too. Breathing heavily, he could only look at her, before stomping upstairs to take his bath, clothed only in his wrath. For her part Grandma came over queer a few more times, then, muttering "Oh, my, oh my!" went upstairs to see whether Grandpa was in the mood for a little hanky-panky.

As it turned out, Grandma's prophecy was correct. The local reporter had got hold of the story of a car seen by the ambulance crew dashing off on a further errand of mercy. In the garbled story from the somewhat tipsy dancers of the evening before, it seemed that Flapper had saved them all from a certain death, asphyxiation in the manure, or at least trampled to death by all those vicious cows in the basement. Father Flapper's picture again graced a special edition of the Tattler, with the caption HERO FLAPPER FLAPS AGAIN. There was a long resume of his previous heroic deeds, greatly exaggerated, together with an embellished account of the previous night's efforts. Bull and Victoria quietly set off to retrieve their dry clothing from the bushes and to make sure it had been properly cleaned before being subjected to too much scrutiny. They kept their own counsel about the evening's events.

CHAPTER 7

Kicking Around the Store

Grandpa Sharp, a giant of a man, was also a taciturn man. He stood six foot four in his stocking feet. Like most giants, he was gentle and humble, a fact clearly understood by Victoria's mother, but by few others. He had waited patiently for fifteen years after the birth of his first daughter, for the second. Clarissa, his first daughter, was a practical, no-nonsense sort. She held no truck with her sentimentalist father, which only gave him sorrow. Her father, believing that all women were born to be protected and nurtured, could not understand his independent older daughter.

Clarissa never learned that her father, the hard-bitten owner of the general store, and mayor of Newnham, was ruled by his heart. Victoria did. She found there was far more profit in letting her mother remonstrate with her father. Victoria gave her father unstinting adoration, with open displays of affection. Consequently, when Victoria dropped her bombshell into the dinner conversation one evening, she did nothing to follow it up, but trusted her mother to look after the matter in private. Her father's bellows, on hearing that his eighteen year old baby wanted to get married, could be heard clear over to the middle of Flapper's swamp.

Victoria prudently retired to bed at the first opportunity. For the next several days she kept a low profile as far as her father was concerned. To her mother she confided that she wanted to get Crawford tied down somewhat lest he meet someone with money at the university. She knew her mother, who had married for love, would understand that argument.

All members of the Sharp family were expected to spend Saturday at the store. Even Clarissa was expected to help, although she was married and pregnant. On that particular Saturday, Clarissa declared that a newly expectant mom was in no shape to work in the store. Clarissa's mother, in the time honoured tradition of all mothers, went off to confer with her eldest daughter on the coming blessed event. Victoria's brother was called out in the pick-up to deliver some fertilizer and a ladder or two. Victoria quickly phoned her beloved as reinforcement to come to help in the store, hoping to prove how worthy Bull was to her father.

Bull arrived on an ancient, disreputable excuse for a bicycle, which he proceeded to place ostentatiously against the front window of the store, a practice that always annoyed Mr. Sharp. Bull then sauntered in, kicking over the six foot high stack of tinned goods so carefully stacked the night before by Mr. Sharp. Discomfited, as always, anywhere near Mr. Sharp, Bull waited for the wrath of the heavens to fall down upon his head. He was in awe and a little afraid of Mr. Sharp. Victoria came out from the back at Bull's entrance, kicked a few tins around and, upon her father's entrance and expression of wrath, told him she had kicked some tins. Bull, wisely, kept silent.

As the day wore on, Bull proved to have less aptitude as a store clerk than as a carpenter. This would not have been a surprise to Mr. Flapper, but it clearly came as a shock to Mr. Sharp, who kept quietly asking Victoria whether she truly intended to marry this bumblehead. Victoria would repair whatever damage Bull had created and assure her father that she did. Grandpa Sharp gave up in defeat and disappeared into the loading ramp to make provision for shipping several rolls of barbed wire. Some moments later there was a great clamour from the back as several hundred pounds of barbed wire fell upon him. There were garbled curses and the sounds of coils of wire being tossed hither and about. Victoria dashed out to find her father bleeding all over, his hands and face gashed. Quickly she hauled out the first aid kit, and wound bales of gauze stripping around his hands to stem the blood. She then did the same for his face, leaving him slits for his eyes, nose and mouth. It was not an expert job, but what she lacked in neatness, she made up for in the quantity of gauze. She then shooed the customers out, locked up the store, installed Bull behind the wheel of the family Volkswagen, with her father in the passenger seat and herself in the rear.

It was always a marvel to Bull how the immense body of Mr. Sharp could bend to get into the car. Seeing him close up, scrumpled into the seat, provided first hand evidence that it was possible. They set out for the city, an hour's drive away, weaving a trifle erratically down the highway. Mr. Sharp, likely still in shock, or, perhaps thinking that his time had apparently come anyway, kept mercifully silent. Victoria gave soft encouragement to both her father and the unnerved Bull in the front, and provided directions to Bull. "No, no," she would say, "that's reverse, Dear, you want first gear, it's at the front." Bull, used to the smooth gear changes in a tractor, wasn't quite so proficient with the more exacting gears of the Volkswagen. For the first three miles the car bucked back and forth until Bull finally got it into second gear. Mr. Sharp, now suffering whiplash as well as his other injuries, remained silent, possibly praying, although no one could tell.

Eventually they arrived at the outskirts of the city and aimed for the hospital, several stop lights along a four lane road. Bull, avoiding the dreaded shift into first gear, tried to arrange it so that he didn't have to stop, by slowing down to a crawl between lights. Inevitably the car would start to jerk back and forth, alarming its occupants and annoying the other drivers no end. Finally a young fellow in a hot rod pulled up in the passing lane beside them. To show off for his gum-chawing girlfriend, Hot Rod leaned over to Bull and made nasty noises. Bull, hoping not to awaken the sleeping cop in the squad car on the corner, quietly ignored the fellow.

It was too much. Enraged, the man got out of his hot rod, and came around with the intention of teaching Bull a thing or too. The girlfriend got out to watch the fun. At this juncture, Grandpa Sharp came to life. With a howl of wrath, or pain, or simply because he had developed cramps from sitting so long, Grandpa uncoiled from the car, all six foot four of him, covered with gauze and blood. His hands outstretched, in front, the loose ends of gauze uncoiling as if from some great mummy, he advanced on Hot Rod. Gumchaw advised Hot Rod of the new player in the game. Then both stood open mouthed, watching the bloodied mummy stumbling towards them with who knows what evil intent. As the apparition closed in for the kill, they came to life. With shrieks of alarm they piled into their car. Rubber peeled off at least two tires as they turned left against the light and took off at high speed in a direction at right angles to where they wanted to go. The cop, awakened by the squealing tires, took off after them. Grandpa Sharp stood and watched the proceedings. Then with a jaunty wave to the assembled crowd, which nevertheless kept well back, climbed back into the Volkswagen and proceeded virtuously, in fits and starts, towards the hospital.

Eventually they arrived, to cough their way jerkily up the drive to the hospital emergency entrance. At Mr. Sharp's first appearance, there were cries of concern from the hospital staff, mainly for their own safety. Father Sharp was helped into the hospital by Victoria, a dainty wisp of a girl, now coated with rivulets of blood. His immense size and bloodied demeanour lending substance to the rumour that zombies had somehow got loose, or something else equally unsavoury. Father Sharp was flanked by what appeared to be a young zombie, not yet fully developed, with long hair, and three or four hairs growing out of his chin, suggesting an attempt at a beard.

As the first alarm went up that zombies had invaded the hospital, general panic ensued. screams of the other patients, combined with the screams of the staff combined to empty the waiting room in short order. When the riot police came charging up the stairs some moments later, they were met by a peaceful scene. By now, Victoria had unwound the gauze from her father so that the doctors could attend to his wounds. They were all three sitting peacefully in the waiting room as the police roared through. Patients not previously apprised of the monster were terrified by the sight of the platoon of police sweeping through the hospital, searching for the hoard of zombies or ancient Egyptians, the police weren't sure which, and didn't care as long as they moved in a cordon together. Patients, uprooted from their beds, streamed out the front doors, some walking, some in wheelchairs and some wheeled along in their beds. Eventually, order was restored.

Grandpa Sharp was attended with all the care due the mayor of a small town. As he was virtually the only patient left in the hospital, he had the combined attention of all the hospital staff. They figured that anyone brave enough to have withstood the onslaught of an invading army of mummies or zombies and obviously routing them, deserved their finest efforts. His battle wounds were soon stitched. The bewildered Bull and Victoria, for a change were looked upon as heros, undeserved to be sure, but heros nonetheless. They went away with an entirely erroneous view of hospital life. For some reason, unfathomable to Bull, this marked the start of a whole new relationship with his intended father-in-law. The engagement was agreed to, just so long as they didn't actually intend to marry for another forty years or so.

CHAPTER 8

Love in the Swamp

Bull had entered engineering at the university. He reasoned that his manual dexterity was questionable, he couldn't draw, his writing was illegible, his logic was faulty or nonexistent, he couldn't speak three languages, or even one very well. In fact, he was indeed useless. With all these attributes, he surprised everyone, including himself, by passing. By the time he got to his third year, he was desperate. It seemed evident that in spite of all odds he might eventually find himself gainfully employed as an engineer. Clearly strict measures were called for.

He decided to get married. But, there was the problem of convincing Victoria's mother. Bull had a long discussion with Victoria on strategy. It was decided that Bull should announce his intentions to join the navy. After all, they reasoned, Mrs. Sharp had never forgiven her brother, Victoria's uncle, for joining the navy, having long since concluded it was his downfall and ruination, not without a certain amount of truth, either. Victoria reasoned that her mother would then allow the marriage to proceed in order to spare Victoria the pain of being married to a sailor.

Victoria announced Bull's decision to join the navy over Sunday dinner, with the whole Sharp clan in attendance. Victoria's mother immediately choked on one of her tender chicken balls, projecting it violently across the table into her startled husband's lap. When the coughing and spluttering were over she was wild-eyed. Clarissa was indignant. Mr. Sharp recovered, discreetly disposed of the wayward chicken ball and harrumphed happily in his chair, pointing out all the advantages of the navy for Bull. He figured there was no way the wedding would come off now: his wife would never agree. Clarissa's husband, as usual, said nothing. He didn't dare. Mr. Sharp left the table a happy man. It was a tactical error.

"Why are you so anxious to rush your engagement to an early end?" enquired Mrs. Sharp of Victoria.

Victoria didn't think her mother would appreciate a discussion on the birds and the bees, so put forth the argument that she and Bull had conjured up. "Poor Bull," she said, "couldn't afford to live in residence. He's slowly starving to death on meagre fare, subsisting from weekend to weekend, waiting for a decent, home cooked meal at our house." (She didn't mention that Bull ate at least five meals a day on weekends, three of them at home and the other two at the Sharp residence.)

Clarissa could see what was coming and set about trying to divert the discussion. "I think they should wait at least a couple of years before getting married," she said. She was afraid her parents couldn't afford both a wedding and a grand party for Clarissa's daughter's first birthday.

"Get married," Grandma Sharp advised. "It's better in the long run to get married than to join the navy." Bull and

Victoria capitulated. They would give up their plans for Bull to join the Navy and instead get married. Clarissa left the discussion with her arguments in tatters.

Unwilling to accept defeat, she sent out for reinforcements. She invited the engaged couple to a party at her house. Also invited were several wealthy potential suitors for Victoria's hand. Much better for Victoria to marry someone with resources than some penniless loafer, with few prospects. The first potential suitor arrived in a Mercedes. He had been well primed on his target. Victoria's weakness was cars. Ignoring Bull, Mercedes took Victoria over, charming her with his small talk and dancing her clear out on to the back lawn before she had a chance to draw breath. Mercedes grabbed her in a passionate embrace. Victoria went into shock. He mistook it for agreement. When he came up for air, she pushed him into the swamp. She waited to observe his technique. It wasn't up to Bull's standard so she went back inside the house to find him. Bull was just beginning to feel lonely, so they thought between them they might repair to the downstairs couch for a little heavy breathing and other stuff. The Mercedes slunk away in the dark. Clarissa, having observed Victoria's departure with Mercedes, drew all the wrong conclusions. When Bull reappeared sometime later with lipstick in unlikely places, she was greatly at a loss to explain it. In future transactions, Mercedes was very reticent about how his evening had ended.

Clarissa's next volley involved a Jag convertible. It was a mean trick, even for Clarissa. Victoria was strongly tempted. She tried manoeuvring Jag into the swamp position. But he had been forewarned by Mercedes. Victoria asked politely whether she might drive the convertible. Jag declined politely. It was just as well. Victoria couldn't drive. But she reasoned that a car that expensive should be able to practically drive itself. It had enough dials and lights and gears, so she thought, if that were any evidence. Victoria said she would think about a ride with Jag. She went off to discuss the matter with Bull. He wasn't too keen on Victoria becoming involved with a Mercedes or a Jag. So Victoria reluctantly gave it up. So did Clarissa.

The entire town of Newnham turned out for the wedding. The reception was held in Farmer Garter's barn, with Gerty Clamper's Band laid on for entertainment afterwards. All was pretty well ready. Acres of food had been prepared by the whole town. Everyone had surreptitiously smuggled in a few bottles, in deference to Grandma Flapper and in case she "came over queer." Uncle Daniel had hidden his still discreetly outside the barn, for a change, hoping to escape detection by the thieving throngs. Everyone expected some incident worthy of Grandpa Flapper's reputation. They weren't to be disappointed.

The ceremony was held in the little white church on the corner, built for a congregation of a hundred, crammed with the entire town and the county around for a radius of forty miles, three hundred gentle souls in all. It was a steamy August day. Neckties were soon pulled loose and the women tried desperately to fan themselves discreetly from underneath. The Reverend McFarlindale, newly appointed to his first ministry, took the occasion to preach a Hell and Brimfire sermon before someone quietly reminded him that it was a wedding. He figured the chance was too good to miss, though. He proceeded to harangue the throng about the perils of the flesh!

The bride and groom were soon wilting, along with everyone else. Vows were exchanged in a constrained whisper. At last the ceremony was over. The town erupted from the church. They barely stopped long enough for pictures. Their thirst was all engulfing. When they got to the barn they sought anything liquid to quench their thirst, soft drinks, juice, coffee, milk, mostly mixed with alcohol. A few of the bravest even tried water, undiluted.

The groom's mother came over queer several times and had to be refreshed. The minister put her subsequent collapse down to a faint from the heat and reproached himself for not foreseeing the consequences of his lengthy sermon. He was patting Grandma Flapper's hand when Grandpa Flapper caught him at it. The minister was mortified. He slipped out through the back door of the barn and hid himself in a small thicket, having gathered that he was not among the town's favourite people at the moment. He discovered that he shared his hiding place with Uncle Daniel's still.

The Reverend McFarlindale was a trifle naive about such things as country stills. Fortunately, it wasn't long before Uncle Daniel appeared, to check on the flame beneath the still, and to make sure there was enough fuel. He discovered the Reverend hiding in the bushes, and in the spirit of camaraderie for which he was famous, invited that worthy to try out the "product." As it appeared to be quite mild, the minister happily agreed. It wasn't long before the Reverend McFarlindale and Uncle Daniel had fallen into a lengthy discourse on the comparative merits of tomato juice and Uncle Daniel's brand of firewater. As time went on, the combination of the heat of the day, the fire under the still, and the firewater proved to be too hot for both parties.

The bushes were stifling. They began to shed clothes until the corpulent Uncle Daniel and the skinny minister of the church were in their skivvies. It is true that they had their shoes and socks on, though.

Grandma Flapper eventually came round as the party proceeded. Gronk and Grandpa, possibly the only sober folks there, were stepping out in time to the music. Gronk's date for the event, Bertha Grimble, a severely buxom lass, was leaping about with such ferocity she all but shook the old barn on its foundations. Most people, remembering a previous occasion in the barn, hung about on the fringes. But the barn held true, having been reinforced throughout with several railroad ties that had mysteriously disappeared from track side one evening a few weeks before.

The newly married couple were pried apart with crowbars. The bride was then held to the ancient tradition of dancing with everybody else there, so the old men could pretend they were young and the young could pretend other things. Gronk, as Best Man, was soon required to perform his duty as well. During this display Gronk, in a fit of chivalry, held Victoria as if she were china. Victoria decided that was no way to rock so dragooned him into an exceptionally fast waltz, by way of exacting compensation. As Gronk lumbered about, he came down on the hem of Victoria's wedding gown. Soon the older generation didn't have to imagine too much.

Gronk, mortified, stood blushing in the centre of the floor. Victoria, grinding her teeth, sweetly suggested he find some pins to reattach the gown. Bull, deciding it was time to leave, whisked his all-but- naked bride off, commandeering the family car for the purpose. The pigsty loomed up invitingly, but he gave it a miss on this occasion, and instead drove the car off into the swamp. Victoria made a bed of the back seat in the privacy of the swamp where they completed the celebration of their nuptials.

After the happy couple had left, the wedding reception became much more relaxed. Grandma, feeling herself come over queer again, set off to find Uncle Daniel, or to be more precise, to find Uncle Daniel's still. Following her nose, she arrived at the thicket behind the barn and plunked herself down behind the bushes with the nearly nude minister and his bosom buddy. Ignoring them, she set about investigating the merits of Uncle Daniel's product. As she felt the first little pinpricks of fire dart through her, she thought that no booze before had ever affected her in quite such a way. Soon the little pinpricks became downright unbearable on the parts of her anatomy that connected directly with the ground. In no time at all she was screaming for help and tearing her clothes off to get rid of the little red ants that had taken exception to her bottom on top of their anthill, biting where they could best gain purchase. That proved to be a sensitive part of Grandma's anatomy.

Uncle Daniel left for other regions in a hurry. The good Reverend McFarlindale tried ineffectually to help. In the scramble, the still was tipped, the fire underneath spreading rapidly, until flames skipped up the side of the barn. Grandpa, alerted by Grandma's screams, came tearing around the barn again just in time to find the nearly naked Reverend patting Grandma's nearly naked bottom. With a bellow of rage, he hurled himself into the fray.

Hearing the commotion, all the wedding guests came charging out to witness Grandpa hoisting the minister up by his underwear and depositing him, none too gently into Farmer Garter's pigsty. They all watched, cheering, while behind them the barn burned merrily, crackling away in time with their clapping for the entertainment laid on.

When the fire was discovered a few moments later, they all realized how near their maker they had come. Attributing their salvation to Grandpa's forethought in providing outside entertainment at the critical moment, they hailed him as a hero and bore him and his nearly bare wife down the main street of town in triumph. The town newspaper, The Tattler had a field day in the next special edition, with giant headlines proclaiming the town hero once again. With remarkably quick thinking, they said, the Flappers had lured their guests outside the barn, having detected the fire. The stratagem worked, no one panicked, no one was injured, and the Reverend McFarlindale, given some credit for his part in the rescue, was quoted as saying that if he had it to do all over again to save the townsfolk, he would. The pictures showed Grandpa being borne aloft triumphantly, and Grandma from a less flattering, but blessedly blurred photograph, beating the heads of her merry bearers with her umbrella.

The next day the Happy Porpoises Lodge and Family Resort called up Grandma to enquire the whereabouts of the missing couple. They hadn't turned up and were presumed missing if not worse. Consternation followed this announcement and all hands set out to search for them. Eventually they were found when the tire tracks were followed around the pigsty, across the ditch, the road and the other ditch, through the cedar forest and into the back of the swamp. By this time, Bull was glassy-eyed and, it was later revealed, Victoria was pregnant. The family car was never the same again.

CHAPTER 9

Giant Cookies and Other Monsters

Victoria and Bull moved to the city, to a little walk-up flat, miles from the University. Bull would set off for classes each day, by public transit, as Victoria walked to her work in a nearby office. They lived in the attic of a house, converted into a flat, reached by a long, very narrow staircase. It was affordable and in a pretty neighbourhood.

The kitchen was also the entrance hall. The sloping roof over the kitchen followed the contour of the roof, but meant that walking was always on an angle. On entering, one walked stoop-shouldered, with head bent off to the right. Turning around was accomplished by moving into the living room first, turning, canting the head to the left, then returning through the kitchen. The living room was the only room affording an upright stance.

A tiny bathroom tucked into a corner, under an extreme slant of the roof, was the only facility. Sitting on it required some dexterity of positioning, head bent towards the left. There was a tiny shower, built for midgets who canted sideways. There was also an oversize sink, built a foot off the floor on the downward slope. Victoria found it somewhat difficult trying to kneel down in front of the mirror over the sink to put on her make-up.

The furniture was shabby, but comfortable. The little chesterfield in the living room was propped up on one corner by a building block. The part in the middle had a spring showing through at a critical position for lovemaking on the settee. Bull discovered this on the first evening in the new home. Having reached an exciting and irreversible stage of hanky-panky, he was suddenly stabbed in one of the cheeks in the lower region, as the spring uncurled. Victoria, on top was thrilled at his mastery and pushed him down with growing excitement. Up they shot again, then down. Bull, by now in agony and gasping. So violent had their hanky-panky become, that the couch fell off its building block. It was a crucial moment. The over-active spring shot upwards violently. So did Bull. So did Victoria. They fell about all over the floor, Victoria clinging to Bull, and making little kissing noises all over him. Bull, relieved from the pain in his rear, sighed in relief. Victoria, misinterpreting the sigh, started all over again. This time Bull enjoyed the hanky-panky, but kept quiet about the previous episode as Victoria seemed to have derived a good deal more pleasure out of it than had he.

Downstairs, the landlord and his wife had been waiting nervously on their couch for some sign that the newlyweds above were going to be happy in their new abode. Hearing the thunk and clatter from above, followed shortly thereafter by the squeaking of the floor boards, they smiled, nodded in satisfaction, and tuned the TV to their favourite soap opera.

While Bull was growing up, it had often happened that his mother had come over queer at a crucial juncture in proceedings before supper. Bull would find himself called upon to save the supper if he wanted any, in consequence of which, he had become a passable, if not entirely proficient cook. Victoria, spoiled rotten by her mother, was not well acquainted with the inside of a kitchen. She did, however, have very definite ideas about what one did in kitchens. Arriving home from work early in the first week after moving into the little apartment, her arms full of groceries, she put the kitchen to rights, then started to make Bull's favourite snack, oatmeal-raisin cookies. Bull arrived home from school just as she was dropping the dough onto a cookie sheet. Noting the ladle she was using to measure the dough onto the cookie sheet, he casually remarked that one more often used a teaspoon. Victoria, fixing him with a glare, and holding the ladle aloft, suggested in a deceptively sweet voice that he might find better things to do with his time.

With a sigh for what might have turned into a cosy time in the kitchen, Bull went reluctantly off to do his homework. Sometime later there was an anguished wail from the kitchen. Bull, fearing for the safety of his beloved, arrived just in time to watch the giant cookie creeping out from the oven. He quietly retreated to the furthest corner of the apartment and hid himself behind the couch. Victoria came in to find him. At first sight he wasn't there. She hauled the couch out and demanded to know what he found so interesting behind it. Bull claimed to be searching for a missing quarter. Victoria didn't believe him. She proceeded to give him a tongue lashing for ruining her cookies. An upset Victoria always blamed Bull, though he might be miles away. Breakfast for several weeks thereafter, was somewhat doughy oatmeal, burned on the outside, dough on the inside. Bull chewed stoically through it, making complimentary noises about her ingenious approach to preparing breakfast, silently blessing the raisins for at least making it palatable.

Bull soon came to the conclusion that it was a good thing he hadn't married his sweetheart for her ability to bake because her next foray into the baking arts was no more successful. She decided on pineapple upside down cake. Bull, creeping up the stairs to surprise Victoria, hopefully in a state of undress, peered over the railing. He was just in time to watch, aghast, as the pineapple upside down cake cascaded all over the oven. Victoria had placed the pan upside down on the shelf in the oven. She carefully ladled dough back into the pan, spied Bull out of the corner of her eye, and leaned over the railing just as he was trying to escape. He didn't make it. The dough caught Bull broadside, a pineapple ring hanging off his left ear. "It wouldn't have happened," Victoria said, "if you hadn't snuck up on me like that." Bull crept back upstairs, dropped to his knees, and waddled into the shower, clothes and all. When he came out he meekly hinted that he had gone off baked goods for awhile.

On the evening Victoria decided to tell Bull of the pending arrival of Michelle, she set about cooking dinner for him. Something simple, she thought, to put him in a mellow mood. Something like spaghetti, followed by a nice pie, purloined from her mother. The package of spaghetti didn't look as if it were enough to feed a starving chicken, let alone her husband. So she added several more packages in an immense pot of boiling water, ignoring the instructions on the side of the packets. Bull arrived home just in time to see the spaghetti monster take over the kitchen. It bubbled over the stove, crept along the counter, on to the table and from there proceeded to march along the floor. Victoria accompanied its progress with screams, between bouts of sickness, dashing off to the washroom to leave Bull in charge of the spaghetti. The landlord, alerted by the screams, arrived at the bottom of the stairs just in time to head the spaghetti off from establishing a beach head in his own flat below. Reinforcements were sent for. A half hour later the spaghetti monster capitulated. It was all over but the mopping up. Victoria went off to do her own mopping up, leaving Bull with the task, along with the neighbours who had showed up to assist in the battle. Afterwards, they all sat around for a beer to compare notes of bravery and courage in the face of enemy sneakiness.

The next morning, Victoria was violently ill, even before getting out of bed. Bull ran off to phone the doctor but never made it. Victoria headed him off at the stairs on the way out and threatened him with his life if he proceeded with the plan. She went off to work, leaving Bull convinced she was trying to shield him from the fact that she had some dreadful disease.

Victoria almost despaired of ever telling her beloved about the blessed event that was about to befall them. She was very sure, though, that it had to be told in the right setting. When her courage returned a few days later, she decided that a simple steak dinner, (What could you do wrong with steak?) with salad, would be ideal, perhaps followed by a simple desert like cherries flambé. At least the recipe made it sound very simple. Warm some cherries in sauce, heat some brandy, pour brandy over the warmed cherries and light it, then pour the lot, burning in a tantalizing blue flame over some ice cream. What could be simpler?

The steak was ready just as Bull came up the stairs from his classes. Just at that moment, Victoria was violently ill. Bull followed Victoria into the bathroom where he scrunched himself under the contour of the ceiling. On his knees, he stood irresolutely around, first on one knee then on the other, offering little murmurs of love and support. Finished, Victoria returned to the kitchen, starving for her steak. Bull, relieved, stood up, cracking his head on the ceiling. Down he fell in a heap on top of Victoria's stiff bristle brush. Up he got cracking his head again, repeating the performance a few more times until he got the rhythm correct and managed to extricate himself. He sat down to supper, completely put off all food. Victoria ate both steaks and most of the salad. Then she pulled out the makings of the cherries flambe. She wouldn't let Bull watch. It was to be a surprise, she said. The amount of brandy wasn't specified, but she figured that half a bottle should be enough.

A short time later there was a great whoosh from the kitchen accompanied by Victoria's screams as the hot brandy ignited. Bull ran in to find the flames licking the ceiling. He grabbed Victoria and ran down stairs to call the fire department. By the time they arrived half the neighbourhood had been evacuated behind a police cordon. Miraculously, there was no damage, except where the firemen had chopped through the roof to get at the fire in the kitchen. By the time they had executed this complicated manoeuvre, the fire had burnt itself out. The newsmen who took pictures of the event wrote it up somewhat differently. According to that version, gleaned from witnesses at the scene, none of whom knew anything about the event, the young hero had defied death to save his beloved wife from the burning conflagration. The subsequent fire had levelled three city blocks. This was reported in the Newnham Tattler with considerably more embellishment, under the headline FLAPPER HEROISM A GENETIC TRAIT. It was accompanied by suitable remarks on the previous heroic endeavours of Grandpa Flapper.

Safely restored to their little flat, with the new skylight over the kitchen, Victoria broke down and confessed to Bull that she was pregnant. "Is that all," he said, "I thought you were crazy, or suffering from plague or ingrown toenails or something." Victoria cried even louder. Bull went off to study.

CHAPTER 10

Marquees and Mudpies

Eventually, the University authorities came to the conclusion that the only effective way to get rid of Bull was to give him a degree and be done with it. On one bright spring morning a great marquee was erected on the front campus to house the graduation reception. The graduation exercise was to be held in the gymnasium, suitably tarted up for the purpose, with the reception to follow in the marquee. The gymnasium was an ancient building suited to the sports of another era, at least a century ago. It was a solemn building, stuffed with its own importance. The centre part was round, lit by a skylight, which could occasionally be opened with a good deal of effort. Normally all such efforts were resisted by the custodian since it required climbing up among the pigeons to push each little window open. Shutting them required a fine sense of balance on the catwalk surrounding the skylight. The pigeons, who had painstakingly entered through all the little cracks around the windows, didn't much care for the human company either. They would fly about muttering imprecations at the intrusion.

In winter the building was draughty and cold. In summer it sweltered. On this hot spring day, the temperature was already climbing. Several hundred touted up graduates, and their families, also in their best spring suits and dresses, contributed to the heating in the building. Everything was more or less in readiness.

Meanwhile out in the marquee, the faculty wives had banded together to make dainty little pate sandwiches and contribute any stale cake they might have had lying around. The tea urns were all filled and somewhat warmed. Professor Grommet, Head of Bull's department, and a great bear of a man, had been through to check on things. It was his delight and pleasure to scare every undergraduate. "Put the fear of God into 'em," he said, "best entertainment around," although few people would have said that Grommet was on speaking terms with God.

To help with his scare tactics, Grommet had a great blathering dog, incongruously, named Harry. It was five feet high at its eyes, with a permanent curl to its lips, just baring its great incisor teeth. Whenever anyone entered Grommet's office, the dog would stand erect, tail pointing skyward, feet braced for combat, beside the Professor's desk. Harry, the dog would then glare, unblinkingly, at the intruder. Undergraduates spent as little time in the office as possible, and then only when sent for. Graduates and secretaries never entered the domain. Consequently, Grommet was able to wield a free hand with his scotch, kept handy in his desk file drawer.

On this graduation occasion, as in the past, Grommet tied the dog to the centre pole of the marquee, then repaired to the gymnasium, leaving the hapless women helpers to skirt twenty feet around the dog to avoid antagonizing him. All that is but the President's wife. In a former existence she had been a sergeant in the armed forces. Even dogs recognized authority when they saw it, including Harry. She didn't like Harry, though, and he reciprocated the feeling, but was careful not to show it.

The senior professors and other dignitaries sat on the centre platform in the gymnasium, all prepared for the convocation exercises, hands folded on their bellies, and comfortably settled in preparation for their afternoon naps. The professors had dusted off their oldest ties for the purpose. Each tie hung in a broad swath down the paunch of its respective owner. Each had a different design. For some it was spotted with ketchup, for others beer or mustard, or both. The odd one showed a bright swirl from some original design, but this was generally frowned upon. The owners of such ties were relegated to the back rows. But each tie was unique and peeped out from beneath the great ceremonial robes while their owners snoozed or listened to the ball game through miniature earplugs attached to radios conveniently stored in jacket pockets for the purpose.

A few politicians were there, those that had managed invitations so they could give impromptu political messages, mostly about how wonderful the government was if they belonged to the party in power, or how misguided and stupid it was, if they belonged to the opposition. The stage was set for a long and torturous afternoon.

The Dean of the faculty held forth for what seemed an hour on the need for life long learning. Next came the President, who managed another hour, or so it seemed, on the same subject. The graduating class, seated together at the centre of the sweltering hall, in their black robes, were by now comatose. Most of the audience was asleep, some making alarming noises. Victoria, very heavy with child, tried desperately to keep cool, fanning herself with her program and uttering little sighs.

The doors were all ajar to allow whatever breezes might find their way in, to stir the air inside. Eventually, the Dean whispered to the building custodian to open the skylight to let in some air. That worthy, thinking of the accumulation of pigeon presence all over the catwalk vigorously shook his head, to no avail. Eventually the custodian started up the ladder, watched by two hundred engineering graduates, one nudging the other awake to ensure no one missed the event. He was also watched by anyone else in the audience who happened to be awake at the time. The custodian slowly made his way around the skylight, muttering oaths about pigeons and professors and other obscene topics, while all of his comments were reflected by the great glass parabolic windows to boom into the ear of the speaker on the podium below, although no one else could hear.

The politician chosen as orator for the day, lugubriously intoned his speech. As he was of the government side, it was all about the wondrous things the government had managed to do with the people's money, and how much had found its way back to the voters, almost five percent or so he would have his audience believe. The politician turned bright red at the implied epithets directed at him from above, sensing even then that he alone could hear them. As no Opposition party had ever stayed him in his speeches before, he bravely ploughed along, refusing to pander to the commentary from on high. Above, the custodian moved along the catwalk dislodging pigeon droppings onto the heads of the faculty below, most of whom slept through it all. The odd one who didn't, and happened to look up at an inopportune moment wished he hadn't.

The pigeons, thoroughly alarmed, began to flap about in the gymnasium, emitting nasty noises. Swooping lower over the centre stage, they got so excited, they did other things too. The class, hung in suspense, took bets with each other on how long it would be before the Dean, the President or the speaker were bombarded by the pigeons. The speaker, by now screaming at the top of his voice to be heard over the cacophony of pigeon calls, was thinking of bringing the proceedings to a quick ending without even finishing his monologue. The President was the first to have his tie decorated, winning a tidy sum for Bull. Next came the Dean. The aroma was almost more than the Dean could bear. And there was still the matter of putting the hoods on the graduates.

Finally the speaker was hit and everyone relaxed as he brought his speech to a rapid conclusion, gasping for breath from the stench, his nostrils and his voice quivering. The class was rapidly formed into twos and run across the stage, each receiving a hood and told in a whisper to put it on themselves, each handed the wrong scroll at the end of the platform and told to sort it out themselves. The valedictorian was allowed to speak for a minute or so before he found himself being thanked, his hand shaken by the President, and ushered offstage at a trot. The recessional, in double time, had the faculty running out to fresh air. Everyone else followed at a more decorous pace.

Outside, the air had become sultry, preparing for a storm. The faculty had already congratulated themselves on their foresight for erecting the marquee. All the guests made for cover in case the storm should break. The professors dashed off to their offices to shake out the dried pigeon presence and wash off the fresh droppings. Afterwards, before joining the reception, they found it necessary to restore themselves with a little drop. Fortunately they didn't have to rely on Grommet for their supplies. Each had his own hidden away somewhere. Eventually, dignity restored, they all returned to the marquee to indulge in a little light chatter before escaping as soon as decently possible.

Victoria, almost fainting with the heat and hunger, made directly for the food, Bull following docilely behind. They ate their way down one table towards the centre of the tent. Grommet appeared in order to take one last opportunity to have a go at Bull. He reckoned without Victoria. He also reckoned without Mrs. Palaver's cat. Victoria took him on first, figuring that he might be another version of her father's species. He wasn't. He didn't back off at all in the face of Victoria's wiles. Victoria, upset by the experience, attempted to put the pole between herself and Grommet. She encountered Grommet's great dog behind the pole. She shrieked and clambered up onto the nearest table. The dog snarled and made to go after her, but reinforcements had arrived.

Mrs. Palaver's cat, a very large, all white Persian, had come to investigate the pate. In the mayhem, with the women all snarling at Grommet, the dog snarling at the very pregnant Victoria, and Grommet, by now sufficiently worried about lawsuits and other equally unsavoury matters, snarling at his dog, the cat joyously swept up onto the nearest tables to investigate the fare. Her tail straight up, she went from dish to dish, oblivious of the noise around.

By now Victoria was screaming, the President was visibly upset, and Bull, diploma safely in hand was threatening all manner of consequences for Grommet if he didn't remove the dog. Bull needn't have worried. The dog had spotted the cat. Just as the storm broke, the dog lunged after the cat. The combination of the dog pulling on the pole, the gale from the storm, and the rain, brought the tent down on everyone and everything.

Freed from the pole, the dog set out after the cat. The cat, not very happy about this state of affairs, set out for higher places. Out of the collapsing tent she lept, crossing the field at a bound. Then she ran inside the gymnasium and up the catwalk to the pigeon roost. There she discovered a haven of another kind. The dog, following in hot pursuit attempted to climb the catwalk. He only succeeded in pitching the rest of the pigeon droppings all over himself, and losing his balance, fell onto the chancellor's chair, winding himself in the process. The cat, stranded among the pigeons, decided to make the best of his opportunities stalking pigeons.

The President, taking a short cut through the building to escape the conflagration outside, found the dog a short time later. He made disparaging remarks about the animal. The dog, waking up, took exception to the remarks. Deprived of its sport with the cat and Victoria, it figured to make do with the President. The President, missing some of the rear of his trousers as a result of his interaction with the dog, joined the cat among the pigeons, which were still all aflutter after their disturbance. The President only noticed that the janitor had removed the ladder after he had made peace with the cat. His cries for help went unheeded. As most of the faculty had already departed for Bermuda immediately following convocation, it was not till the next day before he was discovered. Mrs. President hardly noticed his absence at first, but when he failed to show up as a fourth for their weekly bridge party she sent out a search party for him. He was found roosting among the pigeons who had finally come to accept him. They did not, however, accept Mrs. Palaver's cat, which finally got tired of the sport of pigeon-baiting and set off for home by some devious cat route.

Bull, caught outside the tent at its collapse, with his beloved inside, tried desperately to effect a reunion. Soon it became clear this was not going to be an easy task. It also became clear that he was going to become a father imminently. He could hear Victoria's moaning through the din inside. She was calling for him and he couldn't get there. He could also hear the faculty wives making little helpless cooing noises to try to comfort her. Trying to get inside was a different matter, especially as most of the people were trying to get out.

Grommet, who had suffered some heavy sarcasm from the President and most of the senior wives, had taken refuge under a table. There he rested with his large rear on the ground, almost oblivious to the little rivulets of water and coffee that made their way underneath and around him. Eventually the coffee, near boiling point, let its presence be known to him. He bounced up, hitting his head on the table, swore loudly about second rate institutions, and fell back into the coffee. There was a strained hush as Mrs. President leaned over to enquire whether she had heard him correctly, and whether she might report his feelings at a higher level. He used a few words not commonly found in the dictionary, then quietly resolved to find himself another posting at the earliest opportunity.

By now most of the graduates and their families had set off for private celebrations in drier quarters. Most of the faculty had long since escaped, leaving only Mrs. President and a few other stalwarts, with Grommet, to look after Victoria's interests. Bull, in full panic, finally crawled through the mud to his beloved's side and took charge of her. Mrs. President offered them the use of her car to get to the hospital. Bull accepted, hurrying Victoria, between contractions, to the car. There he unlocked the doors, bounced around to the driver's side and took off at a speed greatly in excess of the regulations. Stopped a few blocks away, he patiently explained the dilemma to the police officer. The latter saw only a mud-spattered miscreant in a crazy black robe with what looked like fake rabbit fur around his neck, obviously in a stolen car, and lent no credence to the theory that the fellow was driving an obviously missing pregnant wife to the hospital. Bull wound up in the clink.

Left on the sidewalk by herself, Victoria sighed and walked the half dozen blocks to the hospital herself. When she arrived at the emergency entrance, the attending physician praised her efforts. "Best thing you could have done," he told her, "I require all the mothers to walk some. Does a marvellous job of speeding up their labour. Today I should be able to get back to my golf game well in time to meet at the nineteenth hole!"

The sergeant on duty at the police station was vastly amused by Bull's incoherent tale of distress. The sergeant kept calling others in to enjoy the story, demanding that Bull recount it endlessly. Each new group went into gales of laughter, while the bewildered Bull tried to decide what to do next.

Bull finally asked to place a call to the President's wife, giving her a garbled tale of arrest and terror. That lady came immediately, descending upon the station with considerable wrath, not having discovered the whereabouts of Victoria, and imagining that Victoria was about to give birth to her baby in a cell. The sergeant stopped laughing at her entrance. He was politeness itself. When she enquired what had happened to the woman having the baby, the sergeant sent his minions out to look over the car again, perhaps in the trunk. Having ascertained that the pregnant lady was not in evidence, he felt on firmer ground. Undaunted, Mrs. President asked Bull's crime. The sergeant, in an effort to impress the old dowager, told her it was car snatch. She asked whose, then identified the car as her own. In vain did the sergeant claim speeding. Mrs. President offered to call a higher authority, her neighbour, the police chief. The sergeant sighed and gave the matter up. Justice had again been thwarted by vested interests and influence.

Bull made it to the hospital just in time for Michelle's birth. When told he had a son, he couldn't cope, and fainted for the first time in his life. When he came to, he was assured it wasn't quads or even twins, but a single, male baby. In later years he was to doubt the assertion that there was only one. However, he never had enough proof to go on. After a quick conference with Victoria, the baby was called Harry, after Grommet's dog. They reasoned he would need that sort of backing to handle all life's little vicissitudes.

CHAPTER 11

Gas, and other Chemistries

Harry always presented a cheerful face to the world, as evidenced by the earliest pictures of him that show him smiling. Even when he first came home from the hospital he was smiling. His mother said it was gas, but his father, never one to accept his wife's pronouncements without a second opinion, felt it more likely that the little fellow had unleashed a brilliant smile to light his father's life. To disprove the gas theory, his father decided to burp him. Father hoisted Harry over his shoulder and tapped Harry's bottom, very gently, muttering something unintelligible when Harry threw up all down the back of his father's new shirt. Harry did other things, too, things that shocked his father no end. Holding the squalling Harry at arm's length, Bull indicated to Victoria that her precious offspring had suddenly started to go rotten. Harry had still not burped.

Neither of Harry's parents could understand their son's inability to burp, little realizing that he was simply storing it up for effect. Bull took Harry upon his knee to bounce him, hoping to dislodge the gas. It worked beyond all Bull's expectations: Harry burped. The walls reverberated with the force of it. Neighbours from three doors away came out to see what had caused the explosion, surprised to see the house still standing. So were Harry's mother and father. Harry immediately went limp. His father cried "Oh my God, I've killed him!" then handed Harry, considerably diminished in size by the loss of his burp, to Victoria. Harry's mother, not knowing what to do with the body put it in the crib. Both parents then tried to find out whether there might be a spark of life left in him.

Bull placed a mirror near Harry's mouth to see whether it might fog up. It didn't. Both Bull and Victoria leaned into the crib to try to hear if Harry was still breathing, but they could hear nothing, no little wheezes, no sighs, no breathing. Eventually they gave up and decided to eat supper first, then attend to the body. It was a sorrowful supper. Neither could eat very well. Their first baby, and they had blown it. Burps could prove fatal: someone should have warned them.

A little while later, when Harry began to scream for food, both parents were ecstatic with joy. That was the last time they were ecstatic with joy over that matter. Over the coming months and years, when Harry decided he wanted to eat, he got instant attention. He hardly had to say more than "UUNGHH" before his mother had him out to be fed. For some months he did nothing but eat, sleep, excrete. He often varied this routine by eating, excreting, excreting again immediately after his diaper was changed, or during the changing, then finishing off by smiling. No one was prepared to take Harry on when he smiled as the previous explosion was all too fresh in their memories.

Harry very early decided that he liked the female form - at least his mother's form - very specifically, her breasts. As

Harry's parents were somewhat ignorant of the scheme of things, they didn't discover his predilection for breasts for some years. Before Harry was born, his parents had decided that the baby should be breast-fed. They worried about how this might be accomplished with minimum discomfort to all. They read books on the subject, but there was much apparently contradictory information. Some of what they read was directed towards "getting the milk to flow." A little bit was directed towards controlling the flow. Very little was devoted to slowing down the flow. Harry's mother turned out to be a natural milk production facility, more than coping with the demand. Neither mother nor father was aware of this until after Harry had arrived. In the meantime, they read about exercises to "induce the flow of milk," and to "stimulate production." They shouldn't have bothered. But it kept them amused for weeks, especially Harry's father. The latter showed great interest in the subject and offered his assistance in the exercises on every conceivable occasion, and some occasions that were inconceivable. "Why use a mechanical pump?" he asked, but Victoria was disinclined to answer. Even if she gave every appearance of enjoying the exercises, she thought it might be morally wrong to enjoy it too much. So, she didn't want to appear too happy about it. Bull was not so inhibited. He was quite anxious to continue the exercises long after they were shown to be superfluous, for several years after.

The result was that Harry became adept at catching a stream of milk from a distance of several feet, or metres if you are French. Harry's mother didn't need to take part in the proceedings at all, a fact that Harry's father would sooner not have discovered, especially in the middle of the night. "Uunghh" would come from Harry's crib. No response from his mother. "UUNGHH," Harry would say. Again no response. Harry's father, wide awake, would wait for Victoria to attend to the matter. She never did. After the third cry, "UUUNGHHH," Harry's father could stand it no more. He would hasten to get Harry from the crib, gently place him next to his mother's breast, lie awake listening to the gurgles and waiting to change sides. He would roll his wife over and repeat the process, all apparently without waking his wife. Harry thrived on the treatment. So did Victoria. But Bull developed a gaunt, haunted look and a twitch in his left eye. Their friends grew very solicitous towards Victoria as Bull's eyes became more bloodshot and his mind began to wander. They didn't believe it was lack of sleep. Harry was obviously thriving. It could only be that Bull had become too fond of strong drink.

When Harry first decided to crawl he showed a certain tendency to do things backwards. His proud mother immediately called all her friends and relatives to come and watch Harry crawling. Victoria placed Harry on the rug in the centre of the room. He then proceeded to crawl backwards at great speed, disappearing underneath the chesterfield in short order. The family pretended not to notice. This was quite difficult because of the wailing from under the couch. It took three men and a boy to lift the couch to free him. Freeing Harry was an exercise in futility. For a moment he sat on the rug and smiled. Everybody ran for cover. By now his smiles, and what followed were famous. Satisfied with the reaction, Harry sat for a minute to get his breath back, then he exited at high speed backwards under the couch again, smiling a broad beaming smile.

No one was anxious to investigate that smile too closely, in consequence of which, it was tacitly agreed that the party should proceed without him. In the resulting hijinks, Harry was forgotten. He was rediscovered about three days later when his father went looking for a quarter lost down the crack of the couch. By this time Harry had missed the party anyway.

Harry was always a lover of music. Even during infancy, he had to have the radio on, all night. He would cry otherwise, or smile, which was worse. The radio stations were undiscriminating when it came to music. So was Harry. Noise of any kind was acceptable. Throughout his life he showed the same singular lack of discrimination in his choices of music. It didn't matter as long as there was noise. Sometimes classical, sometimes hard rock, whether western or blues, it was all the same to him. Noise. Once he complained when someone put on a progressive jazz recording, but he quickly came to accept it when he realized it was just another form of noise. Harry would lie in his crib and go "Uunghh," or on a particularly bad night, "Uuunnnghhh." Once the radio was on, set low, he would merrily go back to sleep. His rump in the air, his face turned sideways, sucking on his dummy, he would sleep happily until moved by hunger or something else. Then "Ungh!" he would say quietly. If there were no response, it would be louder next time, "Uunghh." And finally, "UUUNNGHH!" which always got a response.

Harry was a cheerful child, partly because all he had to do was smile and the world ran to do his bidding. There was some speculation that he had inherited his peculiar habits from his paternal grandfather. The latter maintained it was scurrilous propaganda, passed off onto a gullible family by foreign powers, no doubt imported for the purpose. The spies, according to Grandpa Flapper, had a mandate to destroy the moral fibre of Western Civilization by starting up totally unfounded rumours about upstanding pillars of the community, like him. Discrediting the populace, he maintained, would open doors to all sorts of nasty consequences, the destruction of the family unit, lack of respect for elders, especially Grandpa Flapper, and other things to make one shudder.

It will be quickly realized that Harry came upon his peculiar traits quite honestly, either through the mysterious genetic process, or the equally mysterious environmental process. Influenced by a father whom everyone believed was a nice fellow, maybe, a trifle weird, not too much in the way of good sense, but always good for a laugh; and a grandfather, whose sanity was sometimes questioned, it was a minor miracle that Harry grew up sane. There are some who maintain to this day that sanity is one trait no one would dare ascribe to Harry. Harry's character was no doubt formed, or misformed, depending on the point of view, during his infancy.

CHAPTER 12

Playpens, or Incidents in the Wild

After Harry learned to crawl, his parents obtained a playpen, at great expense. The objective was to keep him enclosed "for his own protection." His mother promptly let down one side of the playpen because "It wasn't fair to keep him penned up." No one consulted his father. This treatment probably coloured Harry's sense of justice and fair play. By now he had discovered that a smile would get him anything he wanted, and probably a great deal he didn't necessarily want at the moment, but that might come in handy later. Sometimes he would smile just to see what it might produce.

The days proceeded into weeks and the weeks into months until, at some stage, Harry decided he could walk. He was a trifle under a year old when he first held on to the side of his playpen and walked around it. He wasn't yet prepared to let anyone know he could talk, but he still smiled a lot. His parents took him for a short holiday into the wilds of North America. Grandfather Flapper's house was as close to the wilds as they could go on their budget, so they made do with that. They installed him in the house, safe and secure in his playpen. Harry's mother had long since given up the idea of leaving the side of the playpen down. She figured it was much better to keep Harry penned up than to let him loose, a sentiment not in any way shared by Harry.

With Harry safely asleep, Victoria and Bull went down to the swamp to watch the beavers, and do other things that required a little privacy. An hour or so later, they returned to the house. There had been no screams to alert them, but Harry had disappeared! Search as they might through the house, from closed door to closed door, no Harry could be found. Several hysterical minutes were wasted discussing the probability that Harry might have become the main item on a bear's menu. Several more minutes were wasted conjecturing the plausibility that he might have led the bears on a raid of Grandpa's garbage box. It was generally agreed that, though plausible knowing Harry, it was unlikely. So by a process of immutable logic they eventually concluded that Harry had gone exploring. His mother, reverting to the theory that he might make a tasty morsel for a hungry bear or raccoon or boll weevil (she wasn't entirely sure what a boll weevil might be, but concluded it must be dangerous as it got so much attention in the press), immediately started wailing for assistance in the search. Fortunately Grandpa and Grandma were out, or Harry might never have been found for all the commotion. Instead, Victoria and Bull decided to go look for him themselves.

Victoria ran screaming off one way to search through the bush at the side of the bog. Harry's father ran the opposite way towards the swamp, yelling "Harry, Har-ry." This was probably not effective under any circumstance, as Harry had never shown any inclination to come when he was called. Twenty minutes later, or perhaps several years, time is difficult to measure under these circumstances, his parents were racing back and forth through the bush at the side of the road calling for Harry. They would race away from each other screaming at the top of their lungs. Then they would turn and race towards each other, still screaming, passing each other to repeat the process.

Finally they were prepared to admit defeat and call in the army, the Navy, the airforce, the firemen, and even the Royal Canadian Mounted Police, on the theory that you could see more from the top of a horse. Just at that moment, Harry came around the bend of the road. He was having an erudite discussion with an old farmer about Revelations, or some other weighty topic, when he spotted his parents, now collapsed by the side of the road. As soon as he saw them Harry clammed up and refused to say another word. The two, farmer and small boy approached Bull and Victoria, the farmer with some degree of curiosity, Harry with some trepidation. Victoria was so relieved to see Harry that she forgot she was angry. Bull, feeling somewhat more guilty than Victoria, wasn't quite so forgiving, until the farmer, deducing that he was face-to-face with Harry's parents, introduced himself. "Ah hopes y'all don' min' de youngun 'n Ah were jist cumparin' notes on t' proper way t'grow rutabagas. T'waren't every un w'at knows how ta grow dem t'ings. But Ah t'inks we'all got it all werked out 'bout now. De young lad wanted ta cum home y'all knows."

Then he waited for some rejoinder. Neither Bull nor Victoria spoke the language, though, so they stood by helplessly, looking at Harry for guidance. Harry didn't have any to offer. The old man went on, "Y'all wantta travel wid a mite o' care now, ya hear, 'cause der be a few bears about. But ya won't cum ta eny harm wid dat youngun as he knows war dey be." Then he turned to Harry and had a brief, but quiet discussion that neither Bull nor Victoria could either hear or fathom. Harry was quite obviously saying something of importance as the old man listened attentively, then they shook hands and parted, the old man making his way slowly back up the road and around the bend.

Harry, now with his parents' full attention, began his own discussion. He folded his hands in front and began a longish discourse on important matters. His parents could tell it was important by the way Harry spoke, but they had no idea what it was that he said. So Victoria grasped his hands firmly and urged him back up the road to his Grandpa Flapper's farm, resolving then and there to curb Harry's propensity for wandering before he might take it into his head to join the Navy, too. Bull went off to other pursuits, still puzzling over the way Harry had managed to communicate with the old man. "Was it possible that Harry was actually talking? Did he only talk to others? How was it that the old man seemed to understand him?" Since Bull couldn't answer the questions he decided to forget the matter, and concentrate on more important things, like fishing.

That was the end of Harry's freedom for some little while. From that time and for many months, he was tethered. This, too, may have coloured his outlook on life. With his harness in place and a stiff leather lead secured to some stationary object, like a house, Harry's meanderings were confined to a ten foot radius. Harry would stand and run as fast as his little fat legs would carry him, towards freedom. Coming to the end of his tether, his legs would shoot straight out. Down he would go on his bottom. His dummy would go spurting off into the distance, and he would begin to smile. With malice.

Crowds gathered to watch the fun. Harry would go on smiling, grimmer and grimmer. With his little arms crossed, he would wait for the world to come to heel. And it usually did. Eventually, when the tension reached unbearable proportions, and the crowd had moved back in case of an explosion, someone would lose heart, usually his father, and return the dummy. Harry would then get up and deliver a sermon on some profound subject in an equally profound language. After that he would wander off to inspect the premises, making disparaging remarks until someone should bring him milk and cookies.

So it was at this crucial stage in his development that Harry's parents decided to introduce him to the wonders of nature and the joy of canoeing. As they loved to go out in the canoe, they reasoned, so should Harry. Off they would go to Newnham for the weekend. Harry was safely tethered, much to his disgust. His Grandmothers and Grandfathers would make a great fuss over him. Harry not only condoned that sort of thing but actively encouraged it.

Victoria and Bull, with a reluctant Harry, would head for the swamp as soon as politeness would allow. Harry's mother loved frogs, especially bullfrogs. With Harry gently ensconced between her knees, and she, gently ensconced between her husband's knees, they would set out in the canoe. Over to the swamp they would go. There, Bull would catch bullfrogs and let them loose in the canoe. Harry's mother cooed with delight. Harry's father, basking in his wife's approval would catch more and more bullfrogs. Harry showed no enthusiasm for the endeavour.

The concentrated noise from the bullfrogs, all issuing from the same place, caused great confusion in the bullfrog community. Soon the bullfrogs would start to swim en masse towards the canoe so they wouldn't miss the party. Bull would scoop them up and hand them to Victoria, who commented on their relative cuteness. The Bullfrogs were much more interested in the food and drink, though, so ignored such compliments. Blowing themselves up to their most impressive size, they would emit the deepest croak they could find, thereby establishing their relative degree of macho in the bullfrog community.

Eventually, with hoppers all over the canoe, Bull and Victoria sat back to enjoy their success. But, it gradually dawned on them that Harry preferred to examine the wildlife one at a time, for preference. He hadn't yet established the order of bullfrogs in his mind, nor had he decided to like them particularly. Some he actively disliked. He especially deplored bullfrogs that were the same size as he was. An especially large specimen greeted Harry with the same warmth as its next dinner. Harry was distinctly uneasy, and took pains to let his parents know in the most effective way he knew. As the smell became more noticeable, Victoria and Bull reluctantly decided to call it quits for the day. They discussed the matter with their bullfrog friends, all of whom agreed that the party was winding down anyway. Besides, the supply of bugs had dried up in the noonday sun.

So Father Flapper gently placed each bullfrog over the side of the canoe. The bullfrogs, released, all returned to their lilypads, "rivetting" or "harumphing," depending on their size and standing in the bullfrog hierarchy. To this day Harry will occasionally "rivet" in sympathy, according to some long forgotten primeval ritual dragged from his subconscious. Over the course of many such trips the bullfrogs came to look forward to the diversion from their daily activities. One weekend towards the end of the season, Bull and Victoria couldn't get their car started, so reluctantly cancelled their trip to the swamp. The bullfrogs, disappointed when they didn't appear, set off for Grandma's back stoop to inquire into the problem.

Grandma, who wasn't expecting about a thousand bullfrogs to descend upon her back stoop, came over queer several times before she got up enough courage to go out and address the throng. Once started, it seemed that she had a natural gift for empathy with the frog community. It wasn't long before she was elected their spokesman on the local swamp committee. Harry wasn't consulted on these matters. He would have disapproved. His attitude to frogs, especially pushy bullfrogs, was always somewhat ambivalent. As a teenager he occasionally wore a frog tee-shirt, saying "Save the frogs." But his heart wasn't in it.

CHAPTER 13

Automobilia

Harry's parents got a car. To be more precise, it was a wreck, disguised as a car, a little 1953 Ford Consul station wagon, "off-white." It used to be white but unspeakable things had happened to the car and its paint. So it was said to be off-white. The car occasionally started when the starter was depressed. More often it didn't. Once started, it rocked violently for the first little while, about an hour, until it was thoroughly warmed up. Then it could be coaxed to go. Harry loved it. Two minutes in the car gently moving up and down in time with the engine, or rocking from side to side according to the car's own premises, and Harry was asleep. He was guaranteed to sleep until the motion of the car ceased.

There were a few idiosyncrasies the car developed over the short time it remained in the Flapper fold. When the car was turned towards the left, the horn would sound. "Aaa-oooo-ga," went the horn as the Flappers turned left into the church parking lot on Sundays. Little old ladies in their Sunday-go-to-meeting best frowned. The two senior Flappers ducked lest they be recognized. Harry shrieked with delight, guaranteeing recognition. The minister would scuttle out of the church, followed by his entire congregation. No one wanted to miss the excitement. The Flappers would give up and exit the car with as much dignity as they could muster. Everyone applauded. No one knew why.

When the car turned right, the lights came on. This rarely presented a problem on sunny days, as few people noticed. When several turns were called for in heavy traffic, people would stop to stare.

On one occasion, Bull was driving in heavy traffic, fortunately alone, when a left turn was called for. He tried to hustle in behind a great, noisy, battered dump trunk. As he made the turn the horn sounded. The truck stopped. A burly, tattooed hulk emerged from the driver's side of the truck. The Hulk didn't so much step down from the cab as step up. Another emerged from the other side. Each rolled up his sleeves. Bull hung on to the steering wheel like grim death, or maybe awaiting that fate. Without a word each grabbed a bumper and hoisted. Up, up went the little off-white car. Down it came crashing onto the flatbed of the truck amongst all the other rubbish. Without a word both men got back into the cab. Half an hour later they backed into the dump, hoisted the flatbed, and let the little car slide into the muck. Teeth clenched together, eyes on the mound in front of him, Bull still clutched the steering wheel. The truck drove off. It took three days to dig out the car, and another two weeks before Victoria would allow Bull into the same room. The aroma, she said, was overpowering.

Keeping the car on the road proved to be an exacting task, well beyond Bull's immediate capabilities. As time passed, the gentle noises from the engine, which lulled Harry to sleep, seemed to become louder. And louder.

Eventually they were a roar rendering conversation in the car impossible. But Harry still slept.

All over the city, there are people who still talk about that car, or its eccentric driver. That was the fellow with dark glasses who wore a hat pulled down over his eyes, and seemed barely able to see over the top of the steering wheel. The only real problem he had was depressing the clutch with his left knee, or the accelerator with his right knee. His wife was dressed similarly, her feet cramped under the dash. No one seemed to recognize them as long as they kept going.

Still, Harry's parents loved the old wreck. "Let's go out in the car," his mother would say, "so Harry will get some sleep." Harry's father, nerves at screaming pitch due to lack of sleep, clutching his coffee between clenched knuckles, would mutely agree. By now they had it down to a fine art. Once in the car, accelerate away from the neighbourhood as quickly as possible. Go in a straight line. After a certain length of time, when Harry was fast asleep, turn the car around, making sure that it was only right turns, so the horn wouldn't sound and wake him. Head back home in a straight line. Turn right into the parking spot. Stick him in bed before he woke up. Turn on the radio. Go to bed, exhausted.

One day Harry took a bit longer than usual to get to sleep. Thirty miles down the highway, he began to show signs of flagging. So did the car. A red light on the dash informed the occupants that the oil pressure had disappeared. The car began to make grinding noises just as the lights on the dash began to flash on and off menacingly. Bull decided it would be better to send Victoria and Harry home by some other means, lest the car explode all around them. Victoria readily agreed, so long as it was by first class. Bull gave up and hired a taxi for them.

Bull was then left to his own devices to get home. By now great clouds of steam were coming out from under the front of the engine. From the rear billowed clouds of black smoke. There was a rather bad smell accompanying the latter. This at least had one desirable effect: it kept the tailgaters at a respectable distance. The little car moved off down the road in its own cloud, confounding onlookers as to its identity.

Bull decided to take the back roads home. The little car, he felt, wasn't up to highway speeds. Also, he didn't want to be in a car travelling too fast when it exploded. The explosion, when it did come, was in the middle of the main intersection in town. The backfire was so strong that it blew the doors open, the hood up, and the hubcaps off, to go meandering along the road all on their own. Bull, blown out through the top, came down through the awning of the corner market, crushing several cartons of live chickens, releasing their occupants.

The chickens set off to enjoy their new-found freedom, cackling and flapping their wings. The customers, frightened half to death by the sight of so many chickens on the hoof, went screaming for the exits. The owner's daughter, caught behind the counter in the resultant melee was screaming oaths at Bull in various languages. Bull, mistaking her cries of rage as cries for help because the building was falling, picked her up over his shoulder and looked for the exit. That was the picture offered as he eventually made his way to the door, the girl's rear end showed over his shoulder, while she pummelled his backbone. The picture, with accompanying story, suitably embellishing this phenomenal act of bravery following the explosion, featured on the front page of the City Times.

According to the report in the Times, an explosion of unknown origin had demolished the car and a substantial portion of the market. The hero of the day had escaped without being identified. The young lady, blinded by the photographer's flash, lost sight of him. Then she had her hands full rounding up the herd of stray chickens before they embarked on another stampede. Bull figured he had better get home to Victoria with his version of the proceedings before someone else gave her a more inaccurate version. Throwing the hubcaps into the trunk and slamming the doors shut, he left for home at a somewhat faster speed than prudence dictated.

Bull decided in the circumstances to sell the car. Not only was it not running true to form, but he was also a little worried lest it be identified with the explosion in town. The first wrecking yard refused to have it on the premises. It was necessary to turn left into the yard. The owner, bending over to extract a stubborn part from some other wreck, clipped his head badly on the wreck's hood as Bull's horn sounded. Bull didn't wait around for outright rejection. He took it as a matter of course.

At the next yard, Bull parked on the street. The toothpick-sucking owner of the yard enquired in a state of disbelief, "Is that thing drivable?"

"Yes" didn't seem truthful, but was given anyway. The owner was suspicious. He hitched up his belt and said "Show me."

Fortunately, it was a bright sunny day. The lights didn't show. The red dash light had long since burned out. Four right turns later, and the owner's suspicions were allayed. "Twenty-five bucks," he grunted.

"Done," said Bull and left quickly, cash in hand.

CHAPTER 14

A Sister, and Other Problems

About two years after Harry's birth, his smile was dented somewhat by the arrival of a sister. The stork wasn't particularly helpful, leaving the matter entirely up to Victoria. Harry discovered that his sister's smile was attended with feverish haste. His parents did not wish to tempt fate a second time. Besides, they had since recovered stock with their neighbours and didn't wish to disturb that happy state.

Both Bull and Victoria were greatly concerned that Harry not be traumatized by the arrival of his baby sister. They agreed to foster as much attention on him as on the baby. Waking Harry out of a sound sleep to change his diapers and burp him along with sister Charlotte, wasn't Harry's idea of a great time. That plan was soon abandoned.

To counter-attack his sister's plan to take over control of the family, Harry decided it was high time he started to speak. He quickly developed a style of speech guaranteed to attract attention. He articulated each syllable so there could be no misunderstanding of what he wanted. Harry's father helped. He would tell Harry to "Say Daddy. Come on, now," Bull would say, "Daddy, Da-a-ad-dy."   Harry might reply,

"I don't want to play with you now, Father, I'm investigating the lower orders of lepidoptera." Harry's father would then wander off to play with someone else, likely Harry's mother.

Harry showed remarkably little interest in his sister. If he couldn't eat it or roll it around the floor he wasn't much interested. Besides, he had other pursuits to follow. He had discovered plastic animals. Tyrannosaurus Rex, Brontosaurus, and other equally horrific demons of another era became his special interest. He would sit on his parents' bed patiently asking the names of each, patiently repeating them until he had got it right. Out of this he developed a remarkable memory. Not much patience, but a truly remarkable memory. On one occasion, his father took him to the doctor for a checkup. Harry's mother was otherwise engaged. She was attempting to stem the flow of milk, with the aid of Charlotte. Harry, then three, sat on his father's lap, greatly amused by the efforts of a gregarious four year old, also waiting. The four-year-old was displaying his knowledge to a very proud daddy. He was pointing out animals in a children's book, "Horsey, cow, ducky, camel."

It was too much for Harry. He leaned over to confront the little fellow. "That's not just a camel," he said, "that's a dromedary." Even then Harry wouldn't suffer fools gladly. A hush descended upon the waiting room. The four-year-old was indignant. The father quietly closed the book. Harry began to discuss the possibility of evolution of camels, dromedaries, llamas, etc. from a common ancestry among the dinosaurs. He enquired of another child whether pterodactyls might have evolved to turkey buzzards. No one, not even his father, was prepared to discuss the matter with him.

When Harry was four he was led astray by a woman. The experience was so traumatic that he never recovered. The little girl down the street took a great liking to Harry's shiny new tricycle. She didn't much like Harry, but she was willing to put up with him for a ride on his tricycle. He suffered from the same vehicle problem for many years. One day she was a little bored. There was no one else to play with, so she commandeered Harry and his tricycle. Harry, ever anxious to please, and not a little flattered by the attentions of this exotic female, agreed. She wanted to visit the stores. The going got a bit sticky through the mud behind the plaza, so they abandoned the vehicle. Harry, in love, showed no judgement whatever. In that respect, he never changed. Off they went without their transportation.

When Father Flapper arrived home from work he was met by a frantic Mother Flapper. It was getting dark, and Harry had been missing for four hours by now. Father Flapper set out across the parking lot towards the fields and the plaza beyond. Eventually he came across Harry, abandoned by his lady love. She had gone off in search of a more exciting companion. He was a tearful shadow of his former self, no bicycle, no ladylove, muddy, dishevelled and distraught. The abandoned tricycle was found some distance away the following day. Apparently his fickle girlfriend had ditched Harry in order to filch his tricycle. Since then, Harry has not often shared his vehicles. Only when he was in love. This occurred at periodic intervals of about six months throughout his early childhood and even thereafter.

Victoria would soon come to recognize the signs. His eyes would develop a far-off look. His usually agile brain would cease to function. He would put his socks on backwards, as well as his underwear. The latter caused him no end of trouble when he went into the washroom. At first he would think that something dreadful had happened to him in the night. He would scream with anguish, bringing his mother on the run. After being reassured, with the problem corrected, he would repeat the whole process again the following day.

CHAPTER 15

Terrorizing the Medics

Harry was always a quiet child, well behaved and friendly, but not too athletic. During one of his frequent bouts with a cold, the family doctor recommended that he see a specialist. The specialist was appalled at the state of his constitution. He recommended the immediate removal of Harry's tonsils. Harry was soon scheduled to go into the hospital. At first he wasn't keen on the idea. He listened with detached interest while his parents attempted to explain the whole procedure to him. After asking some questions, Harry came to the conclusion that it might be a worthwhile venture. He was especially looking forward to the ice cream and custard pudding afterwards.

However, not quite satisfied with the explanations offered, so far, Harry insisted that the entire medical process be thoroughly explained. His parents, not very well educated themselves on medical matters brought home several tomes on medicine, its theory and practice. Harry pored over these, checking out the diagrams to make sure they agreed with his own ideas on the scheme of things. He became engrossed in the study of anatomy, especially of the female form, until his mother caught him at it. She was indignant, but by then it was too late. Harry's knowledge of the subject of reproduction and other such taboo topics had grown in leaps and bounds. His father was all for giving Harry his old copies of Playboy, but Victoria wouldn't allow it.

Without any justification whatever, Victoria decided that Harry was going to be a doctor. Acting on that premise she went out to buy him a little doctor's kit, complete with stethoscope, gown and thermometer. Harry's first attempt to compare the anatomy diagrammed in the book with that of his sister was thwarted when the latter took great exception to the proceedings. Harry took himself off in a huff. His next effort had him examining the little girl next door in rather more detail than her mother wished. Harry was quite indignant that his professional integrity might be impugned. Certainly the little girl, who had actively encouraged him in his examination, showed no reluctance whatever to repeat the experiment in more private circumstances. There is no telling just how far Harry's education might have advanced if the time hadn't arrived for him to be carted off to hospital, with his little doctor's kit and all.

After his mother had been pried loose and shipped home, Harry's first day in the hospital proved to be a revolution. The revolution was not a quiet affair. Harry started by hopping out of bed to examine the charts of each of his neighbours. He had on his little doctor's coat, with his stethoscope around his neck. When the night nurse came on duty, she noticed Harry's empty bed. He was down the ward tut-tutting and hmphing over the charts. She was a trifle unnerved by this behaviour in a four year old, but figured he belonged in the empty bed.

She came swooping down on Harry, but he was ready for her. He fixed her with a beady eye and suggested that the patient he was examining needed attention much more than did himself. The patient, a small tot of about four, in the middle of a seizure, was making little gasping noises. Harry calmly recommended an appropriate medication and suggested that oxygen might be called for. He waited for the nurse to rush about attending to it. Recognizing the voice of authority, she immediately assumed that Harry was a small medical person and dashed off to do his bidding. On returning, she asked him rather diffidently whether he would sign for it. Harry was quite happy to practice his writing at anytime, so scribbled his name all over the page. As his signature was only marginally less legible than any of the other doctors she knew, she thought nothing of it. The crisis over, they continued their round together. She enquired whether he might be a new intern. But Harry was not to be drawn. At the ward door he politely excused himself, leaving the nurse to continue her rounds herself. Harry went to bed.

The following morning, at the handover from night shift to the day shift, there was a very confused account of the crisis of the night before and the strange new intern, only three feet tall, or so. The day nurses took it in their stride when Harry appeared sometime after breakfast had been served. He was in his little coat, armed with his stethoscope around his neck. It seemed that his reputation had gone on before him. He was accorded all due respect as he slipped in to the elevator and asked with a certain modicum of arrogance if the nearest big person would kindly push the surgery floor button for him, please, as he was too short.

And yes, he allowed, it was a darn nuisance being so short, but modern medicine being what it was, would no doubt find a remedy for the condition shortly.

The operating theatre was a revelation to Harry. Here too, his reputation for quick thinking of the night before had gone on before him. There was a restrained murmur of respect as he calmly climbed up to sit on a cart to watch the operation in progress. The attending surgeon, was so startled at his appearance that he slipped. Harry's brief comment, "Oops!" had the surgeon frantically calling for clamps and pressure, here, please. Harry was only too happy to oblige, leaning over to lend a hand and commenting on the clearly distended appendix in the surgeon's clever hands.

Assisting with the operation was about all the time Harry had before he realized he was needed elsewhere. He excused himself. When politely requested to return in the afternoon, he reluctantly declined as, he said, he had a previous commitment. Returning to the ward, he discarded the tools of the medical man and climbed up the end bedpost into his bed, where he was found shortly thereafter by his mother, come to comfort him before his surgery. Harry thought about it for a time and decided he had a very good idea of what was about to happen. However, he declined to send his mother off for fear of hurting her feelings.

Harry wasn't feeling particularly communicative that evening when he accompanied the night nurse on her rounds. He indicated to her that he had a sore throat but that it wasn't catching. He felt he was on safe grounds with that assertion. He recommended a little aspirin here, and a drop of penicillin there. His writing, little more than a scribble was easily deciphered by the nurse, fortunately, as in each case she had a good idea as to what might be required without any input from Harry. In each case he would happily scribble his name, having practised for some time to ensure repeatability. He figured that the letters didn't much matter anyway as he had never learned how to spell his name, let alone write it. Anyhow the nurse seemed quite happy about it.

The following day Harry went home, a different person. He missed the storm that followed his little adventure. The parents of the little fellow saved on Harry's first round thought to commend his performance to the hospital administrator and to give some small donation to the hospital in consequence. The administrator accepted all due praise, then set about to try to find this mysterious small intern who had acted with such promptness. He couldn't decipher Harry's signature. Neither could anyone else. A few unworthies, professionally jealous, of course, thought the writing to be no better than a child's scribble. The night nurse, called in to describe him, had by this time attributed all sorts of miracles to him.

Having made no sense out of the matter, the administrator sought to suppress any suggestion that a Higher Power might have taken a hand. It came as a shock to discover that Harry had also invaded the operating theatre, acting in a timely fashion to assist the attending surgeon to save another life. The grateful patient, previously apprised of his good fortune in having not one, but two outstanding surgeons attending, and that the little visitor had virtually saved his life, leaked the matter to the press. He felt that the city should be justly proud of the talent to be found at their hospital, and meant that everyone should hear about it.

The administrator, called upon to produce this brilliant new intern was quick to note that he had gone on to a another calling, but that they were grateful he had stopped in for a short time. The nurse wasn't quite so reticent. Her story, by now embellished beyond recognition, guaranteed front page coverage. The miraculous wonders that had occurred at the hospital drew donations and gifts, to say nothing of prospective clients, rich and poor, from all over the country.

Victoria wondered aloud to Bull whether this wonderful intern had been responsible for Harry's quick recovery. Harry decided to say nothing about his part in the matter. However, he did show considerably more animation than previously. The quiet child who would sit on the floor watching cartoons in front of the TV, had disappeared. The first his parents discovered this was when Father Flapper walked in the door from work that first day Harry was home and found him climbing the trellis. Trellis-climbing proved to be quite a diversion for both Harry and his parents. Harry quite enjoyed it. His parents didn't show nearly as much enthusiasm for the sport, though. It was preceded by a period of calm, following which he would bolt for the trellis and climb up hand over hand, like a monkey.

The Flapper parents were glad to move when the opportunity presented itself. The trellis proved to be too much of a temptation for Harry. They should have been concerned about the possibility advancing, into the tree stage, say, but they were too short-sighted to consider it.

CHAPTER 16

Harry's Fifth Birthday Party

Harry's hapless mother planned his fifth birthday party with the utmost attention to detail. She determined the progress of the party from start to finish, particularly the finish. She carefully chose the guest list, especially the little girls, one of whom might possibly make a match for Harry. She chose the party favours to complement the children they were intended for. And figured out each game, according to how long it would take and how many prizes might be bestowed to ensure at the end of the day that each child had a favour. It wasn't her fault the party didn't quite match up to the planning.

At the start, a dozen mothers each dropped a little boy at the front door, each one ill at ease in his ill-fitting suit. Each mother waved her offspring away then made good on her escape, thankful for the respite from her offspring for an afternoon. Each little fellow, duly, if somewhat wistfully, handed over to the immediate care of Harry a gaily-wrapped gift. As each present came, Harry would shake it surreptitiously to establish whether or not it could be a puzzle, one of those with two thousand, four hundred and twenty three and a half pieces. Anything that sounded like a puzzle went in one pile, ready for burning, later. All the others went into another pile to be investigated at some more opportune moment, when there might be no other witnesses to the event.

Another dozen or so mothers each deposited a little girl on the doorstep, then fled. Each little girl, each with a bow in her hair, stood about in a party dress, looking innocent. In reality there was in each little girl's psyche, a Machiavellian personality waiting to get out. The boys and girls remained apart until the girls should decide who was to get which boy and for how long. Harry adored girls but was never too sure what one did with them. So he ignored them until he could think of something worthwhile.

Harry's mother, Victoria, tried to find ways to keep the children entertained until all the important relatives had arrived. She sat them all around in a circle on the living room floor to play games. But every time a little girl happened to catch the eye of a little boy, the latter would turn away, blushing with embarrassment. Girls were all right so long as they could be attacked singly, with tadpoles or snakes or spiders, but when it came to girls in bunches, there was no question who would be the losers.

The birthday party might have been a tame affair were it not for the arrival of Great Aunt Claudine. Perhaps that isn't quite true: it was the combination of Aunt Claudine and Grandma Flapper that livened things up. Aunt Claudine stood six feet tall and five feet wide in her old fashioned elasticized stockings. To hide her bulk she wore voluminous dresses, a tactic she had discovered as a teenager and continued unrelentingly for the next sixty years or so.

It was difficult to believe that Grandma and Aunt Claudine were sisters. Even their speech was different. Aunt Claudine rattled along with a rapid jargon few but her close relatives could understand, her choice of language rarely fit for the ears of children. Grandma spoke with dignity in a refined accent. In looks they differed sharply, too. In contrast to Aunt Claudine's barrel shape, Grandma, grey-haired since her late twenties, was skinny and diminutive. Fair-haired Claudine was huge by comparison, outweighing both her parents together by more than fifty pounds. When it came to strong drink, three ounces usually guaranteed that Claudine, would slide under the table in an alcoholic stupor, whereas the same amount would barely register on Grandma.

In a way it was her own fault that Great Aunt Claudine wound up in the back of Grandpa's pick-up truck. When Grandpa had reluctantly asked her if she would like a ride to the party, telling her that she would have to ride in the truck bed, her hearing aid battery was on the point of demise. So Claudine, who always privately considered that Grandpa had married the wrong sister, thought he had said something else entirely, although it had taken him a lot of years to get around to the asking. When Grandpa helped her up the makeshift stairs into the back of the truck, Claudine thought it a bit silly as they could easily have repaired to her king size bed to live it up in comfort. Operating on the premise that it would be an exciting new experience, she went along with the idea until she was safely seated with her back to the cab. When Grandma appeared on the scene, Claudine realized that all was not as it should be, and started to make unlady-like noises. Grandma Flapper, who had noticed Claudine's coy glances at Grandpa on the odd occasion, had a good idea what Claudine had been thinking. She took one look at the indignant Claudine in the back of the truck, then fled in haste to the front cab, ruthlessly suppressing an attack of giggles. There she took out her little mickey of restorative, kept in her purse for just such an occasion. Grandma Flapper felt much better after a hefty swallow.

To get Great Aunt Claudine to the party safely, Grandpa Flapper had wedged her between his mammoth tool box and several cement blocks he carried around "for traction." It might have been more comfortable for her if Grandpa had had the presence of mind to sweep out the remains of last year's Christmas tree first, but the thought had never occurred to him. When they hit the first bump at the bottom of the driveway Aunt Claudine started to holler. She had been wedged in so well that she couldn't get at the pine needles pricking her bottom. The truck rattled and jangled along, the transmission making alarming noises, while the gear box screamed with distemper whenever it was disturbed. Conversation in the cab was almost impossible. Claudine's yelling from the back didn't make too much difference.

The driveway into the junior Flapper household almost proved too much for the truck. As it hit the curb on the way in, Claudine popped loose from her position between the blocks and the tool box, landing with a crash on the tail boards, causing the front wheels to lose contact with the driveway. This effectively destroyed Grandpa's ability to steer the vehicle. The truck bounced over the curb, did a sidewise skitter through Victoria's flower garden, taking out the rose trellis on the way, and came to rest by the big front picture window under the awed eyes of the entire junior Flapper clan. Harry's father stood admiring the way his father handled the truck. Gronk thought the truck might come right on through the window. He retreated to the sanctuary of the back yard with speed. Victoria was the only one who treated the matter calmly. After almost six years of marriage in the family she had come to expect that anything could happen.

Bull and Gronk helped their father to roll Great Aunt Claudine off the tail gate of the truck so that she landed unharmed directly onto the front steps. By this time Claudine had been given to understand by Grandpa that her August presence was needed to establish the correct tone for Harry's birthday party. Somewhat mollified, she allowed herself to be led into the midst of the festivities, while Bull and his father tried ineffectually to restore the roses around the shattered trellis. Grandma, snorting indelicately into her handkerchief to cover her laughter, set off to have a word in private with Harry. Neither Harry nor his Grandmother ever let on the nature of their business, although it likely had something to do with money.

After Grandma and Grandpa Flapper arrived, the party came to life. Great Aunt Claudine was soon ensconced in the corner armchair, while Uncle Gronk, even bigger than Claudine, sat happily rocking beside her in the old platform rocker. Victoria herded the children downstairs to the basement playroom to supervise such birthday games as pin-the-tail-on-the-donkey, leaving the adults for a time to their own devices. It was only later that Victoria realized she should have supervised the adult games and left the children to fend for themselves.

Grandma investigated the birthday punch and decided it had no punch to it. She attempted to remedy the situation by surreptitiously pouring a bottle of vodka into it. It made a pleasant drink that Grandma thought could easily be improved with the addition of another bottle. Well satisfied with her efforts she took up an oversized draught of the concoction for herself, leaving her husband and son to fend for themselves.

Comfortably ensconced back in her chair, Grandma thought it only politic to initiate a conversation with her sister. Such conversations only made sense to the participants, and then rarely as a form of mutual understanding.

"What do you think of the party?" shouted Grandma.

"Parting? Who's leaving?" shouted Claudine.

"No, No!" screamed Grandma in vexation. "The party. The party!"

"Party?" replied Claudine at the top of her lungs. "Which party? Them stoopid Lib'rals or them stoopid Conservat'ves? Them damn Conservat'ves hain't no good fer nuthin', and them damn Lib'rals hain't no good fer nuthin' neither. There ain't no one else! What ch'a want ta go talkin' 'bout pol'tics fer at Harry's birthday party anyway? Whyn'tcha do sumpthin' useful fer a change 'n' get me a drink afore I expire?"

"You old fool," Grandma screamed back. "You wouldn't know a party if you fell in one. Why don't you get yourself a hearing aid that works so you know what's going on around you." And in a quieter tone, she said, "After that I need a small restorative," pouring herself another glass of punch.

She also poured the same amount for Claudine. Handing it to her sister with a small, grim smile, Grandma remarked in dulcet tones, "Try that on for size, you old goat."

"Coat?" screamed Claudine, accepting the glass. "It ain't cold. Why on earth would I need a coat. Sometimes I think you hain't got the brains you was born with. It's summer fer Pete's sake."

She took a great gulp of the punch, then spluttered, "What the Hell did ya put in this stuff anyhow. Who taught you how ta make a drink?"

Grandma, practically hoarse by now, screamed back, "There's two bottle of liquor in it, you old fart!" Then, realizing she had let out a secret she swiftly checked to see whether any of the others had noticed. The references to Liberals and Conservatives had led the men into other byways of conversation by this time. As well, the screaming matches between the two sisters were legendary. They didn't notice Grandma's gaff, so she quietly returned to her chair to await events.

Claudine took another gulp of her drink to check it out, then yelled back, "Whad a ya mean I'm doin' a lot a bickerin'. And it weren't me what farted. It's this damn drink what smells." To prove the point she finished it off and handed it to Gronk. "Make yerself useful fer once in yer worthless life," she hollered. "An' this time make sure its got somethin' in it." Gronk shot off with the glass, refilled it, then handed it back to his aunt with exaggerated care.

Gronk and his father stuck to chilled lime and lemon soda. Grandma, now thoroughly enraged, stalked off to refill her glass, leaving the field wide open for Claudine, who tossed down the last of her punch just as Bull came through the door to gape at her. "Why, Aunt Claudine, I was just about to offer you a real drink. You don't need to settle for non alcoholic punch. I can't remember ever seeing you touch the stuff before."

Only one word made any sense to Claudine, "Alcoholic," she screeched, "I ain't no alcoholic! Just gimme a drink an' I'll prove I can hol' my liquor."

At that instant, from down below came the sound of frightened, childish screams. Everyone except Great Aunt Claudine headed for the basement. That great lady sat in her seat looking offended. "What'd I shay?" she asked. "Why'ed they all go whishout me?" She made valiant efforts to struggle out of the armchair. But the grip of the alcohol proved too strong.

From below, Victoria's screams had now subsided as Harry had whomped the spider with the flat of his hand. Great Aunt Claudine relaxed into the chair, further and further, until finally, unconscious, she accomplished what she couldn't do while conscious, she slid out of the chair with a house-rocking thump and rolled to the centre of the room to stare upwards, catatonically, at the ceiling. The children were first up the stairs to investigate the noise. They all circled around Great Aunt Claudine.

"Ith thee dead?" asked a little girl, hopefully.

Harry approached his Great Aunt Claudine close enough to get a whiff of her breath and quickly backed off. Meeting his mother's eyes he said conspiratorially, "She prob'ly just fell asleep when she was coming downstairs to see the spider." At that instant a stentorian gurgle started in the back of Claudine's throat, rumbled around through her vocal chords for a bit, reaching an ominous crescendo, drowning out all the other noises in the room, before it stopped, leaving an eerie silence. Everyone stopped breathing in sympathy, waiting to see whether Claudine's breathing would resume. And when it did, with a little chirp, everyone began to breathe again, as the rumble started below.

The little girl was not yet willing to concede the point. "Are you thure?" she asked, doubtfully. "Thee thoundth dead, 'n if thee'th athleep why are her eyeth thtill open?"

She continued, "My Grampy fell down while he wath chathing Mith Harrithon aroun' the big tree. He gurgled jutht like that an' thtared up Mith Harrithon'th thkirt with hith eyeth open. Grammy thaid he wath dead an' it were a blethin'. I don't think thee liked Mith Harrithon too much."

Harry, looked to his mother for assistance. However, even Victoria couldn't think of a plausible rejoinder to this revelation. So she tried diversionary tactics: "I know," she said, "why don't we have some cake and cookies and a nice drink."

The children were clearly caught in a quandary. The girls were all for staying to watch Claudine. Food quickly became a higher priority for the boys, though. The girls were torn between the boys and Claudine. Finally, reluctantly, they allowed themselves to be persuaded away.

Harry then proceeded to shepherd all his friends into the living room for cake and cookies and punch. The kids took to the punch right away. Most of them couldn't remember much about the rest of the party. All they could remember was that, except for the headache the next day, it was the greatest birthday party they ever attended.

Later, as each parent came to pick up a child, now asleep in Harry's bedroom, Harry would solemnly offer each a glass of punch. The respective parents had great difficulty assimilating the fact that their normally irrepressible offspring could fall asleep in the middle of a party. After a glass of punch or two, they had a better idea. The parents waited a respectable time after the drinks. Eventually Claudine's wide-eyed sleep unnerved them; and her snore made conversation difficult. They found that they couldn't compete during the rumble, and all conversation ceased as the snore crescendoed to its climax, when everyone held their breath waiting for the snore to start again. So the parents thankfully escaped under the pretext that their still-sleeping offspring needed to be put to bed. Then they dashed home to see what they might be able to do about increasing the family while they had the chance.

Harry wasn't having any punch himself, but was determined to give it all away before he succumbed to temptation. He calmly accepted his role in life: to take charge of events and order them to his own satisfaction. Even at the age of five he had come to recognize that if something were to be done right he had better do it himself, whether it was the killing of spiders or the serving of drinks. He certainly didn't want any help from his parents, especially his father.

CHAPTER 17

Sheep at the Snugglebunny Inn

The summer Harry turned six, his father took a job in Annespoint, out East, "for a year or two, at the most." Victoria consoled herself with the thought that it was only a temporary arrangement and would soon be rectified. Harry's maternal Grandma elicited the promise that it would only be for two years, at most. Everyone believed this little piece of fiction, even Harry's father. For the next ten years or so, Bull was heard to say, "It's a great place to bring up kids." Victoria did not comment on the matter, at least not out loud. Grandmother Sharp did comment on the matter, often. Loudly, too. Or whenever she could convince grandfather to go visiting. That was the one good thing about this venture. It broadened Harry's horizons, also those of his grandparents.   Bull, always short of cash, looked for means to effect the transfer of his family and all his worldly goods over the thousand miles or so of Cross-Canada Highway, as cheaply as possible. The company agreed to pay the freight on the worldly goods, but not the family. So, without consulting Victoria, Bull decided on a plan to "camp out in the car, stopping for nights along the wayside." Victoria, apprised of this plan, consulted with her family on alternatives.

Victoria's father unearthed a tent-trailer that had long since seen its best years of service slip by unnoticed. The trailer arrived on the day of departure, leaving Bull little time to investigate the gift or celebrate his good fortune. However, he did suspect that the trailer might be a little "ratty about the edges," particularly as, when he opened it, he discovered the nests of long-dead mice hidden in the folds of the canvas. He knew they were mice nests because the remains of the mice were also hidden in the folds. Bull discreetly removed the bodies, thinking it politic not to inform Victoria. Although country-bred, when she was near mice Victoria had a certain tendency to scream and leap for high places.

Harry, with his parents and sister, set out for their new province in their two tone pink Plymouth, dragging the ratty old tent trailer behind them. Eighty-three miles outside Newnham, the trailer frame broke. Bull pulled into a service station to have it welded back together. At a hundred and forty-seven miles outside Newnham the tent trailer frame broke again; not only had the previous weld given way, but a whole series of cracks had appeared in the frame. Bull found a welding shop just outside a small town. While the shop foreman tsk-tsked over the trailer, Bull took Victoria and the children out the back to a small marsh. Bulrushes grew in profusion. Ducks could be heard arguing among themselves somewhere in the reeds. Bullfrogs croaked. Bull and Victoria felt right at home. Eventually Bull wandered back to the shop to check on the trailer, leaving his family to admire the marsh. The welder had just begun. Bull offered advice to the welder. The welder wasn't much interested in Bull's advice. Bull persisted, but after awhile the welder seemed to get downright testy.

It was probably inattention that led to the accident. Bull turned his back on the welder at a critical moment just after the welder had his torch up to a nice white heat. Harry and Victoria were amazed to see Bull tearing out of the garage and heading for the marsh, his pants still smoking in the rear. They were even more amazed when Bull threw himself into the water, seat first, with every evidence of relief. As Bull seemed disinclined to seat himself in the car when the welder was finished, the family camped that night on the garage lot, with Bull sleeping, for a change, on his stomach. The welder, on the other hand, seemed the essence of good cheer for the remainder of the day.

When the trailer was re-attached to the pink Plymouth on the following morn, the Flappers set out for the east again, Bull suggesting that Victoria might like to drive while he canted himself sideways on the seat, for diversity, he said. The course Bull had mapped out for their journey took them right through French logging territory, with the Flappers following the yellow stripe down the highway, mile after mile. Bull figured that their goal was the Atlantic Ocean, or somewhere close. Geography did not rank high in his scheme of things.

Eventually, outside a little Quebec restaurant, Bull called a rest break and went in to order, having conferred with Victoria as to how to do so in French. "Quoitra hamburgers, quoitra fries francais und quoitra cokes," seemed safe enough, and not open to misinterpretation.

"Vous désire des 'amburgs comment, monsieur?" politely spoken, but none the less an obvious inquiry for more intelligence, was the response. All Bull recognized was "désire, 'amburg, and monsieur." For a moment he basked in the lofty title "monsieur," until he noticed that the waitress was waiting, pencil in hand. Bull didn't know how to continue. The burly woodcutter on his left interrupted in voluble French, shouting something at the harried waitress behind the counter. She responded in the same manner, so in a few moments they were screaming at each other. Bull was a trifle nervous. He had no idea what the altercation was all about. He waited for a break in the screaming, then interjected with his order again. Now the fellow on the other side entered the fray. He gestured towards Bull, then towards his friend, then at the waitress, his comments getting louder and faster as he went. Bull was distinctly nervous by this time and shrank down into his seat to await events. From the back came the cook to join into the argument. Finally, all turned towards Bull to await some comment from him. Bull repeated his order, rather meekly.

"Oui, oui, monsieur, mais saignant, a point ou bien cuit?" asked the waitress. The burly chap on Bull's left got up to remonstrate with Bull. Although not quite as tall as was Mr. Sharp, the fellow's shoulders were much broader. Then the chap on Bull's right got up to try his luck. Soon everyone in the restaurant was crowded around, all gesturing and shouting to be heard, all huge and threatening, as far as Bull could tell. The waitress stood calmly in the middle, pencil and pad in hand, waiting, occasionally shouting to be heard above the din.

Bull began to back towards the door, almost unnoticed, until one of the two original protagonists saw him making his getaway. He chased after Bull, now in full retreat. Outside he caught up with him. At first he spoke to Bull in voluble French, tapping him on the shoulder, towering over Bull, until Bull finally burst out with, "But all I wanted was fries and hamburgers and coke!"

The woodcutter said very slowly, very distinctly, as if speaking to a child, "Mais monsieur, it eez necessair to tell zee chef 'ow you want eet cooked."

"Oh," said Bull,"medium, then." And meekly allowed himself to be led back into the restaurant. The message was duly relayed. The entire crowd cheered and whistled. The waitress wrote down the instructions and handed the slip to the chef. The chef beamed and retired to his domain. While Bull waited, several customers came up to him, clapped him on the shoulder, and regaled him with completely incomprehensible stories, all in French. They were a remarkably friendly crowd, even if they were entirely unintelligible. Eventually, Bull's order was ready. The entire restaurant turned out to wave the Flappers off. To Victoria's enquiry about why they had done so, Bull could only shrug his shoulders in a typically Gallic gesture. "Je ne sais pas," he said. And he didn't.

That night Bull put up the tent trailer in the rain, with water streaming down the back of his neck. He put up the front fly of the tent and pegged it into the ground, bypassing the puddles, but getting himself well muddied in the process. Then he drove his family up towards the fly, intending them to disembark directly into the shelter. In the process he knocked out the pegs and the fly collapsed. His next effort was no more successful than the first. Sneezing his way through the process a third time, at last he timed it just right. By then the whole family was asleep. Bull carefully placed the mattresses and bedclothes to best advantage, with due attention to his own comfort. Then he carried the sleepers into the tent and tenderly to bed, being ever so considerate not to wake them up lest they might argue with the sleeping arrangements.

Victoria woke up entirely refreshed in the morning. So did the children. They were cheerful and noisy. Bull woke up wet, with a headache, a stuffy nose and a distinct aversion to noise. Fortunately, the only hole in the canvas was directly over Bull. Every one else in the family congratulated themselves on their good luck and thanked Bull for his consideration. Bull, suffering in silence, set about packing up for the remainder of the trip. They eventually set off on the last leg of the journey, Bull sneezing every second mile or so.

Annespoint, a small town, which called itself a city, was in the heart of Baptist country. It spread itself out languidly across the countryside around a bend in the river. The waterway, at once the foundations of the town and its nemesis, divided the upper crust from the lower. And when spring came and the ice went out, every year the bridge had to be closed. The upper crust, on the right side of the river, seemed to take this event in stride. The others, on the wrong side, did not. They saw the bridge, constructed about the turn of the century, as antiquated, inadequate at the best of times, and of no good use to anyone. That was probably due to the ruts along the track of the road and the danger of getting caught in them. Every newcomer to town had at least one little ding on the car as a reminder of his first bridge crossing. At every other time of the year the bridge acted as a traffic stopper, extending the rush hour by at least thirteen minutes, or even more. In this and all other respects, Annespoint was definitely a community with a sense of its own importance. The travellers slowly made their way across the great Eastern Canadian landscape towards this old loyalist stronghold.

On the way into the city, the Flappers came across the Snugglebunny Inn. It was on a quiet sideroad, right on the outskirts of town. They decided to make it their temporary home until they could find more permanent accommodation. Checking in was an experience. The desk clerk was an older woman, heavy with make-up, and garishly dressed in a revealing, bright red, see-through dress, with an expanse of bosom showing through. She seemed surprised to see the Flappers, but agreed that there was a vacancy, and they could have it on a weekly basis, subject to the rules of the house. She then asked them what their specialty was. At a loss how to answer this, Victoria finally said swamps. Without so much as a flick of an eyebrow, the lady promised to refer all swamp inquiries to their unit.

As it turned out, this particular motel catered more for the local trade than to families. The Flappers didn't realize this until the first night, when they discovered that the walls were not very thick and certainly not soundproof. The slamming of the unit doors on either side of them, combined with the squeaking of the respective beds, and other sounds not totally within their experience, served to alert them to the fact that something might be a trifle different. Charlotte and Harry were asleep. Victoria and Bull were reading in bed when there came the distinct sound of a sheep bah-h-ing from the unit behind their bed. Victoria shot up straight in bed. "That was a sheep," she said. "I distinctly heard a sheep!" Not wholly naive about the birds and the bees, their imaginations were none-the-less strained at the prospect of a sheep in the room next door, together with the couple they knew were there. Shortly thereafter, the merry voice of Little Bo Peep could be heard calling her sheep, which went Bah-Bah-h-ing around the room. Bull was all for notifying the desk clerk. Victoria suggested caution as the desk clerk might be involved. In any case, she was very interested to find out what it was all about in case she ever needed to know.

"Bah-h-h, Bah-h-h," went the sheep. "Squeak, squeak," as the sheep leapt onto the bed. As it was a particularly heavy sheep, the bed creaked ominously. Victoria waited breathlessly to see what might come next.

"I'm Little Bo-Peep, and I've lost my sheep. Wherever shall I find him?" crooned a very young, innocent-sounding female voice.

"Bah-h-h, Bah-h-h," came the resonant baritone response. This time there was a great deal of bed creaking, followed by Bo-Peep's young voice. "Oh! There you are, you naughty sheep, whatever shall I do with you?"

Bull's savage whisper echoed round the room. "Whip the blighter back into his paddock. Then lock the gate."

From the other side there came, as if in response, the crack of a whip. "My Goodness," whispered Bull, sinking down into the bed and covering himself clear up to his chin. "I don't particularly like the sound of that." There soon came the sound of chains being dragged over the floor. Victoria quickly doused the light. Both waited in an agony of suspense to see what might then come to pass.

The bah-h-h-ing came to an end as the squeaking accelerated on the one side. From the other there was the sound of chains dragging, now accompanied by moaning. A decidedly bass voice whined, "Oh, Mommy, I've been such a naughty boy!" It was rather a nice voice, a speaker's voice, with that incongruous whine to it.

Next came a woman's voice, loud and forceful, "John, you've been naughty again and I'm really going to have to punish you." This was accompanied by a slapping noise, and more bass moaning. Then the bed on that side began the now familiar song.

Checking out the window, some half hour later, Victoria was surprised to see a very distinguished-looking gentleman with what looked like a stiff black collar leaving quietly from the sheep's room. A very young lady waved him off. Except for the Bo Peep costume she wore, and the little bit of fluff stuck to the back of the gentleman's coat, everything seemed normal. From the other side, came an equally distinguished-looking gentleman. The Amazon who saw him off had on shiny patent leather boots, which came clear up to her hips. On her arms were long black gloves, with gold bands around her biceps. Around her neck she wore a spiked collar. Her other scant clothing didn't merit attention. Shortly afterwards two more gentlemen came along, knocking discreetly at the two doors. The sheep routine was repeated on one side, while the crack of a whip could be heard on the other. Bull, by now, was in a state of shock. Victoria was thinking things over and wondering which approach might yield the best results with Bull. In the end she fell asleep before she could come to any decision.

The Flappers went off to find a restaurant for breakfast in the morning, after which, Bull, his sneeze worsened by lack of sleep, left his family in the unit, the sheep and Little Bo Peep apparently still asleep. That evening, Victoria reported the comings and goings around them. Bo Peep got started early in the afternoon, while the Amazon opened for business shortly thereafter. It turned out that there were a few "regulars" in the other units as well as a few other specialties, not specified. Bull was all for seeking accommodation elsewhere, but Victoria dissuaded him. It was cheap, she said, and Bo Peep was actually rather a nice girl when she wasn't working. The desk clerk seemed very apologetic that no one had enquired about swamps. She admitted there hadn't been a great call for them lately, but hoped that now the Flappers were here, word might get around. Bull was rather hoping word didn't get around.

He started a frantic search for housing. Nothing seemed on offer for rental. There were no apartments available. Things came to a head when Bull had a run-in with Amazon one evening. It wasn't much of an altercation as Bull figured he was outgunned at the outset. She was female. She was bigger than Bull. And she had a whip. Bull quickly retired from the field. He made a head long dash for the door to his unit and for Victoria. He figured Victoria would protect him from one of her own kind. Amazon laughed. Bull decided it was a nasty laugh. Victoria also laughed. That laugh was equally nasty. Bull came to the conclusion that whatever was going around that motel was definitely catching and he had better get Victoria out of there. It was time to move.

CHAPTER 18

Bugs of Various Kinds

The Flappers decided to put themselves in penury for life. They bought a house. To be more specific, Bull bought the house. He arrived back at the unit one day and asked Victoria whether she would like a three bedroom house with a nice big window over the kitchen sink. She wanted to go see it right away before someone else bought it. "No need," said her husband cheerfully, "I already bought it."

"You bought it without checking with me first?" she asked in dulcettones. It was only the excitement of owning her own home with a window over the kitchen sink that kept Victoria from becoming a widow and facing a charge of homicide.

Shortly thereafter the family moved into the new home, where they were to spend the next ten years, or almost that. Harry was ecstatic. His new neighbours had children. Some were his age. Some were even prepared to talk to him on occasion. Harry decided to bide his time to get a feel for the lay of the land. He went back to his study of wildlife. It was just as well. By now Harry had concentrated his attention on the orders of insects. He would follow them around on the patio outside the back door, his nose practically pushing the bug along, so intent was he on examining it at close quarters. After a suitable length of time, and minute investigation of the bug's movements, Harry would decide to dissect the insect. He was never very good at this. His usual method was to womp them with the flat of his hand. It worked very well with most insects, like grasshoppers, aphids and moths, but had little effect on ants. So he learned that good results could be obtained by jumping on them with both feet.

Soon the back patio was littered with the corpses of a great variety of insects. It was colourful, but appeared a trifle unsavoury. Harry's mother suggested that he clean up his bugs. This was such an exciting prospect that Harry decided to make a collection. He sorted the bugs by their anatomical differences, if he could still tell in their squashed state. If he couldn't, he kept them on the theory that they were probably different in some way. Word soon got around about Harry's bug-killing methods. The neighbours began to worry about his bloodthirsty tendency. It wasn't humane, they said. They advised Harry's parents to have him analysed. Harry felt the neighbours could be analysed. He quoted from various eminent authorities on the subject of interfering with the inquisitive nature of children. When he brought Spock into the argument, then capped it with Seuss, the neighbours retreated in disarray.

Grandfather Sharp had a great interest in "bugs," too. Grandpa's bugs were the sort you climbed in and drove. Grandpa insisted that there were no better cars on the road anywhere than the ubiquitous Volkswagen bug. He drove his bug down to visit the eastern branch of the Flapper clan several times. Each time it was a harrowing experience. Not for Grandma, who had never learned how to drive, but for Grandma's daughter who had. Victoria, was fraught with anxiety from the moment the Sharp parents set out from their home until their safe arrival in Annespoint.

The problem was that Grandpa Sharp had never learned to drive either. When questioned on this allegation he freely admitted that he had been driving for several years "before some government idiot decided to issue licenses and driving tests and all that other foolishness." That probably explained the calm acceptance of Bull's erratic performance at the wheel of his beloved Volkswagen.

Victoria was very wary of her father's driving habits. She had had great opportunity to witness them first hand. She was also aware, and, to some extent, shared her father's opinions about driving regulations. After her own event-riddled introduction to driving she had more than an average idea of what might go wrong. From the first time she saw a push-button automatic ("Oh! I see! The R means you turn right, the L means left, and the D means drive on.") until her husband, shaking and trembling, accompanied her on her first practice drive, Victoriahad a very positive approach to driving. This usually meant that when the going got sticky she would simply abandon the vehicle, wherever it was. The first lesson given by Bull to his beloved was in a parking lot. After being severely maltreated for some minutes, the car, the pink Plymouth, rebelled. It started wheezing and gasping in a most alarming manner, even after the key was turned off. Victoria calmly abandoned the vehicle, leaving Bull to cope, if he could. Both of them thought the car was about to explode. But eventually it responded to Bull's tender ministrations and settled silently into the ruts. Bull decided it would be in everyone's best interests if someone else taught Victoria how to drive. That way he had only to sit in the pink Plymouth while Victoria practised. With his eyes shut he would whisper words of encouragement, between prayers, although the words of encouragement were squeezed in very quickly between the prayers.

After one particularly difficult session Victoria exited the car in a fit of rage, leaving it on a hill in the middle of an intersection outside a busy plaza. The car was not automatic. Every time Victoria got it nicely started and attempted to put it in gear to go up the little incline to the plaza, the car would stall. Traffic backed up for miles. Irate men, stuck in the traffic, came along to offer advice and to suggest various improbable places to stick the car if all else failed. Amused spectators from the sidelines offered somewhat more friendly advice without ever mentioning where Bull should put the car, not even once. Naturally, Victoria felt Bull was better equipped to deal with the matter as most of the remarks were directed at him anyway, so she got out, slamming the door and glaring at everyone in her path. They moved hastily out of the way. Bull was trying to remain calm in a sea of embarrassment. Victoria stalked into the nearest store. Her husband stalled the car three times before finally moving it out of the way, under the watchful eyes of a member of the local constabulary who had arrived just after Victoria's grand exit. Muttering to himself about irrelevant matters, the cop took note of the car for future reference.

It was well he did, for his peace of mind. The cop next came across the car with two wheels on the curb and two feet sticking out from underneath. He walked around the car, stopping beside the two feet. The owner of the feet gradually became aware of the very polished, very large brogues. He correctly surmised the occupation of their owner and briefly contemplated feigning sleep or indifference. In the end, when the shoes had started tapping with impatience, Bull gradually withdrew himself from under the car. The police officer took exception to the two wheels on the curb. He then gave his opinion about taking a nap under the car. He finished by threatening all manner of things unless the car was moved forthwith into a private drive.

Bull, with parts of the transmission in his pocket and all over the road, could only stare in disbelief. Since Bull wasn't at all sure of his ground, he mutely agreed in the face of an impending ticket for disabling a vehicle in the middle of the street without provocation. Huffing and puffing, he pushed the car into the drive, then went back and collected the various parts of the transmission left on the street. He next called for professional help to get the car off the ground, or, to be more precise, back on the road.

It seemed that it was always Bull at the wheel when misfortune overtook them. On the next instance, Harry was giving directions to his father from the rear seat, while Victoria smiled indulgently at her son. Harry told his father to switch on the headlights as it was getting dark. Then Harry suggested that it might be wise to obey the policeman's summons to pull over. Bull, who hadn't noticed impending doom, agreed, although with some reticence. Naturally, it was the same cop. He informed the beleaguered Bull that it was a safety check.

The officer checked the brake lights, the turn signals, the parking lights and both high and low beams. He looked under the hood to make sure it looked like an engine, then checked to make sure there were four tires. He asked for the horn to be sounded and listened to see if it registered the correct tone. He checked the trunk to see whether there might be any contraband, or at least a spare tire. Finally, satisfied, he walked around to the front of the car. Somewhat bemused, he pronounced the car fit, then thumped down the hood for emphasis. The front right headlight objected to the treatment. It fell out of its rusted socket in slow motion, finally settling on the pavement under the car, still shining brightly upwards to illuminate the undercarriage. The cop was rendered speechless. He stared at the empty light socket eerily casting its glow, like some sunken-eyed car mummy. He wasn't at all sure whether he might have inadvertently broken the car himself, without ever realizing his own strength. Horrified, he helped Bull to reset the lamp in its rightful socket and gently suggested a spot of fibreglass to secure it.

When next the police officer spotted the car, with Victoria at the wheel, making a highly illegal left turn, he looked the other way and pretended not to notice. Traffic came to a screeching halt in both directions, horns honking and drivers shaking their fists, until they noticed the cop. Victoria continued blithely on her way, with Bull hiding on the floor of the car and Harry leaping up and down and shrieking encouragement. The cop smiled weakly and waved her through. Victoria waved gaily at the policeman and proceeded on her way. Gradually traffic returned to normal.

With this long history of driving acumen now behind her, she knew the hazards of driving, even with a stick shift. She was particularly aware of her father's frightening tendency to back out into the wrong lane of the road outside the Annespoint house, without ever looking to see if the way was clear. Grandpa Sharp would casually search for the right gear, but inevitably get the wrong one. Cars screamed by at impossible angles, the drivers yelling sweet words of encouragement. Grandpa took his own way, in his own good time. His daughter, like her father, her son like his mother. Each took their own time. Each took their own way. None brooked any opposition. Harry's genes were all in order, and impeccable.

CHAPTER 19

Bugs and Glassy Eyes

Even in a nice middle class district, the class system was alive and thriving in Annespoint. If someone sidled up to you on the street, and, with a curl to the upper lip, whispered "Upper Canadian!" you could be assured that you had just been insulted. Harry was ignorant of such things. All that was about to change. Harry was about to discover "Annespoint Society."

The immediate neighbour on the left was a real estate agent who had done well. He was not from "Society." Harry could play with his children. His children didn't particularly want to play with Harry as they thought they were a little too old for him. The daughter of the house was eighteen and looking for boys who knew what life was all about. The six year old Harry didn't seem to offer much in the way of excitement. But then again, she didn't know Harry. Though Harry liked the girl, she didn't treat him seriously. The romance faltered on the question of age.

The son, Albert, or Al, for short, was eighteen and had just discovered motorcycles. When Harry tried to interest Al in his bug collection, that young man's eyes glazed over. Harry had not yet discovered chloroform. Most of the bugs in his collection had met their demise under the heel of his shoe or the flat of his hand. It was presumed that the rest had died of natural causes. Al countered the bug move with the highly strategic motorcycle move. Al and Harry spent the next several weeks discussing motorcycles, taking Al's motorcycle apart, and trying to put it back together in the right order. Harry became intimately acquainted with motor mechanics. They also spent time reviewing the mechanics of motorcycle motion, Harry riding behind and offering Al advice on improving his driving skills.

When Bull returned home from work one evening, he was astounded to see an extremely short motorcyclist, goggles over his eyes, helmet pulled back so he could see, thundering down their quiet street. Muttering a few imprecations about some people's children, Bull went inside to greet his beloved. His beloved wasn't in a great mood. Harry had been missing all afternoon. The spectre of kidnapping loomed up before them. When Harry still hadn't shown up an hour later, both parents decided that some action was required. Running around the house screaming "Harry" bore no fruit. So they set out to scour the neighbourhood. After that, things happened fairly quickly.

Al came over to complain bitterly that Harry was taking advantage of him and it was his turn now. Just at that juncture the phone rang. It was Harry. He had been pulled over on the motorcycle for running a stop sign. When the cop realized that it was a six year old in charge of the machine, he took Harry into protective custody. When asked, Harry readily agreed that he was part of the infamous Flapper Gang and went into a highly coloured description of all the killings he had engaged in, without ever once remarking that his victims were bugs. The cop by this time figured he was on to a major crime ring.

When the Flappers, mother and father, arrived at the police station, it was to find that Harry was in an interrogation room. Apparently, there had been a string of robberies, recently, and the detective in charge of Harry's case was finding Harry's answers more than interesting. The sergeant on the desk, a laconic soul, told the Flappers to wait, while he watched them for signs of something. The sergeant was having difficulty believing that Victoria and Bull were really part of the infamous Flapper Gang. He wasn't too sure who or what the Flapper Gang was either, but knew instinctively they must be up to no good. Victoria was altogether too demure and ingenuous, Bull was obviously too stupid to lead a gang and plan all the crimes attributed to the them. Harry, though, he was a different matter.

Albert arrived to claim his motorcycle. He refused to lay a charge of motorcycle theft on the grounds that he had helped Harry to mount and held the cycle steady until Harry got it going. As Al told the constable, a few practice runs around the block riding pillion, convinced him that Harry was a natural. So he had sent Harry out solo. Why would they think the bike was stolen? The sergeant's eyes boggled. "You sent a six-year old out on a Honda 650 alone?" he asked. "Do you expect me to believe that?"

"Look, Sergeant, do you know Harry Flapper?" The name Flapper did strange things to the sergeant. He sat up straighter and began to fidget, visions of attack from some huge deadly gang flitting across his imagination. The sergeant conceived the idea that they were all part of some new crime syndicate moving into the area. He gave the matter deep thought, then told Al to remove himself and his motorcycle from the premises. Al obliged, while the sergeant went off to have a word with his confreres, and to make plans for keeping the Flappers under surveillance.

Meanwhile, in the interrogation room the detective was having difficulty pinning Harry down. Every time he had a good discussion going on the latest robbery, Harry would change the subject to bugs. Harry described the bugs in such intimate detail that the detective was feeling just a little ill when he decided to call it quits, in frustration, still suspicious. He admonished Harry not to ride a motorcycle for about fifteen more years, preferably fifty, then let him go. The detective decided that he would rather run a grocery store, or at least take a long holiday. The world wasn't making very much sense to him at the moment.

On the way home Victoria asked Harry why he had run the stop sign. "I couldn't reach the ground," said Harry. "Had I stopped, the motorcycle would have fallen over. I wouldn't have been able to start it again. Obviously there is a flaw in the traffic laws about this sort of thing. Short people should be allowed to go through stop signs," he said. And as a small concession to safety, added "slowly" in a whisper, in case anyone might hear and take him seriously. "I tried to tell the detective all that, but he was a little weird. He kept switching the subject to jewellery stores and robberies. I think he's a bit neurotic. He probably needs a holiday."

Harry was admonished by his parents to stick to children closer to his own age for companionship. Harry had no intention of giving his friends up altogether, but thought it good tactics to humour his parents. He approached the children at the top of the street with an offer of friendship. They were from "Society." Harry was judged wanting. By parents and offspring alike, he was judged wanting. The four year old boy enquired whether Harry rode. Harry thought about the motorcycle but decided discretion was the order of the day and hauled out his shiny new tricycle instead. The four-year-old went off in a huff.

Next Harry tried the five year old girl. She was dressed in frills, and patent leather shoes, very shiny. Harry wanted to know if she would play in the sandbox. "Mummy says it's unsanitary." she replied.

"Would you like to see my bugs?" was Harry's next query. She left in a hurry. "That's funny," Harry said, "if you mention bugs, it causes a person's eyes to glaze over, and they lose the power of speech."

By now Harry figured that girls were a lost cause. It was some years before his interest in them again perked up. In the mean time they made good targets for snowballs. This practice invariably caused him some trouble at home. It didn't enhance his chances with the girls either.

From then on, Harry would greet each new acquaintance with, "Would you like to see my bug collection?" His interest in science had now extended to the social sciences, including psychology. Eventually, some of the younger, more daring boys not only agreed to view his collection, but waxed enthusiastic over the bugs. Each would go home vowing to start his own collection.

People began to avoid the Flappers on the street. Soon the Department of Health began to enquire. The gentleman from the Department arrived at the Flapper door one afternoon. Victoria let him in to examine the premises.

He kept asking silly questions about bugs. Finally Victoria figured out that he wanted to see Harry's bugs. As Harry was off on other pursuits at the moment, she took the liberty of showing the bugs to the gentleman. The fellow was visibly shaken when the extent of the collection became evident. He asked what one particularly large gruesome specimen was. Victoria studied it closely. "I think," she pronounced, "that it was a spider, but I can't tell for sure." The gentleman didn't seem inclined to want to study the bugs in more detail.

When Harry arrived, opportunely, and discovered the man was interested in bugs, there was no holding him back. Harry waxed eloquently on the relative squashability of various species of bugs. He then went on to identify each bug in the collection, having discovered a rapt audience. The fellow wasn't so much rapt as in a state of shock. Soon, however, much to Harry's disappointment, the fellow went glassy-eyed. He showed distinct signs of malaise, when Harry offered to bring out another tray of bugs. In fact he made a quite undignified dash for the exit. Harry and his mother observed him driving at top speed, erratically, down the street. Further inquiries to the Department on the subject of Harry's bugs elicited the comment that it was not a subject open to discussion. This was taken to mean that Harry was working on a top-secret government project and his stock in the neighbourhood went up accordingly.

When Harvey was invited to view the collection, he did not go away. Harvey's mother wasn't too concerned about the bugs. Harvey's older sisters had other pursuits. So, Harvey became Harry's best friend. They studied bug collecting together in earnest. They would go out looking for bugs in likely places, and some unlikely places, too. Harry was all for taking Harvey to the Snugglebunny Inn to look for bugs. The only thing stopping him was that he didn't know the way. He was afraid to ask his father because Bull showed every sign of threatened stroke at the mention of the place. Harry's mother wouldn't allow mention of it either. Every time Harry asked the way, his mother said, "Not yet, Dear, you're just a mite too young." So the Snugglebunny Inn's bugs would have to wait for another day. Meanwhile, they concentrated on wildlife closer to home.

CHAPTER 20

Cribs, Cripes!

That first year in the new house was an educational experience for all. Harry shared a bedroom upstairs with his sister. His parents were in the master bedroom on the main floor, next to the warm bathroom. From the time he had first learned to crawl, Harry had shown no inclination to remain in bed after waking. He rose each morning at the first eye opening. Unknown to his parents, he was also teaching Charlotte the art of early rising.

One Saturday morning as Victoria and Bull were studying the intricacies of early morning hanky-panky, there came to their ears a great screaming. Before this event no one had thought to test Charlotte's capacity for producing sound. Afterwards there was never any doubt. At the first whimper, move. Harry's screams were drowned by those of his sister. On investigation (It probably took half a second for both parents to scale the stairs, not touching any of them on the way up.) Charlotte was found hanging upside down by one foot from the side of her crib. Harry had been "helping" her to escape. Charlotte wasn't as proficient at hoisting her leg over the side as Harry. Harry had started screaming so that Charlotte wouldn't have to do it all by herself. He had little effect beside Charlotte. His heart wasn't in it. Charlotte, though, had by now perfected a magnificent wail that could be heard three counties away, and, as it turned out, was.

The neighbours flocked to the Flapper household from miles around to enjoy the excitement and dig up any scandals not previously unearthed concerning the new family on the block, and perhaps make up a few if the current ones weren't to their liking. Anyhow, they reasoned, now that they were all there, they may as well have breakfast. Getting rid of the police who came to investigate the use of an unauthorized siren was not so easily done either. The police remained convinced that no child could possibly make that sort of noise, so nosed about the house to find out the actual cause. The firemen from the three fire trucks that responded to the "fire alarm," were also convinced that the Flappers were trying to hide something suspicious. Victoria had long since given up the thought of comparing the Amazon's technique with that of Little Bo Peep. Besides, the police and firemen had converged on her bedroom, convinced that if anything illicit was going on in the house, that was the most likely room to find evidence.

Breakfast turned out to be a merry affair for all the guests, most of whom were still in their robes and pyjamas. Bull and Victoria were kept busy running back and forth with plates of food until everyone was fed, except the police, who by now were searching the basement with flashlights. In vain, Bull had tried to switch on the lights for them, but they were having none of that bait and switch technique. So Bull gave it up and left for work. Victoria spent the rest of the day shooing her unwanted guests out of the pantry or the closets, and for one intrepid soul, from underneath the bathroom vanity cupboard. She didn't discover him until she was almost ready for her shower. She started to scream but thought better of it, remembering Charlotte. After all, she reasoned, Charlotte had to get her abilities in that direction from somewhere, and Victoria had never yet tried a flat out scream. So instead, she patiently shooed her guest out of the bathroom, and this time checked all over, including the toilet reservoir before stepping into her shower.

Harry showed little inclination to play with Charlotte further that day. He went back to his investigation of bugs. Charlotte decided she wasn't all that athletic. Instead, she practised how to sulk.

The firemen had other pursuits, so left before the week was out. In general, it was a slow time for the police so they decided to make the best of their investigation and kept at it for the better part of a month. Unfortunately one officer happened to be in the broom closet when Bull burst in one evening and talked about lopping off the ears before it was too late. The misunderstanding was never cleared away entirely to the police satisfaction. Bull had some difficulty too. He couldn't understand why the police might be interested in his corn crop. He had never thought of himself as a "dangerous offender" before. Somehow the thought gave him a certain pride that anyone, even in error, might call him dangerous. His stock in the neighbourhood went back up again.

The weather remained balmy until the end of September. One evening after driving home from the office in the rain, Bull was working in what he called the study. It was actually a closet but Victoria didn't have the heart to tell him that. Bull was listening to the radio while he worked. The announcer came on to tell his listeners that they could expect "continuing clear weather." Bull walked outside, held his hands up to the heavens to catch the unusually heavy dew, then returned inside to telephone the radio station. He thought they might have missed the torrential downpour in consequence of the other momentous news. After all, the mayor's wife's cat, Petunia, had been missing for three days now. It was a case, according to the police, of suspected catnapping.

Petunia turned up two weeks later with seven little Petunias, but meanwhile, it was front page news, pushing everything else into a position of relative unimportance. Petunia's life story was relayed several times in various versions, each more colourful than the last. Mayor Bert, thinking of the coming election, aided and abetted the process, so his life story was also told in great detail, concentrating on his status as a war hero, among other things. The story was so good and so well told that most people forgot he was only nine years old at the end of the war and, by nature, not the sort to indulge in acts of bravery. In the first place, he had always run to a little too much fat. In the second, he was just a trifle vain. Only his hair dresser and his wife knew he wore a toupee. It looked quite natural, giving him a rather distinguished look. Perhaps it was the distinguished look that people confused with bravery.

When the circumstances are known, it is quite understandable that a weather forecast, even an erroneous weather forecast would not be a matter of concern. "Anyway," as the announcer told Bull over the phone, "anyone with half an eye, and that partially blind, could see or at least feel that it was raining outside." What did it matter anyway? Eventually he sighed, though, and promised an updated forecast. When it came, it was a surprise to everyone, including the announcer. According to the weather office, four hundred miles away, it was "Cloudy tonight, clearing tomorrow." It should have been taken as an omen.

Harry saw his first real snow storm a few months later. One bright morning early in November, there were a few snowflakes coming down, just as the radio announcer was saying "Partly cloudy." Harry's Dad drove to work in the gathering storm, but getting home at the end of the day was another matter. By then there were 30.9 inches of partly cloudy all over the ground. The parking lot had disappeared. The streets had disappeared. Some houses had disappeared. Even Petunia had disappeared. That was probably because she was indistinguishable from the snow, being snow white, except her eyes, which weren't.

It took four hours for Harry's father to drive the few miles home. Drive is not a good word to use in these circumstances. Bull had been forewarned about the weather out east by a friendly neighbour. "Ten months of winter and two months of tough sledding," he was told. So the first thing Bull did after moving to Annespoint was to buy an electric snowblower. It stood about a foot high at the business end of the machine. With Harry at his side, all primed to help, little red shovel at the ready, Bull opened the garage door, standing expectantly, snowblower all ready to go. Snowblower, Harry and his father were all buried under the resulting avalanche. It was tacitly agreed that the snow would need to be shovelled down to manageable proportions. This proved to be a depth of about two inches of snow before the snowblower would work. Harry helped with his little red shovel. He loved the snow. His father hated it. Together they shovelled, and shovelled. For days they shovelled. The driveway was never cleared out completely from the mound of snow until the following August. Late August.

The Flapper's immediate neighbour to the right, Jerry Blomwidge, had a tougher time of it. Apparently, he, too, had bought his house in summer. During every major snowfall, and every snowfall in that part of the world turned out to be major, Jerry's house would be covered entirely. The children in the neighbourhood loved it. They would come from all over the district to ski down the new "hill." The only evidence that there might be a house underneath was the stream of smoke issuing from a little hole near the top of the hill. It was all right for the children to indulge. But the Flappers thought it a bit callous when some folks made a snowmobile jump out of it. About a week after the snowfall Jerry would manage to dig himself out from inside. If there were a fresh snowfall in the interim, and there usually was, it would take longer. One year it took until mid August. Bull located the chimney and dropped supplies down it. Jerry became a firm friend as a result.

They formed a neighbourhood poker club. But there were problems with the weekly poker game, what with Jerry getting himself snowed in. The problems were solved when Harry took over Jerry's seat and communicated in a whisper with Jerry over a walky-talky. They would discuss strategy and work out the best odds. Jerry, with nothing better to do, would sit in front of his computer terminal checking for the most advantageous strategy. Harry would implement Jerry's instructions. Soon the pair became a winning combination. Harry's earnings grew. So did the earnings of the absent Jerry. Harry came to anticipate Jerry's instructions after awhile. One of the neighbours, becoming jealous of their success, and not a little abashed at losing to a six-year-old, sabotaged the walky-talky one day. Harry doubled his earnings. The walky-talky was quickly restored.

Harry and Jerry decided to enter the stock market game on their winnings. Since Jerry was still snow bound, Harry did the leg work. Harry decided to visit the stock broker in person. Gideon Gallrock was amazed one day to find a small person on the other side of his desk. At first he took it for a six-year-old who had strayed from the playground. He tried to send him off to return to the playground. Harry was having none of that. He remarked on investment opportunities and stock options. The little fellow enquired whether Mr. Gallrock thought Upper Cobalt Mining might split two for one, in view of the projected take-over by Abitibi Smeltering. Mr. Gallrock was interested to know where Harry had picked up his information. Harry told him how he had figured it out. Together they mapped out a scheme for them both to get rich, along with Harry's silent partner.

Jerry made plans with his share of the loot. As soon as he got out from under the snow, he vowed to move South. When August finally arrived that year, Jerry was a rich man. He thought about moving South again. On due reflection, he decided it was wrong to break up a winning partnership. Victoria and Bull, knowing nothing about the investment world, were entirely ignorant of Harry's success in financial circles. He took care not to let them know too much. He thought there was no really good reason to jeopardize his weekly allowance. Harry figured that he would tell them of his good fortune soon enough, when he was old and grey, maybe on his thirtieth birthday. Meanwhile he would enjoy himself.

CHAPTER 21

Taxis and Baby Sisters

The fourth year after Charlotte's appearance proved to be eventful for Harry. Traumatic for his parents, but just eventful for Harry. The old pink Plymouth met its demise in the middle of a snow storm. Bull had got stuck, then abandoned it in favour of a warmer spot, deciding to walk the last few hundred yards home. In the middle of the snow storm most drivers had abandoned their vehicles. Before morning all the cars had disappeared under the gentle cold blanket. But all the other owners got up early to dig their vehicles out before the snowplough came. Except Bull. Bull slept in. The snowplough deposited the pink Plymouth somewhere on the fringes of the city. By the time Bull found it again, three years later, all need for it had disappeared. Besides, there was nothing much left to salvage that rust or scavengers hadn't made off with. Meanwhile, with no car, the Flappers walked everywhere.

"Exercise," Harry's parents intoned, "is very beneficial." It seemed very strange to Harry how quickly their attitude towards walking had changed now that they could no longer afford to run a car. When Harry broached the subject to his mother, Victoria said simply that she didn't want to talk about it. Charlotte, on the other hand, was quite voluble in her distress over this state of affairs. Naturally, when they went shopping or visiting, it was Harry who wound up pulling Charlotte in her wagon or sleigh. Everyone said the two of them made a cute picture. Harry had other thoughts on the matter and occasionally expressed them. However, the activity and fresh air probably accounted for their good health over the next few years. It also convinced Charlotte that she really wasn't cut out to be an athlete, or if she had to indulge in sport it had better be cross country skiing, in which, she imagined, one needed only to strap the skis on, then magically they would take you wherever you wanted. It was some years before she could test that theory, and by then all need for the magic carpet had passed.

Harry's life progressed on an even tenor, more or less, until he was about seven, when he received a portent that his life was about to change. Victoria asked him casually one day whether he might like a little brother or sister. Harry thought about it for a while then allowed as how a little brother, say about six years old, would be nice. He didn't want an older brother: but he felt one slightly younger would provide companionship, while still being at his beck and call. His mother only smiled and suggested he wait and see when he gave in his order.

In the meantime, the family still wrestled with the problem of transportation. As Victoria was finding it increasingly difficult to get around, this became a matter of concern. The Annespoint Coal, Steam and Tugboat Company ran the bus service in the town. Erratic it was at best. And as the Flappers lived "on the Hill," which was not considered part of the town, service was probably not the best word to describe the operation. So Victoria occasionally took a taxi. That was another matter. As the APCSTCo. ran what passed for a bus service, the taxi companies ran a competing bus service. The taxis were more flexible, more expensive, and considerably more exciting. One never knew what might happen.

The taxi would cruise around to look for fares. Having captured one, the driver would continue to cruise. The drivers played a game among themselves. The object was to fill the cab. The driver who could fill his cab quickest and keep the passengers the longest would win a trip to Moose Junction. Once the cab was filled, the driver would take the most circuitous route possible, to the destination the furthest away. Reluctantly he would let the passenger go. In the course of the day, the driver might drive home for dinner, leaving the passengers in the taxi. While the driver ate, the passengers would have a party. The intervention of the police to quell the disturbance would bring the driver back, according to the rules of the game. Then the driver would have to continue to ply his trade. Sometimes it took a passenger up to three days to get to his destination.

Most regular users were members of the frequent travellers club. They saved milage points based upon the length of time they spent in the cab and the distance travelled. They could either trade their points for a quick-release program to get to their destinations quicker when they were in a hurry, or have a holiday trip to Moose Junction when they had accumulated enough points. The taxi ride in Annespoint was generally recognized as the best guided tour of any city in North America, if not the world. Possibly Avignon in France could compete, but few others.

Victoria, very pregnant, one September afternoon, allowed as how she wasn't up to keeping her appointment with her doctor. Even though the doctor's office was only a mile or so away, Victoria knew from past experience that she had better leave at least three hours to travel by taxi. Bull, leaving the decision to Victoria, went to work. He walked, as usual. When Victoria phoned her doctor, she was convinced by the nurse to keep her appointment. After another hour and a half in the doctor's office, a somewhat jaded Victoria finally got in to see the doctor. She suspected something might be amiss when he immediately advised his nurse to postpone his remaining appointments. Sure enough, Victoria was advised that she should hasten to the hospital. She thought she should go home to collect her suitcase, but her doctor dissuaded her on the grounds that she was in advanced labour.

Victoria stepped outside the clinic to hail a cab. The clinic was a favourite collecting spot for the taxis. The cab that responded already had several people stacked in it. The enlarged Mother Flapper lumbered in, just as her water broke. The cabby hadn't finished collecting passengers yet. He tried to entice more people in. But they weren't all dummies. None of those outside wanted a baby born in their laps. Those inside weren't too anxious to share the birth experience either, but they were already trapped. Whispered prayers could be heard during lulls in the Cabby's entreaties to coax just one more fare inside. Victoria leaned over and smiled at him. That should have been a warning, but, then, he didn't know Harry. Victoria's smile was infinitely more powerful. "I wouldn't delay too much if I were you," she said, "not unless you want the baby born in your cab."

The Cabby had never even witnessed a birth, let alone assisted at one. He thought better of his actions. He figured he had lost the game for that day anyway. It was a toss-up between delaying his passengers with a birth in his cab and suffering the trauma of making the delivery himself. On balance, he decided that for once a passenger should be dropped at her location as rapidly as possible. He hadn't accounted for Annespoint's fifteen minute rush hour. By now he was in the middle of it. All going his way. He must have spent time learning to drive in England, for most of the trip was spent on the wrong side of the road as he passed everything in sight. Even without turning, his horn was blaring. He flashed his lights on and off and made wailing noises in his throat, like a siren, he later said.

By now some passengers had joined him in this exercise, wailing with increasing distress as it became apparent they might never reach the hospital in time, and most had better things to do that afternoon than to attend at the birth of a child. Arrived at the hospital, the driver attempted to get rid of Victoria as quickly as possible so he could rejoin the game with all possible speed. She exited slowly, with dignity. The remaining passengers all breathed easier as they sped off for their nightly party.

Johanna made her appearance moments after her mother's arrival at the hospital. Even after she grew up Johanna showed a decided disinclination to use taxis. It's also possibly the last time Johanna was on time for anything.

Johanna became Jo-Jo, a name invented by Charlotte, who started out by adoring her. Charlotte mothered Jo-Jo for several months. Then the rot set in. Jo-Jo would take one look at Charlotte and begin to wail. Strangely, all it took was a gentle word from Harry to calm her. Battle lines between Charlotte and Jo-Jo were drawn the first time Jo-Jo crawled onto Charlotte's patch and swiped the latter's favourite toy. Harry became the exasperated peacemaker.

Harry was now seriously outnumbered by females in the household. Up to this point he had displayed typically possessive characteristics about his belongings. After Johanna's arrival, he gave up. She was not a respecter of the territory of others. As soon as Jo-Jo could crawl into Harry's room, she did so. She showed none of the Flapper characteristics to back into situations first. She marched in frontwards, on all fours. Her first problem was to find a way to carry off her stolen booty, whatever Harry had left neatly piled in his room. She usually stuck it in her mouth. Harry looked with horror at his brand new leather baseball glove after Jo-Jo's treatment of it. She had gummed it to death, drowning it in saliva. It was necessary to sterilize the glove before Harry would touch it. Then he handled it gingerly. This was his first problem with baseball and one of the reasons it became, for him, a spectator sport.

Afterwards, when Jo-Jo's collection of Harry's toys had grown, she took to dragging them around in a sack. At first Harry responded by developing tendencies of excessive neatness. As Jo-Jo's ability to ferret out Harry's favourite toys increased, Harry finally gave up. In an excess of zeal, he began to help Jo-Jo to mess up his room. No one ever successfully figured out his reasoning. Overnight he changed from the neat and tidy soul he had always been. His room became a disaster area. It remained that way. Anyone brave enough to cross the threshold took his life in his hands. Few were brave enough to try. Even Jo-Jo gave up. In the end Harry's tactics were successful. Controlled disorder, he called it. It was a philosophy he was to practice all his life.

C H A P T E R   2 2

Potatoes and Other Inedible Foods

It may have been the arrival of Jo-Jo and the return of Harry's "breast fixation complex." It may have been other natural causes. Whatever the reason, Harry's eating habits underwent a radical change. He began a set of experiments with white rats to determine which foods were edible and which should be left alone. He started by surreptitiously feeding his spinach to the rats but quickly abandoned that when it appeared as if the rats were thriving on it. He explained this aberration in the edibility of spinach between humans and rats by noting differences in physiology.

His next experiment with spinach involved his sisters in an attempt to prove that it was unfit for human consumption. After hearing the terms of the experiment, his sisters objected, strenuously. After Charlotte whacked him in the stomach with her giant panda, he abandoned that experiment too. It took him a week to get over the incident. He gave Charlotte a wide berth for much longer. He also developed a complex about giant pandas. Fortunately, in his daily life, he rarely had to cope with giant pandas, stuffed or otherwise. Harry went back to the rats. He fed them nothing but potatoes for several months. Eventually, they died of boredom.

Until this time, Harry had cheerfully devoured his potatoes. "Smashed" as he called them, French fried, baked, or scalloped, he loved them all, particularly scalloped potatoes. After his experiments, he would complain bitterly that potatoes were entirely inedible and shouldn't be used for human consumption. "They are poisonous" he averred. "I fed potatoes to my rats and the rats died." His mother had fixed on the rats. She hadn't heard anything after that. She wanted to know where he kept them and why. Harry patiently explained, but she wasn't really listening. There would be no rats in her house, she said. They arrived at a compromise. Harry would eat his potatoes. He would also take his rats out of the house. Victoria was a tough negotiator.

Harry figured that sausages must be bad for you. They tasted bad enough. Potatoes, according to Harry, were inedible. Sausages, on the other hand, were an abomination and a blight on the entire existence of mankind. He fed them to the remaining rat colony, now housed at the end of the garden. The rats thrived. Harry figured something must have gone awry with his experiment. Some other test was called for as he knew intuitively that sausages couldn't be good for you. He decided to try them out on the canary. So whenever Harry was served sausages, he furtively dropped them into the canary's cage. The canary objected, but lost the battle. The canary decided resistance was called for. It took up weight lifting.

When it had built up its chest muscles it went in for kung fu. The canary discovered that sausages were an excellent source of protein, among other things. But it still didn't like them much. So it practised its kung fu until it felt confident. One day, when Harry was casually discarding some unwanted peas into the canary's cage, the canary flipped him. The canary dusted off its wings and flew back into its cage. Harry maintained that he had slipped. But he avoided going too close to the canary from that point on, lest the canary get a strangle hold on him. Harry decided that sausages were definitely not good for him. He wasn't too sure about peas either. And canaries were definitely crossed off his list of associates.

Chocolate was the only other foodstuff to cause Harry any serious problem. It wasn't that he was allergic to it. Rather, it was associated with a childhood trauma. At one point, when Harry was just a toddler, he was encouraged to meet with the Easter Bunny. Harry's feelings on rabbits were not known at the time. However, when he was confronted by a massive rabbit over six feet tall in a mall one day, he decided that the rabbits could have the field. They could have anything else their hearts were set on too. This particular rabbit was dispensing chocolate Easter eggs. The rabbit decided that Harry should have a chocolate egg. That was fine with Harry until he got close enough to realize that this creature from the wilds was not only acting out of character, but was a very great deal larger than Harry. Harry backed off. The rabbit advanced. Harry began to smile. The rabbit, misinterpreting the smile, advanced, chocolate egg in hand. It was a pity that Harry was the only child around for the rabbit to attack. Harry thought so too.

The standoff might have gone on for days. If the rabbit had lain down, with its feet in the air, and played dead, Harry might today still eat chocolate. The rabbit apparently didn't know that game. So Harry screamed. His father rescued him. From that point on Harry associated chocolate with man-eating rabbits, or as in this case, child-eating rabbits. Chocolate ceased to be of any interest to him.

CHAPTER 23

Pets and Pratfalls

arry decided he should have a pet, a real honest-to-goodness pet. Rats weren't classified as pets in his books. They were merely necessary adjuncts to his experiments, or so he averred. No one seemed inclined to take his wishes seriously. Certainly not his mother, who visibly shuddered at the thought. His father passed the remark that every boy should have a dog, but left it at that. Harry decided to take the matter into his own hands. As it turned out, it was even easier than he thought. On one of his treks into the bush, he came across a kitten that was starving to death. That was what Harry believed when the poor little thing tried to eat him. So Harry rushed home to find food for the kitty. He figured that steak would do for the time being. The kitten agreed. Mother Flapper objected strenuously when supper turned up missing. So Harry decided to keep his activities quiet. Getting a supply of fresh meat for the kitty proved less a problem than Harry had thought, although it ate deeply into both his supper and his pocket money.

In the meantime, Bull and Victoria argued privately about whether Harry should have a pet. Bull was all for getting a dog. It would be protection, he said. Victoria demanded to know who would look after the animal. Bull finally broke down and agreed that if Harry failed at the task, and neither Charlotte nor Jo-Jo would take it on, then he would step into the breach. The next step was to agree on a breed. Victoria suggested a cocker spaniel. Bull's eyebrows almost met his hairline. He counter offered at a doberman pincer. They compromised on a dog from the pound that "wouldn't grow too big," in Victoria's words. "Too big" was not defined. They decided to surprise Harry with his own pet dog on an appropriate occasion.

Harry was making great strides with the kitty. Eventually it came to look forward to Harry's visits, until one magical day when it leapt onto his shoulder, purring. Harry decided to call the kitty "Claws." He thought the name suited it. When the kitty started to come out to meet him, Harry decided it was time to take it home. He walked in the door with the kitty balanced on his shoulders. There he met his parent's surprise, the new dog. Dog saw the kitty. Claws saw the dog in the same instant. Claws kept a wary eye on Dog but remained where it was, curled around Harry's neck, purring. The dog figured all cats should be chased so tried to get something going. Claws ignored Dog, which only infuriated Dog the more. What with all the barking, and Harry hollering, the rest of the family emerged to see what might be the matter.

Dog was leaping up to try to get at the cat. The cat was just switching her tail back and forth. Harry, in the middle, so to speak, was yelling at the dog. Bull grabbed the dog's collar just as the cat decided to come down. The dog lunged for the cat, so Bull let go. The cat turned to face the dog, flicking its tail angrily back and forth as the dog rushed, baring its fangs. Claws waited until a judicious moment when the dog was within range. Then it reared up, grabbed the dog's nose with its claws to steady itself and bit, all in a flash. The dog tried to back off, getting its nose scraped for its pains as it escaped from the cat. The dog ran for Bull, hiding behind him and trembling.

Victoria, who had a soft spot for kittens, scooped up Claws and took her into the kitchen to feed, leaving Bull, Harry and Dog to sort things out among themselves. Harry and Bull came to an agreement: Bull would feed Dog. Bull would walk Dog. Bull would clean up any little indiscretions Dog might leave around. If Dog needed attention, Bull would give it. Harry was a tough negotiator.

Harry meandered out to the kitchen to help his mother with Claws. The cat was lapping at some milk when he arrived. "She likes meat," Harry informed his mother. Victoria had already discovered that fact. Turning her back to get the milk from the fridge, Claws had downed the chicken meant for supper in a flash. Victoria had a discussion with Claws about the propriety of stealing chickens and the life expectancy of a cat that stole chickens. Claws was prepared to negotiate, but not to give up her point altogether. If Victoria supplied her with fresh meat, she wouldn't steal the family supper. Claws knew how to negotiate.

Victoria turned her attention to Harry. She agreed Harry could keep Claws on certain conditions. Harry would supply Claws with fresh meat. Harry would let Claws out and in when necessary. Harry would clean up Claws' litter box. If Claws needed any attention, Harry would give it. Victoria was a tough negotiator.

Claws and Dog came to an agreement. Claws could do anything she wanted, go anywhere, hiss, spit if necessary, and walk unhindered where she liked. In return, Dog would cower whenever Claws appeared. This seemed to work very satisfactorily until the day Claws walked off the stairs onto Dog's back without warning. She had a fair ride from one end of the house to the other and back, with the dog yelping all the way. Finally Dog slowed down, Claws loosened her hold. Having found a warm spot, Claws seemed determined to take advantage of it. She curled up on the dog's back and went to sleep. Dog was afraid to move for fear of waking Claws. He stood rigidly to attention for several hours until someone noticed the cat and started to pet her. It was almost the death of Dog as Claws unsheathed her claws and dug them into the dog, making dough for sheer enjoyment.

Dog and Claws grew together, Dog to an immense size for a dog, much to the alarm of Victoria, Claws to an immense size for a cat, much to the alarm of Dog. Claws began to prowl the neighbourhood looking for stray dogs to terrify. On finding a likely candidate she would flaunt her tail until the dog noticed and gave chase. Depending upon her mood, Claws would then either bite it on the nose or leap on its back if she were feeling lazy and wanted a ride somewhere. She wasn't quiet about it either. When she was out hunting for a dog she would roar like a wildcat. It wasn't long before someone noticed that she looked like a wildcat, too. The older she got, the more ferocious she looked.

Mrs. Pumphrey lived up the street. Her hound took exception to the cat. As the hound was always tethered, Claws figured it wasn't fair to bite it on the nose. Instead she would gauge the length of the rope fairly accurately, then lie on the verge a foot or so beyond. The dog would come yapping down at her, taking a flying leap as he closed in. He would come up short on his lead in mid-air, practically strangling as his body whipped end for end. Down the hound would smash onto the ground, winded, at the cat's feet. Claws would get up, yawn, stretch, then clean herself. The dog would go crazy.

Hound had never really had the pleasure of a face to face confrontation with Claws until one day he slipped his lead. It started with Hound sunning himself on the front porch, dreaming of cats and other things and occasionally whimpering and kicking his left hind leg. Down the street came Claws, somewhat bored and looking to annoy Hound. She lay down at the end of Hound's drive and awaited events. When the scent of cat reached Hound, it was like triggering an alarm clock. Down off the porch he flew, taking a giant leap towards Claws, who barely twitched a muscle. It was a surprise to both Hound and Claws when the dog made contact with his quarry.

Claws made a quick recovery and settled herself on Hound's hindquarters, well dug in. Baying at full lung, Hound made a quick about face to find his owner, and comfort. He found her in the back garden, hanging out the wash. The poor lady had her mouth full of clothespins, and her arms full of washing just as they rounded the corner of the house. Hound leapt for his mistress' arms. She wasn't proof against the weight of an eighty pound dog at full gallop. Down they all went, Mrs. Pumphrey spitting out clothespins, or as many as she could and chewing up the rest. To make matters worse, Hound got himself tangled in the sheets, rolling over and over, and in the process attaching

Claws even more firmly to his backside. Pushing his feet through the sheet, the hound regained his feet. Now blinded by the sheet, he set off through the back gardens, eventually making it out on to the main street, heading into town, baying and growling by turns, while Claws began to shriek her objections too.

The duo might have made it safely out of town if Mayor Bert hadn't come out to see what was the matter. As the apparition bore down on him, he completely forgot his war record for bravery. He turned and ran. Hound, looking for direction, followed Mayor Bert's footsteps. The faster Mayor Bert ran, the faster ran Hound. Three miles out of town they came to Fester's Pond, the local beauty spot and swimming hole. In went Mayor Bert, followed by Hound and Claws. Hound got himself disengaged from the action, transferring sheet and cat to Mayor Bert. With his arms pinned to his side by the sheet, now wrapped around him from neck to crotch, Mayor Bert started back for town at the same breakneck speed. A wet, spitting, snarling Claws clung grimly to his scalp, not quite dislodging Mayor Bert's toupee.

They made it clear back into town before Mayor Bert finally got rid of Claws. And then, he only managed because Claws had something better to do. The whole town had gathered to witness the commotion, standing around in little groups waiting for enlightenment, or gossip, whichever came first. The Hot Dog stand had set up on the corner and was doing a booming business when they arrived.

Claws, smelling the meat, was reminded that it had been some time since she ate. Swimming gave her an appetite almost as much as people-riding. She disembarked from her transport to amble across the road to the Hot Dog stand. Along the way, she flicked the toupee from her left hind foot. Mayor Bert made a dash to retrieve it, but without hands it proved futile. Besides, he got into an argument over it with a group of pigeons. The pigeons thought the toupee might be edible or something, and proceeded to peck it to death. Mayor Bert gave it a good try but his pecking ability was no match for the greater experience of the pigeons. Claws leapt onto the Hot Dog stand and was rewarded with a wiener, no relish, no ketchup, no mustard. The stand owner was delighted. Claws, recovered from her ride, was delighted. The town folk were delighted. Everyone was delighted, except Mayor Bert. He went home to get antiseptic on his scalp and on his pigeon-pecked nose. He also hoped Mrs. Bert would unwind the sheet so he could scratch a little. Hound had sent him another set of passengers who were just beginning to make their presence felt.

C H A P T E R   2 4

Meeses, Tame and Wild

Harry was greatly interested in animal wildlife, usually the larger, the better. His complement of white rats had improved to the extent that he had a couple of dozen, all individually named. He had carefully introduced each to Claws who had tacitly agreed to leave them alone while steak was on the menu. Harry reckoned that what his mother didn't know wouldn't hurt her, and she definitely didn't need to know about the rats. And Harry did love to gambol about with all his animals. So much was he interested in the animals that he would seek their company whenever the opportunity presented.

It was fortunate it was so, because the wildlife in Annespoint was coloured and varied. Harry got to know the habits of many little furry visitors, and some that were decidedly not little. The occasional transient wolf would trot into town to check out the local dog population and keep them on their toes, usually in the middle of the night. When the wolf had made it to the centre of town, it would set down in the middle of the park to try a few exploratory howls, just enough to alert every canine in town. The dogs would all answer back. Then, satisfied, the transient would

153

slip out of town again before the constabulary could locate it. Meanwhile the dogs would continue to give tongue, frantically howling at each other, the moon, and every passing noise until the first tentative rays of dawn progressed across the sky.

Dog was not immune to these fits. In fact it was the one thing he did very well, howling at the moon, or anything else, for that matter. Now, given a live chipmunk, three feet from the end of his nose, Dog didn't do so well. It was all right if the chipmunk were headed in the right direction when the chase started. But if the chipmunk were headed towards Dog, it was a different story. Dog simply didn't know what to do with the animal. So Dog never caught any creatures to speak of. That is, excepting one stuffed toy rabbit that had been discarded by its owner beside the path through the park. Dog seized it and shook it with such vigour that the stuffing fell out, or rather, shot out. Dog was so surprised to find the animal was nothing but a piece of cloth that he dropped it. As luck would have it, the remains of the rabbit fell into a creek, and drifted out of Dog's reach. Dog, reluctant to give chase into the wet, stood and barked at it until it was out of sight. The rabbit got away by this little stratagem.

Other animals besides wolves wandered into town occasionally. A moose or two could often be seen browsing beside the roads, or cropping the water lilies in backyard ornamental pools. For the most part they were gentle creatures, despite their great size. The chief problem was that they often got their great antlers caught in someone's wash, hooked it clean away, line and all, then dragged it through town snorting and shaking to try to get rid of it.

By this means, everyone would soon discover Mayor Bert's favourite make of briefs, or the size of Miss Cruikshank's brassiere. Otherwise no harm would be done.

But, in the fall it was a different story. The bull moose, in rutting season, would snort and bellow and paw the earth looking for other bull meese to challenge and drive off. As the creatures were remarkably short sighted, they couldn't distinguish between another bull moose and, say, a Ford station wagon. In a head on battle, the Ford was no match for a bull moose. So after charging and goring the car to death, the moose would shake its massive antlers, trumpet in triumph over the car, and jog off to find a more worthy opponent. The crippled car would hiss steam all over the place out of the crushed radiator, drip oil out of the cracked crankcase, and emit distinctly whining noises from its starter.

The driver would shake his head in exasperation, call up his insurance agent, and increase the moose damage clause on the next policy. Tourists, principally from south of the border, when afforded the moose treatment, would go home with a real story about the Great Canadian Northland.

It so happened one fall day that a lady moose on one side of the bush in the park, let it be known to the gentleman moose on the other, that she expected to be courted, and soon! Harry and Dog were out strolling through the bush, admiring the autumn colours. They didn't know they were in a direct line between the meese. But Harry knew what season it was, and when he heard old Mr. Bull Moose come charging through the bush snorting and bellowing its version of "Wait for me Nelly, by the old oak tree," Harry figured it was time to clear out of the way.

He tried to call Dog to heel. That had never worked before, and, sure enough, it didn't work this time either. Dog kept on chasing a rabbit, taking great care never to get close enough to catch it. The rabbit ran into a bush. Dog's tongue was hanging out with the excitement of it all, that is when he wasn't howling. The moose came upon him just when Dog figured he had got the rabbit cornered in the bush. The howling, combined with Dog's motion, convinced the moose that it had a contender for the lady moose's hand, or rather, hoof. Harry saw what was coming and decided that he could see the action better from up a tree. Preferably a long way up a very large maple tree.

Dog's eyesight was much better than the moose's. He had no trouble distinguishing size, about ten feet from hoof to antler tip and 1800 pounds; velocity, about 20 miles per hour; direction, straight for Dog; willingness to negotiate, zero. Since the moose burst out of the bush the rabbit had disappeared into, Dog took it into his head that this was a grown-up rabbit. He decided that rabbits, especially eighteen hundred pound rabbits, were not on his menu that day. Dog located Harry up the tree and elected to join him. He gained purchase on a low limb and scrambled up to the enormous branch Harry balanced on. There he stood quivering with fear until the moose, somewhat surprised to find his adversary climbing out of sight, charged the tree for good measure. Whereupon Dog leapt onto Harry's shoulders, clutching him around the head and effectively blinding him.

Unbeknown to both Harry and Dog, the fork in the branch had been the home of countless generations of squirrels over the hears. When the moose charged the tree, the branch gave way. Harry, Dog and branch careening down out of the tree straight onto the moose's upturned head, knocking him out. Harry lay stunned beside the moose for a few minutes while Dog picked himself up, sniffed all around the moose, then howled for sheer joy. The lady moose, who knew the rules of the game, decided that the spoils went to the victor. As she was the spoils she pranced over, all 1200 pounds of her, and tried to make love, moose fashion, to Dog. Dog left town with the cow moose in hot pursuit. He arrived home very battered and bruised about midnight the following night, but wouldn't discuss his adventures at all. On the other hand the rabbit population was quite safe from his efforts for some time thereafter.

Meanwhile, Harry awoke to find himself eye-to-bleary-eye with a very large, very old, amorous moose. The moose, still in something of a stupor, decided that Harry was his lovely lady moose and set off to consummate the union. Harry lit out for home, outstripping all land records for human speed in his passage, the moose chugging away behind. In later years Harry was heard to remark that he could easily win the thousand metre dash in the Olympics. However, the trouble to get the moose in position wasn't worth the pain involved. And for him, the pain was all too well remembered, as the moose took away a sample of Harry's briefs with it to display to the moose fraternity in recounting the story about the one that got away.

Victoria's meese were altogether a different breed. They were much smaller, their horns, if they had any, were invisible to the human eye, and they scuttled in and out of holes in the wall. Victoria, normally a lover of all creatures, large and small, took exception to the meese over-running her kitchen.

She decided it was time to call in the big guns and declare all-out war. Claws was enlisted for service. Claws was soon given to understand that it was "get rid of the meese or stop eating." Claws definitely wanted to continue eating. She only insisted that if Victoria was to be the commander in charge of operations, then Claws should be second in command. Victoria agreed. So they mapped out a campaign for battle between them.

The plan called for cooperation from Harry. Harry's white rats were to be called up for service as foot soldiers. Harry figured that the rats could infiltrate the enemy. The rats could crawl into the little meese holes and scout out the opposition. Then, being somewhat larger than the meese, the rats could intimidate the smaller beasties and herd them out of their cramped quarters into the waiting jaws of Claws. Harry had the job of training the rats in their roles. For Harry, it would be redemption for his little white friends, and perhaps a place for them in the bosom of the family, excluding Claws' bosom, of course.

Harry began an active training program to teach the rats how to herd. He started by getting them to herd a bunch of ping pong balls into a corner. Then they graduated to live critters. Harry took them out to the garden. They started with insects, but Harry gave up on the ants. They didn't cooperate at all, running off in seven directions all at the same time. Before long, however, Harry had the rats herding rabbits around. It is a little known fact that rabbits do not herd easily, so this turned out to be a real accomplishment. The rats were so proud of their skills that they thought to herd the neighbourhood cats out of the neighbourhood. Harry convinced them it might be a dangerous exercise.

Instead, he promised them a go at the meese, and protection from Claws. The operation proved to be a great success. After all the meese had been dispatched, Harry showed that he had not inherited his carpentry skills from his father, by remoulding the base boards to exclude meese holes. And his efforts were highly effective, too. Claws had an enormous feast, while the rats got the run of the house, under supervision, of course, and only when Claws was otherwise occupied.

CHAPTER 25

Selling Jo-Jo

arry and his older sister went to school. Harry's younger sister stayed home to annoy the neighbours. Jo-Jo discovered that she could make a great deal of noise on the hardwood floor by smashing her toys down. The neighbours came to complain. Victoria tried covering the floor with a rug and replacing the wooden toys with soft animals. After the first fit of sulks, Jo-Jo discovered a new trick. By stomping with her three year old heels across the floor, even barefoot, she could rouse her mother's wrath if not the neighbours'. Harry didn't mind the neighbours' wrath descending on his sisters. By this time he would cheerfully have sold them. He wasn't yet prepared to give them away, but he was prepared to make a profit on the deal. The first effort, to trade Charlotte for a garter snake, failed due to Victoria's untimely intervention.

The problem was never entirely resolved that year. Jo-Jo continued to stomp. Harry offered her for sale or trade. No one else showed quite the same enthusiasm to have her around as her parents. Harry invested a good deal of time in trying to convince his parents that trading Jo-Jo for some other wildlife was to everyone's advantage. Nothing ever came of it though. In desperation he tried trading her for a baby brother. Jo-Jo's parents showed no great enthusiasm for that deal either. When he suggested trading her in for a new car there was some resurgence of interest, but not enough to warrant any decisive action. Harry's parents were clearly weighing the advantages of a new car versus the disadvantages of children as a whole, when Harry decided to cancel his campaign for the time being.

The idea of owning another car had taken some root among the Flappers. Bull was agreeable so long as it wasn't pink and had a viable transmission. Victoria thought a nice shade of chartreuse would be ideal for a new car. She didn't much care about the inner workings, so long as the car didn't clash with the exterior paint job on the house. She thought the interior of the car shouldn't clash with her either. Together, Bull and Victoria sat down to write out the specifications for the ideal car for the Flapper clan. Including the cost of the wading pool suggested by Jo-Jo, who had recently discovered the benefits of bathing in the summer, and the scanning electron microscope for Harry, so he could examine whatever he wished, at microscopic level. The proposed car came to thirty-two feet long and only cost Bull thirty-seven years' salary.

They pared down their requirements. They settled for a stripped down station wagon, make, colour and options to be negotiated. They decided to visit various car emporia, those within walking distance, anyway. Eventually they found a dealer who could supply them with the car, not quite of their dreams and certainly not at a price they could afford. But it was a car that would match their requirements.

The family decided that as soon as the car arrived they should all go off on holiday.

Towards the end of June the car arrived. The family gathered in their new Ford station wagon. Then, dragging their ratty old tent trailer behind them, they set off for British Columbia. Bull showed them points of interest along the way, the Saint Lawrence River, which Victoria thought looked a lot like Spencer's Creek. The Chaudiere Falls at Quebec reminded Harry of Grand Falls, New Brunswick, which he had seen illustrated in a book. He decided to keep quiet. Mother thought that Lake Superior was a bit small. She didn't think you could see all the way across Lake Superior quite so easily. Then off they went across the prairies to the mountains beyond. Victoria privately thought the mountains were a bit small to be made so much fuss over. Six weeks later they wound up on the East coast again. There was some mention of a wrong turning six miles out of Annespoint but Harry and Victoria hadn't kept careful notes. So no one ever proved it.

Bull insisted that they got all the way to Vancouver island and produced a picture to prove it. Everyone else insisted that it was really Prince Edward Island and he had just got a little confused as to which ocean he was looking at. Either that, or he had a nice disregard for the truth.

CHAPTER 26

Harry as an Athlete

Harry decided when he was about eleven that he was a born athlete. He announced the fact over supper one evening, with the stated intention of joining the all-star hockey team the following season. His father opined that he might be a bit premature. In the normal course of events one should learn to skate first. Although Harry felt it was pandering to his father's unreasonable whims, he eventually gave in. Skating lessons were arranged at considerable financial sacrifice. Harry's parents did not, at first, realize there was another, much more important sacrifice involved. Sleep. Harry's mother was the first to find out. She kept it a secret for some weeks. Harry's father fell into the trap. He took Harry and Charlotte to their lessons. One hundred children were placed on the ice for the first lesson by their loving, though misguided, parents. There the children stood, clutching the boards, while the skating coach demonstrated the mechanics of ice skating. How to push off was the first lesson. On the command, one hundred children pushed off from the boards. One hundred children fell all over the ice. Hundreds of children's relatives screamed in anguish. All the children screamed with delight. Some were so well padded they couldn't get up again. The rest of the lesson was spent by the helpers in placing children on their feet. The children thought it was a great game: they promptly fell down again.

The second lesson was a little better. A few children actually let go of the boards before they began to fall. After the first year or so, most could make it all the way across the ice. The drop-outs went on to better things, like football or table tennis.

There was a rule in the skating club: the better you got, the earlier you had to skate. Eventually, the Flapper clan were rising at four in the morning for a five o'clock ice time. All, that is, except Mother Flapper. She claimed exemption. No one cared to dispute her claim. Mother Flapper in the early morning was a force to be reckoned with. None of the other Flappers were keen to do any reckoning at that hour, especially Father Flapper. He showed the least inclination to waken his wife.

Harry was eventually judged a competent skater. His father enrolled him in hockey school one summer. Hockey schools out East are invariably held in the summer, just before the snow has all melted. Harry's love of hockey was not inherited through the genes of his father. At best it could be said that his father tolerated the game. It was his mother who was the fanatic. She would avidly watch every game televised. Those that weren't, she heard on the radio. She would scream with delight or dismay, depending on what was happening to her team. The neighbours at first thought she was being beaten. When assured that she was just watching a hockey game, they would stay to watch her watching the hockey game.

Stories about her dedication to the game, and her antics during it grew. On one occasion, Bull's boss 'phoned just after supper, when a game had just begun. The boss, an older, very polite, very dignified gentleman enquired whether he might be disturbing the family by calling at that hour. Assured that he was not, he had begun to describe his problem, when a member of the opposing team did something nasty to one of Mrs. Flapper's players. "Kill the bum!" she shouted. "Clobber him, hit the no good wretch," or words to that effect could clearly be heard on the other end of the line.

Misinterpreting the situation, the boss said, "Oh dear! I have called at an inopportune time." Then he hung up quickly. Bull was quite mystified to find an unusually large raise in his pay packet that week.

Harry eventually reached the ripe old age of nine. His interest in hockey was known far and wide. It was exceeded only by his interest in baseball, another of his mother's armchair pursuits. During summer, with the snow pushed to the side of the field, the neighbouring children would gather for a game of softball in the park.

Harry was usually the catcher. On one particularly fine day he forgot to duck. A bat caught him on the side of his head. Harry went into the hospital again, this time without anything like the enthusiasm of the previous occasion. When it was apparent that he would recover, his parents sighed their relief, and promised him the world. Charlotte and Jo-Jo weren't quite so enthusiastic. They figured that Harry would want his toys back.

The official medical opinion enjoined Harry from playing team sports. He immediately took up chess. His father taught him. Harry loved the game. He read avidly every book he could find to help him improve. Soon, his father's enthusiasm for the game waned. "Well, I let him win another game," he would tell his wife. Victoria denied that she had any interest in the game. She was prepared to play with Bull, depending on what he was prepared to put up for stakes or what she might have to forfeit. As she was once heard to remark, she didn't think her game would ever improve as long as the forfeits were so much fun. Victoria had long since concluded that the best way to stay ahead of Harry was always to be playing at a different table, or to be in charge of making up the rules. She didn't think that she could get away with that in chess, so didn't attempt to play with Harry. Forfeiting to Harry wasn't nearly the fun it was forfeiting to Bull.

Harry's father vicariously enjoyed his son's success in chess. If Harry couldn't be a hockey star, perhaps he could gain international fame in chess, Bull boasted to his friends and neighbours. He would button-hole complete strangers on the street to exclaim on his son's prowess at the board. One of his colleagues proclaimed himself a chess master. He offered to teach Harry some of the finer points of chess.

Mr. Whitten-Brown was of the old English school. He reckoned himself an expert at chess, having once been junior lower school champion. Harry agreed to play Mr. Whitten-Brown, so long as it didn't interfere with more serious pursuits. Mr. Whitten-Brown arrived one Saturday morning unheralded. "It is our obligation," he said, "to encourage our youth and by so doing to set an example so that they will better understand their duties and obligations in life." Then he proceeded to lecture the Flappers, and especially

Harry, on the finer points of the game, proceeding at some length from the methods of movement of the various pieces to standard openings and then, illustrating each move, to showing the endgame. He very kindly offered to take the black pieces for the first game. Then Harry and Whitten-Brown set to for their clash on the playing field of chess. Several games later, under the indulgent eyes of the senior Flappers, Whitten-Brown gave as his opinion that Harry must be a genius. Only a genius could ever beat him. He then went on to lecture the Flappers on their responsibilities towards their genius son. Harry listened with curiosity to this little discourse, showing remarkable discretion, for a change. He didn't once gloat, although he thought about it a lot.

CHAPTER 27

Difficulties with Heaven

Harry decided to take up the study of chemistry the year he turned ten. He thought it prudent not to inform his parents about his latest pursuits. It is true that he had some trouble getting supplies. However, he was able to get his hands on an old chemistry set left over from his father's youth. He reasoned that his father didn't need it any more. At least Father had not shown any inclination to use it for at least twenty years. There were explicit directions on making various things. Of special interest were a few gases which smelled awesomely dreadful, some people might have said obnoxious. Consequently Harry spent some time learning how to make them. Victoria became increasingly worried about Jo-Jo's digestion over the course of the next few days. Since Jo-Jo showed no ill effects, Victoria shrugged and finally gave it up.

Harry thought he might try making a little gunpowder, since he had a little excess sulphur and some carbon. All he needed was some saltpetre. He tried a pharmacist. "Where do you keep your saltpetre?" he enquired.

The pharmacist couldn't see quite why a ten-year-old might want saltpetre. "There isn't much of a market for it these days, but I do have some put away. Why would you be needing saltpetre?"

Harry hemmed and hawed for a few minutes, but finally admitted, "Well, I'm really desperate to obtain some."

When Harry said he was desperate to obtain some, the pharmacist looked upon him with new respect. He said, "You know it's really a myth that it would work the way you want. Have you tried cold showers?" Harry couldn't see how cold showers would help in the manufacture of gunpowder, but promised to give it a whirl. He returned the following day to report that cold showers hadn't achieved much except to get everything wet. The druggist hastily gave him a small vial of saltpetre, then closed up shop and went home to his wife.

That good lady couldn't understand what had come over her husband. Here he was home in the middle of the afternoon, for goodness sake. There were some things one didn't do in the middle of the afternoon, she informed him. She was from Annespoint Society where such goings on were frowned upon, especially in the afternoon. The poor fellow went off to seek solace with Bo-Peep, who, he felt sure, would understand. He also felt sure that Bo-Peep wouldn't think anything about doing such things in the afternoon, although he hesitated to approach her anytime before noon.

Harry went off to his own work. His first batch of gunpowder represented a tiny effort. Harry packed it into a little cylinder and went off to collect Harvey. The boys headed out of town to a secluded spot to try it out. The resulting bang seemed quite satisfactory. They got back on their bicycles and headed for home. Strangely, there seemed to be excitement all over the place. People were standing about discussing the recent earthquake, and that in a zone that had never in its three hundred years of recorded history had an earthquake before. The boys quickly got down to work to reproduce their next little miracle. In their excitement, the saltpetre was spilled. It fell down the cracks of the floor in Harry's bedroom. After some fruitless efforts they gave up trying to rescue it and made plans to purchase more.

The pharmacist was quite shaken the next afternoon when two little faces appeared over his counter after school to demand saltpetre. He wanted to know what dose they were using. Harry told him. "Oh my!" that good man said. "Perhaps you are using a little too much." Harry agreed that was possible and inquired of the correct dosage. The pharmacist told him. Then both parties went off on their separate pursuits, Harry and Harvey to their manufacturing operation and the pharmacist, giving his wife a miss, went straight on to Bo-Peep.

This batch proved even better than the last. They secreted some quantity of it away under Harry's bed. Then set off for their testing range. The resultant bang could be heard for miles around. On their return to town folks enquired of them whether someone might be setting off dynamite The boys declined comment and set off home to lie low for a while. Bo-Peep got a rest for a few days from the attentions of the pharmacist, too. All remained quiet as the boys settled down to a relatively composed existence.

The Reverend Beverly Gordon took his calling seriously. In between discussions with God, he talked with his flock. He was always on the look out to save as many of the populace from their sins as convenient. One day while ministering to one of his flock who had strayed from the proven path too often, not attending his church and so not contributing to uphold that institution and its leader, he decided to canvass the neighbourhood. Victoria was at home, but quite busy with her own flock to worry overmuch about the Reverend's flock. Her response to the minister's query about which church she attended, was "Well, my husband, Bull, usually looks after such things, but he's not home right now."

The Reverend wasn't too sure about anyone named Bull but thought as he still had his foot in the door, he wouldn't remove it until he had something more substantial to go on. Victoria sighed and gave in, besides he looked like somebody she should know, but the puzzle hadn't resolved itself. "Bull won't be home until supper time," she volunteered.

"Perhaps I could return then," he suggested.

Vitoria gave up. Seeing as how he was a man of the cloth, she invited him to supper.

Charlotte enquired very solicitously of the Good Man that evening "Mister, did you know you have your collar on back to front? I wouldn't put my collar on back to front! Why did you do that?"

The Reverend sighed and thought about other children he had met and hoped they might be put to bed somewhat early that night. Victoria and Bull, watching, decided that the children might benefit from the discussion. But it quickly became clear that was a mistake. The children were not amused and proceeded to make things difficult, especially Harry, as his new batch of gunpowder, he figured, had about dried, and he wanted to put it away somewhere. Mother and Father Flapper held on grimly, refusing to be intimidated. The Reverend Gordon hung on grimly too. They all sat around the table and listened to the Reverend intone against sin.

Soon Jo-Jo began to nod. Victoria, sensing a means to escape, excused herself to put the youngest to bed. Charlotte and Harry looked at each other, then skittered after her. Both repaired to Harry's room where Harry took great pains to inform Charlotte about his newest venture.

Below, the Reverend Gordon was just getting wound up. He had decided to try out his last sermon again on a captive audience, to find out why some folks had snored towards the end of it last Sunday. He began quietly enough, declaiming against excess, and decrying sin. Bull wasn't too sure what he meant by "original sin" and asked the question, stopping Reverend Gordon in mid sentence. The Reverend's reply was still rather vague. So Bull tried again, reminding the Reverend that he did have a family and he hadn't noticed any storks around on their arrival. It stopped the Reverend, but only for a moment. He gathered his forces, thinking that here, anyway, he had found an exceptional enclave of sinners.

When Reverend Gordon got rolling again, he was truly magnificent. His voice rose and fell as he gathered steam. He pounded the table to accentuate his points and looked his captive sinner in the eyes. Upstairs, Harry had just decided that his last batch was not behaving in the approved manner. Downstairs the Reverend had just got to the good part, where, in thunderous tones, he called down upon the heads of all sinners the wrath of God. The unstable mass under Harry's bed went off with a bang, dropping most of the ceiling on the good Reverend's shiny bald head.

The Reverend sat amongst the mess. Mother and Father remained untouched, while all around the Reverend lay the remains of the ceiling. At last, he got up quietly, with dignity and moved toward the door "I am sorry to leave you so early, but I don't feel too well," he said.

Mother agreed that he did look a little peaked, then she solicitously, happily, saw him out the door. The Reverend made his way in a daze to his car, started it up, then peeled rubber out of the drive and all the way down the street as he made for the Snugglebunny Inn and the tender ministrations of his Amazon. Victoria, with some satisfaction, having glimpsed the Reverend from behind, knew exactly where she had seen him before, and filed the information away for future reference.

Victoria went to investigate the more earthly origins of the bang, starting with Harry's room. The room smelt rather badly of gunpowder. Harry sat on his dishevelled bed and tried to bluff it out. Mother was a hard negotiator, though, and insisted on having the details, before the fire engines arrived. Harry told her that a little experiment had gone awry, but it was all right now. Mother thought that Harry wasn't telling all. Harry decided that what Mother didn't know was good for him and held his counsel. When the doorbell chimed, Mother went down to admit the firemen and the police, both excited about the prospect of a return to the Flapper gang's hideout. Bull hid while Victoria barred the door, refusing admittance. "If you all are wanting breakfast," she intoned, "you will have to wait until morning."

They left, but reluctantly. Harry decided to take up the study of chemistry that same year. He thought it prudent not to inform his parents about his latest pursuits. It is true that he had some trouble getting supplies. However, he was able to get his hands on an old chemistry set left over from his father's youth. He reasoned that his father didn't need it any more. At least Father had not shown any inclination to use it for at least twenty years. There were explicit directions on making the most interesting things. Of special interest were a few gases which smelled particularly interesting, some people might have said obnoxious. Consequently Harry spent some time learning how to make them. Victoria became increasingly worried about Jo-Jo's digestion over the course of the next few days. Since Jo-Jo showed no ill effects, Victoria shrugged and finally gave it up.

Harry thought he might try making a little gunpowder, since he had a little excess sulphur and some carbon. All he needed was some saltpetre. He tried a pharmacist. The pharmacist couldn't see quite why a nine-year-old might want saltpetre. When Harry said he was desperate to obtain some, the pharmacist looked upon him with new respect. He asked Harry whether he hadn't tried cold showers. Harry couldn't see how cold showers would help in the manufacture of gunpowder, but promised to give it a whirl. He returned the following day to report that cold showers hadn't achieved much except to get everything wet.

The druggist hastily gave him some saltpetre, then closed up shop and went home to his wife. That good lady couldn't understand what had come over her husband. Here he was home in the middle of the afternoon, for goodness sake. There were some things one didn't do in the middle of the afternoon, she informed him. She was from Annespoint Society where such goings on were frowned upon, especially in the afternoon. The poor fellow went off to seek solace with Bo-Peep, who, he felt sure, would understand. He also felt sure that Bo-Peep wouldn't think anything about doing such things in the afternoon, although he hesitated to approach her anytime before noon.

Harry went off to his own work. His first batch of gunpowder represented a tiny effort. Harry packed it into a little cylinder and went off to collect Harvey. The boys headed out of town to a secluded spot to try it out. The resulting bang seemed quite satisfactory. They got back on their bicycles and headed for home. Strangely, there seemed to be excitement all over the place. People were standing about discussing the recent earthquake, and that in a zone that had never in its three hundred years of recorded history had an earthquake before. The boys quickly got down to work to produce their next little miracle. In their excitement, the saltpetre was spilled. It fell down the cracks of the floor in Harry's bedroom. After some fruitless efforts they gave up trying to rescue it and made plans to purchase more.

The pharmacist was quite shaken the next afternoon when two little faces appeared over his counter after school to demand saltpetre. He wanted to know what dose they were using. Harry told him. "Oh my!" that good man said. "Perhaps you are using a little too much." Harry agreed that was possible and inquired of the correct dosage. The pharmacist told him. Then both parties went off on their separate pursuits, Harry and Harvey to their manufacturing operation and the pharmacist, giving his wife a miss, went straight on to Bo-Peep.

This batch proved even better than the last. They secreted some quantity of it away under Harry's bed. Then set off for their testing range. The resultant bang could be heard for miles around. On their return to town folks enquired of them whether someone might be setting off dynamite The boys declined comment and set off home to lie low for a while. Bo-Peep got a rest for a few days from the attentions of the pharmacist, too. All remained quiet as the boys settled down to a relatively composed existence.

The Reverend Beverly Gordon took his calling seriously. In between discussions with God, he talked with his flock. He was always on the look out to save as many of the populace from their sins as convenient. One day while ministering to one of his flock who had strayed from the proven path too often, not attending his church and so not contributing to uphold that institution and its leader, he decided to canvass the neighbourhood. Victoria was at home, but quite busy with her own flock to worry overmuch about the Reverend's flock. Slyly she suggested that he might return when Bull was home because Bull knew more about those things than did she. The Reverend wasn't too sure about anyone named Bull but thought as he still had his foot in the door, he wouldn't remove it until he had something more substantial to go on than that. Victoria sighed and gave in, besides he looked like somebody she should know, but the puzzle hadn't resolved itself. She invited him to supper.

Charlotte enquired very solicitously of the Good Man that evening whether he knew that he had his collar on back to front. She couldn't quite make out how he had made such a mistake and told him so. The Reverend sighed and thought about other children he had met and hoped they might be put to bed somewhat early that night. Victoria and Bull, watching, decided that the children might benefit from the discussion. But it quickly became clear that was a mistake. The children were not amused and proceeded to make things difficult, especially Harry, as his new batch of gunpowder, he figured, had about dried, and he wanted to put it away somewhere.

Mother and Father Flapper held on grimly, refusing to be intimidated. The Reverend Gordon hung on grimly too. They all sat around the table and listened to the Reverend intone against sin. Soon Jo-Jo began to nod. Victoria, sensing a means to escape, excused herself to put the youngest to bed. Charlotte and Harry looked at each other, then skittered after her. Both repaired to Harry's room where Harry took great pains to inform Charlotte about his newest venture.

Below, the Reverend Gordon was just getting wound up. He had decided to try out his last sermon again on a captive audience, to find out why some folks had snored towards the end of it last Sunday. He began quietly enough, declaiming against excess, and decrying sin. Bull wasn't too sure what he meant by "original sin" and asked the question, stopping Reverend Gordon in mid sentence. The Reverend's reply was still rather vague. So Bull tried again, reminding the Reverend that he did have a family and he hadn't noticed any storks around on their arrival. It stopped the Reverend, but only for a moment. He gathered his forces, thinking that here, anyway, he had found an exceptional enclave of sinners.

When Reverend Gordon got rolling again, he was truly magnificent. His voice rose and fell as he gathered steam. He pounded the table to accentuate his points and looked his captive sinner in the eyes. Upstairs, Harry had just decided that his last batch was not behaving in the approved manner. Downstairs the Reverend had just got to the good part, where, in thunderous tones, he called down upon the heads of all sinners the wrath of God. The unstable mass under Harry's bed went off with a bang, dropping most of the ceiling on the good Reverend's shiny bald head.

The Reverend sat amongst the mess.

Mother and Father remained untouched, while all around the Reverend lay the remains of the ceiling. At last, he got up quietly, with dignity. He thanked Mother Flapper for the meal, but said that he didn't feel too good any more. Mother agreed that he did look a little peaked, the she solicitously, happily, saw him out the door. The Reverend made his way in a daze to his car, started it up, then peeled rubber out of the drive and all the way down the street as he made for the Snugglebunny Inn and the tender ministrations of his Amazon. Victoria, with some satisfaction, having glimpsed the Reverend from behind, knew exactly where she had seen him before, and filed the information away for future reference.

Victoria went to investigate the more earthly origins of the bang, starting with Harry's room. The room smelt rather badly of gunpowder. Harry sat on his dishevelled bed and tried to bluff it out. Mother was a hard negotiator, though, and insisted on having the details, before the fire engines arrived. Harry told her that a little experiment had gone awry, but it was all right now. Mother thought that Harry wasn't telling all. Harry decided that what Mother didn't know was good for him and held his counsel. When the doorbell chimed, Mother went down to admit the firemen and the police, both excited about the prospect of a return to the Flapper gang's hideout. Bull hid while Victoria barred the door, refusing admittance. If they wanted breakfast, she said, they ought to return in the morning. They left, but reluctantly.

CHAPTER 28

Birthdays

Harry's twelfth birthday started out as any ordinary day. Since most of the population of Annespoint was entirely ignorant of the genius lurking in their midst, it was not surprising that they ignored that momentous occasion. The rest of the populace showed up that day at one time or another, on one pretext or another. The invited guests included their neighbours, Jerry Blomwidge, who drove his Ferrari the fifty-six feet over to the Flapper's driveway. Al arrived with his sister on the rear seat of his motorcycle. Harvey, and sundry other odd assorted friends from the district, young and old, were also invited. Gideon Gallrock was there. Even old Mrs. Pumphrey from up the street came to the great gala. Grandpa and Grandma Flapper made the long journey down to Annespoint, especially for the occasion. Grandpa drove with his usual abandon, totally ignoring the other drivers on the road. He reasoned that if he pretended he was the only driver on the road, then he could drive as he liked. So he did. Other drivers could get out of his way as he blithely ignored them.

Grandma came over queer several times on the way down. It was very difficult for her as she was reluctant to upend her flask in front of Grandpa. Instead, she would plead with him to stop so she could go into the bushes. Grandpa was amazed at the poor state of Grandma's bladder and resolved to do something about it on their return home. Meanwhile, he humoured her by stopping. While Grandma was in the bushes, Grandpa spent the time swearing at the drivers passing him. After all the trouble he had taken to get out in front of them, now they were all passing him again. Grandpa figured there should be a law about that sort of thing. Out on the road again he would hurry to get back into position again, scaring the life out of the more conscientious drivers as he roared past at breakneck speed with little attention to the possibility there might be oncoming traffic. He was oblivious to the trail of destruction left in his wake.

Pulling up to within a few inches of someone's bumper, he would swear feelingly. "Why on earth do they allow turkey-brained idiots like that on the road?" he would enquire. "What does he use instead of brains," he would ask, "coddled eggs?" Then honking his horn with vehemence, he would dart out on the upswing of a hill, passing that "piddle-farted contraption with the wart-brain for a driver." The poor driver would almost suffer a heart attack as Grandpa ruthlessly cut him off in the face of a huge tractor trailer bearing down on them. The little man behind would stand on his brakes, pull to the side of the road mopping his brow, and decide that he had missed altogether too many Sundays at church.

Once Grandpa had passed someone they stayed behind him, even pulling to the side of the road if necessary to allow Grandpa his privilege. Grandpa almost became a statistic in Quebec. However, a passing patrol car, recognizing a man of importance, gave Grandpa a police escort to the border, where they had a hilarious discussion in two languages, neither having any clue what the other was saying. Grandma and Grandpa continued on their way after Grandma had taken another trip into the bush. When they finally arrived, Grandpa was in a mellow mood. So was Grandma, due to entirely different reasons. They were all set for an exciting vacation, free of the cares of home.

The uninvited guests included the Reverend Gordon. The prospect of a free meal was an inducement that couldn't be ignored. Great was the Reverend Gordon's surprise to discover a minister from another persuasion already at the fete. The Reverend McGonachie was also surprised to find the Reverend Gordon among the guests. Victoria was delighted that Mr. McGonachie could come, but less than enthusiastic to discover Mr. Gordon. She figured Harry must have invited the latter as comic relief and that the matter would sort itself out later.

Harry had prepared for his birthday with care. He started with his birthday cake. He reasoned that an twelfth birthday demanded special consideration, with more than the usual flame on the candles. In the early morning of his birthday, he rooted around in the kitchen until he found his mother's stock of birthday candles. Next he resurrected his recipe for gunpowder and prepared a fresh batch. There remained only the job of remoulding the candles with gunpowder applied to the wick down the centre. With just enough time to spare before his mother might go looking for them, Harry returned the candles to their hiding place.

Harry thought gunpowder might provide more sparkle. Taking one of the new candles with him to try out, he then quietly disappeared from the house. Claws and Dog accompanied him for a jaunt through the park. It might be more correct to say that it was Dog who took Claws, as the feline had curled up on Dog's back, keeping one eye open for some mischief to get into, and several claws anchored to Dog's pelt. Once among the trees, Claws went off to terrify the local squirrel population, while Dog went off to provide a little light relief for the rabbits.

Harry lit his candle, then stepped back to see how it might perform. It was almost too good to be true. The candle burned with a white heat, spitting and sparkling as it went, leaving only a small puddle of hot wax after a few moments. Harry spent the rest of the afternoon looking for bugs and other items of interest, in happy contemplation of the millions he could make after marketing his new candle. Eventually, tired out, he joined up with Dog to begin the trek home. Claws appeared from above, dropping lightly onto her transport, lightly that is, for a twenty-five pound cat.

Grandpa Flapper was having trouble adjusting to the fact that there was no swamp nearby. He stood with hands in pocket, a lonesome expression written across his face. When Harry, Dog and Claws appeared at the end of the drive, Grandpa went off to join them. He thought that either Harry or Claws might know where to find a swamp. Dog, he figured, was too besotted with Harry to know much of anything. It was almost party time before the group reappeared, Grandpa restored to a better humour, and Dog entirely exhausted, either from chasing rabbits or carrying Claws.

Sometime afterwards, Jo-Jo was pounding the piano in the corner with feeling, but not much control. Charlotte, no one ever called her anything but Charlotte, was sitting halfway up the stairs composing a sonnet on the mysteries of life, Claws on her lap, oblivious to the world. Grandpa was arguing ferociously with Mr. Gordon, and had just concluded that the minister must be one of "them spies sent over to destroy the fabric of the Canadian way of life." Dog was trotting around wagging his tail, wriggling ecstatically around the legs of his human friends, and ingratiating himself with everyone, while Victoria was preparing to bring out the birthday cake.

With a coordinated effort, Bull turned out the lights just as Victoria lit the candles and marched into the living room, with everyone singing Happy Birthday. The candles appeared to be glowing brighter and brighter, hissing and sparkling noisily. Dog was petrified, making a dash for the stairs and safety. Claws woke up in alarm, thinking that her time had come. She thought she might take Dog with her. As Dog came within range she launched herself onto his back. Dog retreated down the stairs. Harry figured he had better blow the candles out quickly and positioned himself at the side, taking a big breath just as the cake exploded. Mr. Gordon took the brunt of the blast. In the darkness, Dog's howls combined with Claws' growls to instil terror into Mr. Gordon's breast. As the lights came on, the white, cake-covered apparition that the minister had become, took to his heels in terror, his deep, sonorous voice now several octaves higher.

Dog thought the Reverend Gordon might be the cause of his unhappiness and, in a rare moment of aggression, attempted to relieve the minister of a portion of his backside. Claws hung on to Dog, snarling and screeching in turn. As

Mr. Gordon made it to the front door, Grandpa remarked to McGonachie that the fellow had seemed a bit on the weird side. McGonachie, who knew a good deal more about his colleague than was common knowledge, held his counsel. Dog followed Mr. Gordon outside and kept going at a steady pace. The minister made a few tentative forays to get into his car, but was thwarted each time by Dog. Finally, the minister headed for the one place he could hope for comfort. Dog and Claws followed to see where that might be.

Amazon already had a client and advised the minister to keep circling until it was his turn. Claws disembarked on one of the revolutions, to try a different strategy. In typically feline twisted logic, Claws had decided that the minister must be the enemy. On his next round, Mr. Gordon discovered his way barred by a spitting, snarling wild cat. He left the grounds of the Snugglebunny Inn at high speed, eventually finding relief in the middle of Fester's Pond. Dog and Claws circled the pond in opposite directions, stopping to confer every now and then. The Reverend Gordon decided he might leave town whenever he got out.

Harry, in retrospect, decided it was the best birthday party he had ever attended. He discussed the matter at great length with Grandpa, who agreed with Harry's assessment. Together they plotted the course of Harry's next birthday.

CHAPTER 29

Ping-Pong and Other Body Contact Sports

Harry figured he needed some regular form of exercise, so he persuaded his father to build a ping-pong table. The project was undertaken with the same degree of alacrity Bull had shown on other occasions requiring his skills as a craftsman. For example, some people might have thought that Bull should have used plywood just a little thicker for the top. But Bull figured the table didn't need to bear any weight, so opted instead to use a very thin plywood, quarter inch thick, if you are a conservative, six millimetres if you are a liberal. By bracing each section in the middle, Bull hoped it would do. Besides, the wood was cheap, obtained as surplus from his employer, who had used it to protect the bicycle rack from the weather.

Bull figured the warp wouldn't matter much once the table was braced. Unfortunately, this gave all sorts of scope for error, since it meant that five legs had to be cut to the right length on each section of the table, the fifth leg intended for the middle of the section. Right there the project got off to a bad start when Bull couldn't make the legs even. He applied a level to the top of the table, not taking into account the fact that the table tended to sag under the weight of the level. When finished, the table was a masterpiece. It is true that one section of the table was higher by half an inch than the other. It is also true that the warps in the table made little dips and hills somewhat greater than Bull had envisioned. On the other hand there was the minor consideration that the plywood was known as "good one side." That side happened to be the side facing the floor. The bad side, face up, was marred somewhat by the lack of a smooth finish and the presence of several potholes that might swallow the ball quite unexpectedly. But as Bull pointed out to Harry, it made for a really exciting game when you had to account for a dip of half an inch when making a shot. Or if you had to avoid a pothole so as not to lose the ball.

It was agreed that a pothole shot was a foul. The receiver needed lightning reflexes to return a serve, as one never knew just how the ball might carom off the table. This was a decided advantage for anyone familiar with the table. And Harry rapidly became proficient. He could carom off a hill or the edge of a pothole with remarkable accuracy. Even his slow shots were difficult to return. The state of the table led to the defeat of many an excellent player, cajoled by Harry into playing, with a few small bets on the side "to add a bit of incentive," as if that were necessary.

Bull, initially enthusiastic about playing with Harry, soon showed a lack of enthusiasm for the sport. Harry, never a good loser, was always magnanimous in victory. "Boy, that was a great shot you made, Dad. I almost didn't get it," he would say. His father rarely responded.

Harry had a good coach. It turned out that his grandfather was an expert on a poor table. Harry and Grandpa Flapper would practise for hours, discovering all the little nuances the table had to offer, neither gaining much advantage over the other, but both developing an ability to crush lesser opposition, like Bull.

They decided that it might be fun to implement a Ping-Pong ladder, with themselves as the top-ranked players, naturally. Everyone, family and friends alike were invited to join. It might have become a focal point for the entire neighbourhood if Claws hadn't taken an interest in the game too. One day she was lying, stretched at her full impressive length along a rafter, in the ceiling of the basement, eyeing the play below. It was a minor tournament attended by a good many erstwhile players, and quite a few spectators, who had come along for the express purpose of heckling. Among the spectators was Hilbert Spifflebanger, renowned for his home videos, one of which had even been shown on local television. Grandpa considered it a great treat to have such a celebrity in their midst.

Claws hadn't quite fallen asleep, she was in that somnambulistic state somewhere between waking and sleeping, well into the world of dreams, the erratic swish, click, thok, swish, click, thok below, barely impinging on her consciousness when her dream state evoked some far off primeval memory. Dog slept peacefully under the table, occasionally whimpering and jerking his right hind leg as if chasing a rabbit to ground, a very small rabbit. Perhaps, when the errant ball hit her, Claws believed she was a vengeful mother defending her young, or a great lion attacking a huge beast in the desert, to feed her cubs. She never did say what started it off. But suddenly there she was, right in the middle of play, swooping down like a vulture, she landed right on the lower section of the table, thereby causing its immediate collapse, while she destroyed the ball by the simple expedient of crushing it in her jaws.

Claws, now fully awake stood, spitting out bits of ping-pong ball while Grandpa hopped about on one foot groaning, muttering imprecations about that "darn fool animal that had the temerity to belong to the feline species." Dog, believing the rabbit had come after him with reinforcements as the table collapsed all over him, took off towards the other end, right through the legs of Grandpa's opponent, Jerry Blomwidge, bringing him down smartly on his rear. Not satisfied with matters so far, Dog then went through the bleachers, upending the entire lot. Then, baying at full tongue, he lit up the basement stairs.

Meanwhile, everyone, participants and spectators were in an uproar. This brought Grandma and Victoria down on the double quick to see what the ruckus was all about. Grandpa, by this time limping about, swearing, had finally taken in the complete state of desecration of the basement. Jerry was standing, rubbing his backside and thinking to himself that it would be some time before he could sit down comfortably. Claws, her tail fluffed out to its full extent and raised in as much a salute as a question mark, was stalking with great dignity towards the stairs and escape to a saner world.

Victoria dashed over to help her father, who would just as soon not have suffered her ministrations, while Grandma rushed upstairs to make some of her special coffee, and hoping that her secret supply of booze would withstand the demand long enough for her to replenish it. The spectators, finding no major injuries among them, decided it was probably the most entertaining game they had seen in a long time. They begged Grandpa and Harry to repeat the performance. Hilbert Spifflebanger had managed to capture the entire episode on video tape. So everyone, except Grandpa, trooped upstairs to view the tape and try out Grandma's special coffee. Grandpa stayed downstairs to swear some more.

Perhaps mellowed by Grandma's coffee, the preview of the tape turned out to be a great success. Between bouts of the action on top of the table, Hilbert had caught a picture of Dog, peacefully asleep under the table. While following the flight path of an errant ball that had caught the edge of a pothole and airlifted towards the skies, he had caught Claws peacefully drifting off to sleep among the rafters. At the precise moment the ball had careened into Claws, he had caught the cat's reaction. It was a masterpiece of filming, including all the sound effects of the occasion. Even as Hilbert was being tumbled to the floor by Dog's mad rush under him, he had kept the camera going. He had caught Grandpa hopping about, clutching his foot where the table had creased it, and swearing. "Goll darned thimble-brained cat," Grandpa said, and other such spifulous commentary. Hilbert made capital out of the episode. It was shown on prime time television that evening, complete with sound effects and a voice-over commentary describing the action as if it were a football game, all meant to be hilarious. Overnight Grandpa became a celebrity in his own right. It wasn't at all the sort of celebrity status, though, that would warm Grandpa's heart. He went off on another swearing fit, disdaining to take Claws with him into the wilds where he felt free to give vent to his feelings. Claws, miffed, followed him anyway, to make sure he came to no harm.

The RCMP, notified by the local police of increasingly suspicious activity in the neighbourhood, demanded a copy of the tape from the television station to check out the activities of the notorious Flapper gang. They weren't altogether sure about the notoriety of the gang, going strictly on the local police appraisal. Still, in the interests of public safety, they put a tail on Grandpa, as he strolled through the woods just outside of town. Grandpa knew nothing of this. Claws did. Claws decided the tail, dressed like a raspberry bush, was up to no good. As the trail meandered along Fester's Creek towards the pond, Claws followed. Every time the bush turned around to check behind him, Claws pretended to be an innocent pussy cat out for a stroll.

Eventually the path wound around to the cliff overlooking Fester's pond. At least the locals called it a cliff, though it was only ten feet, three inches high. They called it a cliff after poor old Mike, the town drunk, fell off and would have drowned, had he not had enough strength to stand up in the three feet of water below. Even at that there were discrepancies in the story, as Mike insisted he had been pushed by a kangaroo. Though the kangaroo had never been found, some people believed it was roaming around just waiting to find another victim to push off the cliff. Grandpa was greatly surprised when the raspberry bush screamed and leapt into the pool from only a few feet away. He was even more surprised to see Claws slink off into the undergrowth.

The hapless constable was the most surprised, however. He had been brooding about the story of the kangaroo, only to have one rise up right behind him and bite him in a very awkward place. The constable made for the opposite bank at great speed, leaving Grandpa staring after him. It seemed so odd to Grandpa, that the raspberry bush would leap into the pond in the first place. But to hear it swearing out loud, and to see it swim across the pond and emerge on the other side, running at full tilt for the trees, stretched even Grandpa Flapper's credulity. He decided to say nothing of the episode to anyone, although he thought it might be judicious to get back on the good side of Claws again. With that thought, he called the cat and they set off together for home, Claws restored to Grandpa's good esteem, and Grandpa firmly entrenched in Claws' good affections.

The constable's report on the matter was a model of restraint and diplomacy. He thought it impolitic to mention the episode of the kangaroo. He also felt it would be wise not to say anything about his swim in the creek. Not having seen Grandpa thereafter, due to matters beyond his control, he described what he thought might have happened, making Grandpa out to be a Godfather who met his subordinates in the woods during what others might think was merely a peaceful stroll with Mother Nature. Grandpa knew nothing of this turn of events, but thought it right strange that there always seemed to be a crowd of people behind him wherever he went. There was something incongruous about a couple of painters, a telephone repairman, a waitress from a restaurant, and a fire hydrant all strolling through the woods behind him, all apparently unaware of each other or him.

C H A P T E R 3 0

Grandpa Flapper Takes a Walk

Grandpa Flapper wore suspenders, wide, bright red suspenders. The suspenders were mainly for effect, although they served the secondary purpose of keeping his trousers from encircling his ankles. Grandpa had discovered that by sticking his hands through the front of his suspenders, and leaning back on his heels, that people tended to forget he was short and nondescript. They listened to him, or so he thought. Actually they were trying to gauge how far he could lean backwards before overbalancing, or imagining the consequences if he did fall. The red suspenders matched his knee socks very well. But few people knew that. Grandpa had worn lace up leather boots for fifty years and had no intention of changing just because they might have gone out of fashion fifty years ago. The boots kept his socks from showing. They were also useful for anchoring the ends of his winter longjohns.

Grandpa had settled on a routine for the duration of his visit. He would get up at five o'clock in the morning, making as much noise as he felt suited the occasion. After trying to impress Victoria by knocking pots and pans around the kitchen for ten or fifteen minutes, he would give up that pursuit. (Victoria had never been much impressed with early risers. No one had ever established whether she slept through the din, or merely ignored it.) Grandpa would then collect Claws and Dog and the three would go out to make their rounds, Grandpa to wake the neighbourhood if at all possible, Claws to get into whatever mischief might be going, and Dog to cower and quiver.

Grandpa would stomp and grunt his way to the end of the driveway, then stomp along the street towards the park. He was always a little amazed at the sort of thing he saw in the neighbourhood at five o'clock in the morning. For example, he would sometimes see Mr. Osmond, the neighbour from down the street, sneak in through his front door, with shoes in hand. Mr. Osmond didn't notice Grandpa, possibly because Grandpa was hiding behind a very large tree at the time. Grandpa was nothing if not curious. He wondered why Mr. Osmond would sneak into his own home. Grandpa thought it might be connected with the lipstick all over Mr. Osmond's face and neck, and possibly other places. It might also have had something to do with his buttons, none of which connected with their respective holes. Mr. Osmond's tie hung out of his back pocket. On the other hand, Mr Osmond was very cheerful, almost smirking as he would step inside. This was in direct contrast with Jake Howy, directly across the street. Jake would return home very gloomy indeed, muttering to himself, almost as if he were afraid to enter his house. In his case his pockets were hanging right out.

Most of these little diversions didn't last long. Claws wasn't much interested and Dog's whimpering threatened to give the game away. So Grandpa would stomp along again towards the park. There Grandpa and Claws would discuss nature while Dog slathered about chasing leaves or insects or squirrels or whatever else took his fancy. The routine was broken only once, the time Grandpa saw a couple of suspicious looking characters skulking about Mrs. Pumphrey's house. Grandpa didn't really think that deliveries would be made at five o'clock in the morning. Not only that, but the two delivery people seemed to be removing things from Mrs. Pumphrey's house, not putting them in. Grandpa, Claws and Dog scrunched behind a willow tree, well hidden by the foliage, to watch. Stealthily the two thugs brought out furniture, appliances and boxes of things. Grandpa, with Dog following closely, behind, set out stealthily to investigate matters a little more. It is probably not accurate to say that Dog followed closely, unless by that one means a euphemism for being glued to Grandpa's ankles, quivering, either with excitement or fear, likely the latter.

Claws, on the other hand, decided to investigate at close range in case Hound might be around, and offer up a little sport. While Grandpa and Dog snuck around to the rear of the house, Claws followed the thugs inside, to investigate matters there. Grandpa found Mrs. Pumphrey tied to her bed and rendered effectively voiceless by the expedient of having her false teeth removed. Grandpa didn't know what to do next, so stealthily tried to raise the window. It didn't budge. By this time Claws had found Hound tied up to the table in the kitchen, feasting on a huge, juicy steak. Claws immediately took over the steak, while Hound howled in protest. When Claws marched out of the kitchen with the steak, Hound dragged the table after, attended with blood-curdling howls and a great clatter from the table as it up-ended, freeing Hound. The two thugs arrived to try to subdue Hound again, but all their ammunition (steak) was gone. Hound was free and angry. He set after them with murderous intent. Grandpa, frustrated with his inability to open the window, lost his temper. With a great cry of rage, he smashed the window open, admitting himself and Dog, whimpering at his heels. They rushed to free Mrs. Pumphrey while the ruckus in the kitchen escalated.

Claws, having polished off the steak, returned to see what the excitement was all about. As the first thug emerged from the kitchen, Claws took him out with a flying cat grab, landing on the fellow's face, clutching his neck and ears with the claws on all four feet extended. Mrs. Pumphrey emerged from the bedroom, wielding her cane at just that moment. As the thug, blinded by Claws, tried to pass between Mrs. Pumphrey and the cellar stairs, that good lady clobbered him across the shins with her cane. "Stak at, you phrtlin' nummy," she screamed. The thug pitched down the stairs. His buddy, attacked in the rear by Hound, came high-stepping out of the kitchen, tripped over Dog, lying a quivering mass in his path, and pitched down the stairs too.

"Shee how uu lik' i'nown lair," Mrs. Pumphry screamed after the second one. Grandpa stood by admiring Mrs. Pumphry's use of language, determining to add some of her swear words to his own vocabulary. Mrs. Pumphry slammed the cellar door, marched over to the phone, and dialled 911. "Wheez got shom shtoopid Krooksh in zse sheller," she screamed into the mouthpiece. Grandpa gently took the phone from her to direct the police to her house. The noise level from the cellar had increased rather than decreasing, with the two thugs now screaming for mercy.

Claws was apparently in a temper. When the police careened up in platoons a few minutes later, they had somehow got it into their heads that the Flapper gang had been caught red-handed in the cellar. Greatly disappointed they were to discover that it was only the thugs responsible for half the thefts in town. The thugs, however, demanded to be rescued from Claws' tender ministrations. When released from the cellar they hurtled out, forearms extended for the cuffs, looking fearfully over their shoulders. Claws was much more dignified. Her fur still ruffled, she stalked up the stairs, ignored the police, collected Dog, and rode out the front door into the sunrise and a new day. The police chief recovered himself to say, "Wall stroke my beard and stomp my feathers, I ain't never seen anythin' like 'at befo'."

The Annespoint Ancient and Venerable Newspaper reported the incident in very subdued fashion, on the fifth page in the bottom left hand column, directly under the daily bridge column. CANS, the local radio station capitalized on it, filling in details not generally known, even by the participants. Eventually the story made its way back to Newnham, where it was blown out of all reasonable proportion under the headline "The Great Flapper Teams Up With Jungle Cat to Foil Thugs," spread across the entire front page. When the Annespoint Police were apprised that they had let a genuine hero slip through their hands, they were much chagrined.

Grandma came over queer a few times that day, aided somewhat by Victoria, who thought it was a quaint custom. When Grandpa and Claws sashayed into the kitchen, expecting lunch, they were met by the sight of Grandma and Victoria both asleep, propped up by the kitchen table.

Grandpa rattled a few pots to get their attention, but neither one seemed inclined to do their duty. Grandpa, thoroughly out of countenance, decided it was time to get back home again where he had only one female to contend with. Grandpa and Grandma left the next morning, Grandma dreading the trip, Grandpa with a gleam of anticipation in his eye. His final pronouncement to Bull was that he should hie himself off home so that Harry could grow up in more congenial surroundings, where he might be finding himself in more civilized company. It was generally felt that the civilized company in question was Grandpa Flapper.

Bull felt there was some merit in Grandpa's suggestion. He was beginning to suspect that his career would never get under way at his present spot. His first suspicions came after he had put an extraordinary effort into one of his projects, only to have it rejected on the grounds that since he was from Upper Canada, he couldn't possibly comprehend the situation fully. A few weeks later at a department meeting, his chief excused him on the same grounds, "You can hardly expect Old Bull to realize his plans aren't worth a pinch of groundhog doodoo, he's from Upper Canada, you know." Bull never did establish the relative worth of his plans in groundhog doodoo, but decided that it might be worth considering a return to the land of his birth. He had a decided preference for bullfrogs over ground hogs, anyway.

CHAPTER 31

Finding Work, and Other Expensive Pleasures

Bull started a frantic effort to find a job in Upper Canada. He was aided and abetted by a friend in the big city. Arthur Hapsbillingcut, of the Hapsbillingcut family of merchants, was a friend and drinking companion from Bull's university days. He phoned Bull one day to complain about the lack of civilized company around, by which he meant there was no one among his current acquaintances who understood that single malt scotch should be drunk neat, or at most with just a drop of water. Arthur was still shuddering from his last encounter with a fellow who insisted on having ginger ale with his single malt scotch. Arthur recounted the story, suitably enlivened for Bull's benefit. Then as an afterthought, he enquired "Are you thinking of moving?"

"Yes, where to?" asked Bull.

Arthur was quick to notice the hesitation in Bull's voice and capitalize on it, "To Cootesville. We don't really have a job for you. But if you want to come now, we should be able to find something for you to do, as long as you don't expect too much." Bull hadn't been expecting much at all lately. He was grateful for any tid-bits that fell his way. The job sounded entirely reasonable to Bull. "I'll check with Victoria and let you know." he said. Bull went on to explain, "They don't drink scotch here anyway. They don't even drink screech, at least not in public. The men do all their drinking out behind the barn. I never found it very comfortable. Besides, there's snow there most of the year around." Bull figured he finally had a fast track back to Upper Canada.

Bull went home from work that evening in a jaunty mood. After supper, he broached the subject with Victoria. "Arthur says if I come to Cootesville now, he might possibly find a job for me, maybe next year. It may be a bit risky. What do you think? Victoria? Victor-i-a?" But it was no use; she had disappeared. He found her a little while later, tearing clothes out of the closet andthrowing them on the bed. "What are you doing?" he inquired, quite calmly for Bull.

"Packing!" said Victoria.

Bull stood back in amazement. "But," he said, "Arthur only called me today. It will take some time before we know for sure."

Tight lipped, Victoria looked at him. Then with something close to pity she said, "Bull, there is a tide in the affairs of women. And in this case, I'm going to be in my boat and moving when the tide turns. If you don't intend to be on board, you could at least shove from behind." Bull figured Victoria knew something he didn't. When Victoria next glanced around, she found him filling his own suitcase.

Arthur was not satisfied that Bull had taken his offer seriously. Not wanting to leave anything to chance, he arranged to fly into Annespoint to apply a little more totally unnecessary pressure. Arthur arrived two days later, by taxi. Had he walked, he said, he would have been there a day sooner. But at least he had seen Annespoint junction, forty miles outside town. Forty miles, it might be noted, on the other side of town. "I didn't mind the ride out," he said. "There were two beautiful women, one on either side of me, and I might have made some time with them, given about ten more miles. But the ride back was conducted with a great fat lumberjack on one side, and his equally large wife on the other. They were fighting, with me in between. And not only that,"he complained, "but neither had seen a bathtub for the better part of the winter and all spring. Added to that, the taxi driver had the heat on full." He said, "It was an interesting ride. But I hope not to repeat it, at least this century."

Fed a couple of double scotches, Arthur had mellowed somewhat. By the third, he had decided that life was all right, after all. He explained what was entailed in the job. The main element seemed to have something to do with scotch, but by this time Bull couldn't quite make out what Arthur was saying. So they had a discussion on Greek philosophy instead, acting on the premise that neither knew anything about it so couldn't very well be contradicted.

Bull took the non-existent job. Victoria was delighted. The two years in the Maritimes, which had grown to ten, had come to a merciful end for her. Before Arthur left, the house was all but packed, even though the scheduled move wasn't for another three months yet. When the removal men arrived, there wasn't much to do except stack all the Flapper goods in the truck. Harry bid Harvey good-bye. With the keen insight of a fourteen year old, he also promised to write every week. So did Harvey. As neither could hold a pen longer than twenty seconds without developing writer's cramp, the promises, fervently delivered, were never meant to be taken seriously, by either of them.

Parting with Jerry Blomwidge proved more difficult. Jerry, friend, mentor, business partner, and confidante, was shattered when he heard the news that Harry was leaving. Bull, Jerry maintained, had never learned how to play cards anyway, so his presence would never be missed. But without Harry, Jerry would have to take up working again for a living. So Jerry did the only honourable thing he could think of: he offered Harry a home. Victoria, when the question was put to her, pointed out to Harry that Claws, Dog and the white rat community were all travelling west. If Harry wanted to come with them, he could. In the face of such telling arguments, Harry decided that he might be better off with his family. Victoria failed to mention the canary and Harry didn't think to ask. It probably would have been better for him to have settled the question of the bird at the outset. Jerry decided to retire to the sunny climes southward and live on his investments.

Harry decided that his bug collection might travel better in the car with him, along with Dog, Claws and the white rats. Neither Jo-Jo nor Charlotte were overly delighted with this arrangement. Jo-Jo figured Dog ought to run along behind. She was perfectly happy to accommodate Claws, on her lap if necessary. She was indifferent towards the rats. Claws was agreeable to the arrangement, but Mother Flapper queered the deal when she noted that Claws would undoubtedly either squash Jo-Jo or suffocate her. So Claws took up her position on the long-suffering Dog, who curled up on the floor at the children's feet. The canary sat in its cage just behind Harry's head, causing the latter a good deal of pain, one way or another. Harry got a crick in the neck trying to keep an eye on the canary lest the bird take it into its head to practise its judo on him. Claws and the canary, in close quarters, didn't make for comfortable travelling companions.

Just before Quebec City the canary led the rats in revolt against Claws. The uprising was ruthlessly suppressed. After the feathers and fur had settled, Harry claimed that one of the rats had disappeared. The canary, restored to its cage, indignant that anyone might suspect it of cannibalism, muttered to itself for the rest of the trip. Dog, not exactly a participant, but as his back served as the battlefield, displayed every evidence of relief at the end of hostilities. Charlotte read throughout the altercation, entirely oblivious to Claws' growls, Dog's howls, and Victoria swatting the combatants with a newspaper, none too gently.

Bull stopped every now and again to stretch, a relief especially welcomed by Dog. Dog, afraid to move lest he incur the wrath of Claws, lay on the floor of the car, shivering under the tender ministrations of Claws. Let out, Dog went wild with joy. The white rats and the canary stayed in the car. Claws, Dog and everyone else got out for a walk around, or in Dog's case, a frantic run around, dribbling on every tree and bush. Claws either followed Harry or rode on his shoulders. When Bull signalled, with a sharp whistle, everyone reassembled in their allotted places. They would drive on for another hundred miles or so, then repeat the process all over again. Otherwise, the trip passed in relative calm as they made their way in the Flapper rattletrap towards Cootesville.

CHAPTER 32

Cootesville

Cootesville sleeps in a valley some distance from Newnham. It is at least far enough away that neither Victoria nor Bull would expect a surprise visit from their respective parents. The area is surrounded by natural attractions, waterfalls sparkling off the sides of the cliffs that ring the town, wooded trails interspersed with the rich farmlands Southern Ontario is noted for. Next door to the moderately sized city of Hamilton, Cootesville has all the amenities of a city, while retaining the charm of an elderly, dignified, small town, and all the disadvantages too. The Flappers were used to the congenial life of a small town. They hankered after it. They were prepared to enjoy their new life.

When the Flappers arrived in town they had a week to spare to find a house before their furniture arrived from out east. There was no such thing as a Snugglebunny Inn to call home until a home could be found. Much to Bull's surprise, there wasn't an inn or motel in the entire thriving centre of commerce, excepting the local drinking emporium, a spartan establishment used by the itinerant male drinking population when they had a dollar or two to spare for a drink or a night's lodging.

The family put up at a motel six miles from Cootesville on the main highway from Here to There. There were several disadvantages to the place. It was miles from anywhere. The traffic ignored the posted speed limit of 80 kilometres per hour, attaining speeds of well over a hundred in either direction. This was probably due to the traffic light down the road. The drivers were either in a big hurry to get through the light before it turned, or in a greater hurry to escape from it if they were on their way to There. The traffic brought with it the usual layer of dust that settled in a fine film over everything. Perhaps that was the reason no one ever wanted to stay longer than a single night, and at that, most of the tenants were commercial travellers.

As far as Jo-Jo was concerned there was one mitigating factor that outweighed all other considerations: immediately beside the motel, in the middle of nowhere, was an ice-cream parlour, specializing in every type of chocolate flavour imaginable. Jo-Jo and Charlotte were in heaven, all the TV they could watch, and as much chocolate ice-cream as they could cajole from their parents. Harry was in the depths of despair. He didn't really want to watch the cartoons, which the girls favoured. The girls, who voted against him in a solid block, wouldn't switch to the sports network. And to insult him further, the ice-cream was all tainted with chocolate, which he detested.

Victoria and Bull began a frantic search for housing, egged on by a tough real estate agent, Mrs. Moynihan, who was determined to sell them a house, any house. First thing in the morning she arrived, to share breakfast and review the day's planned excursion through the houses of Cootesville. She spoke rapidly, with the peculiar monotone clip of the dedicated purveyor of houses, her teeth clamped shut as the words were forced out between them. Bull, who rarely managed more than a grunt until after his second cup of coffee, was caught with his cup to his lips on the first sip, as Mrs. Moynihan launched into her spiel on the relative merits of this house over that one. He had time for a taste of toast and a sip of his second cup before Mrs. Moynihan managed to pry him loose from his chair and got two grunts for her efforts. From that point on she figured Bull was a dullard and turned to Victoria for translation, running a lengthy monologue, so Victoria didn't need to bother. The first house, clinging in cobwebs, the hardwood floors curling up at the board ends, not only did not match their pocket books, but also would have taxed Bull's carpentry skills beyond their legal limits.

"This would be a beautiful home for the right owners." said Mrs. Moynihan.

Bull, who had no doubt that it could be turned into a magnificent showpiece, turned to Victoria to discuss the matter in private. Victoria looked at Bull in disbelief, then reminded him of past efforts, and swept out without any further consideration. As far as Victoria was concerned, the Flapper clan were definitely not the right owners. The house was missing the most essential feature; a window over the kitchen sink. The next house, just built, was surrounded by mud. The Flappers walked along a narrow board walk to get to it. Inside were pristine, newly carpeted floors hiding the plywood flooring below. The banisters were a vision in dramatic white and black paint. Bull could tell that Victoria was weakening when she saw the kitchen, a gourmet cook's delight, spacious and convenient, and windowed all around. Bull, disgruntled, decided it might be better to hide in the basement for a while. He was knee deep in water before he realized that the basement, as such, did not really exist.

Mrs. Moynihan assured him that it was just the normal damp basement found in a new house and would dry out in a week or two at the most. The crack in the far basement wall, newly patched, suggested some other cause for the water. Bull invited Victoria to view the basement with him, failing to warn her about the flood as she preceded him down into the gloom. She descended the stairs, her eyes not yet adjusted to the limited light, trying to identify the objects in the basement. She was knee deep in water before she had a chance to draw breath. Startled, she screamed. When that didn't help, she turned on Bull, to belt him with her handbag. Bull, not quite stifling his giggles, helped Victoria out of the mire. Victoria, not greatly amused, left in a huff. As Bull consoled her later, "It's much better to keep the swamp out of the basement. Dad tried bringing it indoors but didn't find it very convenient."

Monday gave way to Tuesday, then Wednesday to Thursday. The Flappers returned exhausted each evening from house hunting. Friday came and they became desperate. Mrs. Moynihan clenched her teeth tighter and tried harder. Passing the end of a long winding street up the side of the valley, Victoria saw a For Sale sign on a house sitting on a plateau on the side of the hill. Victoria looked at the house basking in the afternoon sunshine in serene glory. She fell in love with it in the instant. On the opposite side from her house, and a few hundred yards down the road, sat a picturesque, abandoned farmhouse looking down on the valley. Victoria called Mrs. Moynihan's attention to what she already thought of as "her house." Mrs. Moynihan wasn't too enthusiastic about pursuing the matter, because it wasn't her listing. But Victoria persisted. Mrs. Moynihan, in resignation, agreed to get permission to see the house.

Later that same day, Mrs. Moynihan arrived at the motel to escort Bull and Victoria to see the property. The house, built in the late nineteenth century by an incurable eccentric, was not old enough to be interesting, nor modern enough to be desirable. The big rambling kitchen faced out over the hill on one side, with a large window giving view to the spectacular scenery of the valley below. Also on the main floor there was a large, formal dining room and an equally large living room, complete with a huge, working fireplace. The four roomy bedrooms upstairs were serviced by a single bathroom, obviously constructed out of what at one time was another, smaller bedroom. The great old-fashioned, wood-framed windows let in the light, as well as the weather. The hardwood floors were stained and faded, badly in need of attention. The cellar, with no pretensions to being a basement, had massive stone walls surrounding a cobbled stone floor. The house was heated by an elderly oil furnace. Faded and peeling wallpaper, several layers thick, covered the walls, promising a massive job of renovation for anyone foolish enough to try.

On the way in, Mrs. Moynihan deftly guided them around the loose floor board in the entrance hall, pointing out as she went, the effect of the stained glass window, reflecting the last rays of the setting sun in a riot of vivid colour all over the ceiling. Then, as they passed underneath the stairwell, rotted out at the third step from the top, she pointed out the beautiful wainscotting around the bottom half of the dining room. They proceeded from room to room, Bull hanging behind to touch the wall or try to turn on an ancient tap, or even to try flushing the toilet.

Bull discovered that the plumbing was ancient, and highly acoustic in its performance, reverberating throughout the house when in operation. When the toilet upstairs was flushed, the noise began in the basement, rumbled up to the first floor, then finally erupted into the confines of the second-floor washroom, screaming like a herd of banshees on the loose. Filling the bathtub was an exercise in itself. The plumbing rattled away during the process, rendering speech in any part of the first floor impossible until the taps were finally turned off. Then when the plug was pulled, the great sucking noise sounded like a cyclone let loose in the house.

Victoria's good common sense deserted her, just when she needed it most. She forgot that her husband's abilities as a handyman were next to negligible. She forgot that the cost of renovating such an ancient fortress could be enormous. She saw only what it could be, in her mind's eye, not what it was. "We'll take it." she said. Bull looked around himself with mounting disbelief. He looked at Victoria, then down at his hands, as if willing them to an expertise in carpentry and repair of which they were wholly incapable.

Bull attempted to tell Victoria that she was making a mistake. But by then, she was halfway down the stairs, happily planning for his future, all his evenings, weekends and holidays for years to come. He could see it and feel it. He could already taste the plaster as it flaked off the walls, and smell the dust from decades past. He could already feel the slime of newly mixed wallpaper paste, and feel the paint dripping into his hair.

In that moment Bull realized that the entire rest of his days would be consumed by the house. He ran after Victoria to tell her to forget it. He landed on the fateful third step from the top and crashed right on through to the ground floor, never missing a beat as he hurried to catch up his beloved to save them all from penury and servitude for the rest of their natural days. It was the loose floorboard in the entrance hall that got him. As he stepped on the front part, depressing it down towards the cellar, the back end rose up like a live thing and smote him in the back of the head.

Bull woke up three days later in hospital to find Victoria anxiously hovering. When his eyes popped open she gave a sigh of relief, told him that she had just the thing to get him back on his feet again, then cheerfully went off to find the nurse. Returning some time later, Victoria told her husband that she had bought the house. She apologized for not waiting for him to recover, but as there was another offer pending, she had to act forthwith. Happily for all concerned, Bull's memories of the house had evaporated. So Victoria's enthusiasm had him smiling and agreeably falling in with her plan to move into the house immediately, as Victoria said, to save money. She also pointed out that Bull could begin the "little bit of renovation necessary while he recovered from his wounds." Bull, entirely ignorant of the scale of the renovations, happily agreed.

The furniture arrived and was carefully placed in the new abode. Bull, still suffering from his massive concussion, had no say in the matter. At last the great day arrived when

Bull was reintroduced to his new home. Victoria collected him from the hospital and drove home. She led his tremulous frame through the front door, carefully avoiding the loose board. Bull wasn't so lucky. But this time he saw the board coming up at him and took avoidance manoeuvres, dragging the surprised Victoria along with him. Victoria recovered in time to assist the ailing Bull up the stairs. She was surprised when Bull disappeared at the third stair from the top.

Figuring out what had happened, she skipped back down to collect the dazed Bull from underneath the stairs and start the trip all over again. Bull allowed himself to be led up the stairs again, but this time, he avoided the trick stair and made it all the way to his bed. Victoria's skill with a hammer matched those of her father-in-law. Although the bed would capably hold the lithe frame of Victoria, it succumbed to the much heavier Bull, tipping him out all over the floor as it collapsed with a crash. Victoria rearranged the mattress on the floor then deposited the shaken Bull on it. Bull then listened with mounting apprehension as he heard the noises of the house, the rumbling of the flush, starting in the cellar and working its way up to the little facility next door; the bathtub, when not in use, dripping, dripping, incessantly dripping, in use, a howling holocaust. He heard the wind creaking through the siding, and he heard the squirrels in the attic. And with it all, his spirit grew more and more restless, and his mind less able to cope, until he arrived at the only possible decision: he sent for his father, and relapsed into his former comatose state.

CHAPTER 33

Secret Rooms

Harry viewed his new domain with none of his father's trepidation. He set about exploring, starting from the cellar and working up. The cellar didn't appear to offer much in the way of possibilities for forming an empire or building a fort. It was barren except for the fruit cellar at one end and the furnace at the other. Moving on to the first floor, Harry checked out the pantry and would have taken up residence except that his mother didn't appear to be too thrilled about that prospect. So he continued his search. The stone fireplace seemed to offer all sorts of possibilities. He figured there must be a secret room off it some place if only he could find the hidden switch to activate it. A day and a half later and Harry was willing to throw in the towel. After going outside to investigate the wall behind the fireplace, he finally concluded that the secret room could be no more than eight inches wide, which meant that if he ever did find the secret switch, he wouldn't be able to fit anyway. Obviously the secret room in this particular house was built for very small people.

The second floor seemed to offer no further excitement. Harry was reluctant to infringe on the domain of his parents.

Besides, his father was still recovering in bed and was rather irascible at times. The girls wouldn't have him snooping around in their rooms, so Harry stood outside on the landing and cast an eye out for other possibilities. He might never have noticed the door hidden in a small recess had the wind not rattled through at that precise moment. It was a very small door, papered over with wallpaper to conceal it, and held closed by a piece of wood carved to match the decoration around it. Harry turned the wooden latch and found himself in a tiny passage with a set of stairs ahead of him, almost concealed in the gloom. He returned to his room for his special issue, deluxe, focussing flashlight to light his way up the stairs. Then, heart pounding, he began ascending. The stairs creaked, the cobwebs caught around his face and neck and the wind whistled eerily through the rafters. But when Harry emerged into the crowded attic, he immediately saw the possibilities for creating another empire.

In the old broken furniture, the discarded remnants of another era, he saw in imagination the stuff of dreams. He set about building his own little nook. A huge old trunk formed the back wall of his aerie, while the side walls were formed out of the backs of old sofas, chairs on their sides, and decorated with discarded pictures. So long as he stayed towards the centre on the wood flooring there was no danger of falling between the beams and so through the lapstrake and plaster to the floor below. One gable window provided light in the daytime, while an abomination disguised as a lamp provided light in the evening. Leaning against the wall furthest from the window, wrapped carefully in paper to protect it from the grime of ages, was something. Harry was anxious to check out the something. He unwrapped it with care, only to find an old painting. He was about to discard it as of no interest when all of a sudden his fourteen year old libido suffered a blow. This was no ordinary painting - it was one of the most beautiful women Harry had ever seen. The artist had captured her seated on a plush chair, her full skirts billowing out around her in virginal white, her long blond tresses draped over her shoulder as she gazed dreamily into the future. She clutched her robe to her bosom, revealing just enough to fire Harry's fancy. Harry immediately decided he was in love.

Downstairs, Grandpa Flapper had arrived in his truck, bringing all his tools, including his level. Grandma Flapper, somewhat slowed by advancing years, crawled out of the passenger side, slowly lowering herself to the ground. Grandpa set about exploring this new domain, level in hand, exclaiming about the marvellous workmanship here or decrying the poor repairs there. He tested everything with his level, tsking as he went, while Victoria trailed around behind him, anxious as ever to make a good impression, copying down Grandpa's every word on her pad as if they were pronouncements from a Higher Authority.

Grandma hmphed along after them for a bit, then set off on her own pursuits, seeking a hiding place for her small stash of booze. It couldn't be long before she found Harry's hideaway. Harry, somewhat appalled at first when his grandmother made her appearance, was soon dashing about to do her bidding, resurrecting a reclining chair for her comfort, washing it down, then wiping it clean and polishing it until the old leather on the chair fairly gleamed. Then, Harry at her feet, Grandma told him the stories of her youth, and with him relived another time, fired by the occasional medicinal snort, but mostly fired by nostalgia. Together they dragged out the old trunk and went through it piece by piece. There were old lace collars and high button shoes, long lengths of beads and boas and great ostrich feathers and underneath it all, at the very bottom of the trunk there was a pile of letters, neatly tied in a faded blue ribbon.

The letters dated from the eighteen eighties. But the thick paper had been well preserved in the bottom of the trunk. And the old copperplate writing, with its elegant flourishes was only a little faded. Harry and Grandma decided that they would read the letters, but only one a day. In that way, said Grandma, they could really appreciate the letters and the writer. So they opened the first one, which was as love letter from Alfred to Sophie. Alfred had apparently left Sophie for some reason.

Grandma lay back in her recliner and gazed out the window, not at the scenery but at another place and another time, the letter, for now forgotten on her lap. Harry looked at the picture of his beloved lady, hanging on the wall and noticed that she was not quite as young as he had thought at first glance. Perhaps it was the sad expression that played around her mouth. He thought to ask his grandmother's opinion and opened his mouth to do so when he noticed her expression. Comparing it with the expression on the lady in the picture, he thought maybe they were the same. Harry tiptoed down the stairs, leaving Grandma to her dreams. At the back of his mind he wondered about the mystery of why Alfred went away. What did he blame himself for? Why hadn't Sophy gone with him? Were they married? Were they lovers? Harry wasn't altogether sure what lovers actually did, but all the best books talked about them, without giving all the explicit detail necessary to understand the mechanics of the operation.

The following day they were back up in their nest, Grandma, Harry and Claws. Claws was intrigued. She prowled around investigating the various nooks and crannies in the attic. But it was summer and the squirrels had vacated the premises. Eventually Claws sought out Harry's warm lap and draped herself across him, first softening the area by digging her claws in and pulling them out one by one, much to Harry's discomfort. The second letter was read and pondered over, giving no new clues. Again Grandma went into her dreamy state. Harry, perfectly comfortable at her feet, gazed at his lady for a little while longer, his eyes slowly closing as he found himself in another world, slaying dragons for his lady and trying to bring a smile to her lips. It wasn't the tree limb scraping against the roof that woke Harry, but his own particular dragon. Claws, hearing the scraping, believed they were being inundated by a swarm of furry little animals. Digging in her claws in unmentionable parts of Harry's anatomy in preparation for a running start, Claws punctured Harry's dreams at the exciting part. Harry woke up suddenly, disgruntled, in pain, and conscious of a very peculiar feeling.

With the combined noise of the branch on the roof, Harry's moans of pain, and Claws knocking over various articles of furniture in the dark recesses of the attic, Grandma woke up with a start, coming over queer in the process. She retrieved her flask from her handbag for a medicinal snort. Noticing that Harry seemed to be in some kind of fit or in pain, she offered him a snort too. Harry, with all the trust of a child for his Grandmother, took a great swallow, then wished mightily that he had taken only a small taste. His first taste of alcohol proved a powerful restorative. In his struggle to get his breath again, Harry forgot all about his other problems. The fiery liquid burned a hole straight through to his stomach, part of it going the other direction towards his lungs. He went into a fit of coughing, his eyes streaming. "Gee, Grandma," he said when he had recovered, "your medicine sure is potent." Grandma, a small gleam of humour lurking in the depths of her eyes allowed as how it should only be used for emergencies. In any case, she said, there seemed to be enough emergencies in a day to keep her going. Harry wasn't altogether sure he understood what she was talking about.

In the following days, Grandma and Harry, by mutual consent, excluded Claws from proceedings. The letter reading went on without the assistance of Claws. Harry was beginning to dislike the letter writer heartily; this Alfred, he thought, was altogether too soppy. No new information came to light in the next several days. Harry's lady still wore her dreamy expression. Harry still dreamed of her at night, waking up at odd hours with the most peculiar sensations, parts of his anatomy, it seemed to him, no longer under complete control.

Finally the inevitable happened. Harry woke very early one morning after one of the most delectable dreams. He couldn't quite remember all the details. He only knew it was exquisite. And then he became aware of other less pleasant sensations. The sheets were sticking to him in the lower regions. They were wet through. He didn't think he had wet the bed. It didn't smell as if he had wet the bed. Still there was the possibility. So he dressed with all haste, balled his sheets up and snuck down the stairs with them, carting them to the pond in the field a half mile away. He rinsed them through, trying to prevent the green slime of the pond from infiltrating the sheets. His efforts were in vain. The sheets came out with a green sheen clearly visible in the early morning sun.

Harry strung the sheets over the bushes to dry and sat down to ponder life's strange mysteries. When everyone else had gone about their business in the early afternoon, Harry snuck his green sheets, now dried, back into the house and made his bed. The smell was a little overpowering, but he figured he could live with it. The problem now was to keep his mother away. He wasn't sure why he had to keep his mother away, he didn't think it would matter too much if it were his father doing the sheets. But somehow it didn't seem right that his mother should know about his little problem.

On the Monday following, Victoria discovered that Harry had a problem. She didn't know what the problem was, she only knew that Harry's sheets were green and smelled dreadful. She immediately assumed that her firstborn had come down with some dreaded disease causing Harry to wet his bed and turning his urine green. Extremely distraught, she immediately got Harry into the car to cart him to the doctor or the hospital or somewhere for help. At emergency she waited in an agony, trying not to let Harry know that his days were numbered, the tears seeping slowly out of the corners of her eyes and dribbling down off the end of her nose. Harry, mystified by his mother's behaviour, seeing her unhappiness, decided to humour her until he could get to the bottom of the problem. When finally their turn came, Victoria had a whispered conversation with the doctor. Harry, on the other side of the room heard only a few words. The doctor, his eyebrows arching along the top of his hairline, saying, "Good God! Green, you say." And, "Smells like what?"

Victoria tried to whisper, but in her agitation and exasperation said quite distinctly, "---smells like a swamp. I know swamp smell when I smell it. And believe me, so should Harry, because he was conceived in a swamp." This was the first Harry had heard of his origins and he found it not a little unsettling. The doctor was beyond words. He merely stared at Victoria for several seconds, wondering about primeval swamps and the origins of life before coming back to reality again and gently but firmly easing Victoria out of the cubicle. He had a whispered conversation with a nurse in which the words hallucinating and delusion figured prominently. The nurse took Victoria gently off to calm her and see whether she might be admitted to the psychiatric ward that day.

Harry decided that if anyone could fill him in on the mysteries of what had happened to him, it had to be the doctor. So he told all. When he got to the part about rinsing the sheets in the swamp the doctor could hold it in no longer. He started out with a chuckle that quickly grew to a full blown belly laugh. The doctor laughed until the tears came to his eyes. Then every time he tried to talk to Harry he burst out in laughter all over again. Harry had figured by now that whatever was wrong it wasn't life threatening. So he waited patiently for the doctor to regain his composure. "Nothing to worry about, Son. You just had a wet dream," was all he said. Harry could see that the doctor thought he had explained the matter clearly enough. But Harry was no further ahead. He left the cubicle in a puzzle to find his mother. It wasn't until Harry was outside that Victoria's other remark about conception in the swamp penetrated the doctor's consciousness. He chalked it up to experience and sent for the next patient.

Meanwhile, Harry was wandering about the hospital looking for his mother. He asked several people who gestured vaguely in one direction or another until Harry finally got to the psychiatric ward. When he asked there he was told that his mother was nicely sedated and couldn't talk to him right then. Harry briefly thought of stealing a robe and prising his mother free, but abandoned the idea at conception. This was a job for his father, he thought.

Bull was still hiding in his bedroom, awaiting events, possibly the collapse of the house. He figured it wouldn't be too long now, with his father on the job. He could hear the elder Flapper downstairs whistling jauntily between hammer blows and sawing noises. When the phone rang, Bull stretched lazily to answer it. But his son's revelations had him recovering a lot faster than he had intended. "Hold it," he screamed down the lengths of the phone wires, "what's this about your mother going crazy in a swamp?" Harry's explanation had come out a little garbled. Bull gathered that his beloved had somehow transported herself from the swamp to a psychiatric ward and was now in immediate danger of being committed for life. Bull looked around himself, seeing the faded wallpaper, the curling floorboards, and, reminded at that moment by the noise of the plumbing, figured that he had better rescue Victoria forthwith or he would be stuck with the whole mess himself.

He took off down the stairs, stuffing his shirt tails into his trousers, careening through the fated third step to reach the ground floor, avoiding the trick board, though it had long since been pounded into submission by his father with six inch spikes. Out the door he dashed only to skid to a stop as he realized that Victoria had taken the car. Back inside dashed Bull, screaming for his father to help as Victoria had gone nuts and Bull wanted to go and join her.

Grandpa, his hammer tucked down between a couple of belt loops, a pencil behind his ear, figured that his younger son had finally gone completely around the bend and if Victoria was in that unmentionable place, the quicker Bull joined her, the better it would be for all concerned. So they set off in Grandpa's old truck towards the hospital, the truck belching steam and smoke by turns. Grandma came over queer and retired to the attic to escape contamination from the crazies while she took several snorts to help dispel the anxiety.

When the old truck finally rolled to a stop by the hospital doors, Bull was beside himself with anxiety. He was through the hospital doors in a flash as he spotted Harry lurking on the other side. Grandpa caught up as they set off for the psychiatric ward. They arrived on the scene, Bull wild eyed, half dressed, unshaven and unkempt, demanding that his wife be produced forthwith or Heaven only knew what foul deeds would surely follow. The duty nurse took one look at him and sent for reinforcements, big strong burly reinforcements. Meanwhile, Grandpa had discovered his hammer and was battering at the door for entrance. Harry stood by and watched. He figured that once in, he would have to rescue the lot of them and he wasn't too keen on making the effort at that moment. Fortunately, the attending physician, hearing the babble, arrived to quell the disturbance. After a quick word with Harry, he calmed Bull's spirits, took Grandpa aside for a grandfatherly discussion, and gave orders for Victoria's release into the arms of her loving family.

When Victoria appeared some minutes later, it was a Victoria Bull had never seen before. Her eyes were dreamy: she sort of floated over to Bull, draped an arm about his neck and looked longingly into his eyes. Bull decided to get her out of there with all good speed..

Harry rode home with Grandpa, giving him an expurgated version of events, especially avoiding the discussion about green sheets. Sooner or later, he thought, his mother would be after him for that story anyway. On arrival home, the invalids headed for bed, Bull carrying Victoria upstairs as she clung dreamily around his neck. They disappeared for the rest of the afternoon, refusing later to even discuss events or explanations. However, Victoria gained a new lease on life, and Bull responded to the treatment with astonishing results. The following day he joined his father to effect the remainder of the renovations as rapidly as possible.

Harry took his Grandma into his confidence, relaying the whole tale to her, hoping for another taste of her remedy. After Grandma had finally finished wiping the tears of laughter away, she obliged. Harry discovered a basic fact of drinking from a half empty flask: it is impossible to sip, you can only glug. He glugged, going into the same fit of coughing as before. When he had finally recovered, Grandma and Harry read through the last letter. It seemed that Alfred was on his way home to Sophy with many words of endearment, having only just discovered that she was now with child. Their fortunes repaired, he promised to refrain from gambling their nest egg away again.

CHAPTER 34

Christmas, Bees and Other Quirks of Nature

Eventually Grandpa decided it was time to get back to his own patch of swampland. Besides, he reasoned, his son's house was now habitable. That was a matter of debate, but Victoria was equally keen to have her in-laws on their way. It wasn't that she didn't appreciate her father-in-law or his dedication to improving her lot. It was the thought of having her home to herself. Harry was sorry to see his grandmother go. He had come to appreciate her finer qualities, a recognition shared by his father. Grandma had begun to treat Harry as an adult and an equal because of their experiences together. Harry felt that he had achieved adult status and looked for appropriate recognition. His mother treated him with indulgence. But his father, now privy to Harry's secrets, looked upon him, though not quite as an adult, at least as more than a child.

Harry, Charlotte and Jo-Jo each tested out the new school system in their own ways. Charlotte, quiet, more brilliant than all her teachers combined, had never found it expedient to let anyone know what lurked all secret in her mind. She hid her flair behind Harry's bright impudence and waited for things to transpire, occasionally assisting them with a deft, but unseen hand. Jo-Jo didn't wait like a shrinking violet for recognition. She went out to actively cultivate it. Jo-Jo took the primary school system by storm, while Charlotte captured the junior high by stealth. Harry went along for the ride, discovering in the process that younger sisters were occasionally a boon. Their girl friends, invited to the Flapper household to play, soon began to swoon all over Harry. Harry, just beginning to realize the great potential in feminine company, kept his own counsel, with a slightly superior air about him.

Claws and Dog still walked the autumn forests, investigating anything that required their attention and a great deal that would have profited better without it. The rabbit population multiplied, making Dog's life a joy. The rodent population decreased, making Claws' life a misery. Through the red-maple days of autumn, Harry, Dog and Claws roamed through the little forest behind their home. Then one morning it was no longer autumn. The snow lay thick on the ground and on the branches of trees and even on the telephone wires as they looped in long arches from pole to pole. Dog was in ecstasy; Claws was in torment. They all went out to admire the new look of the countryside. Harry thought Dog and Claws might enjoy tobogganing downhill with him. Dog, his tongue lolling out to one side, showed every evidence of enjoying the new sensation in spite of Claws clinging on his back. Claws, well dug in, hunched down to avoid the wind and wait for the torment to end. Eventually Harry and Dog tired of the sport and headed for home, Dog galumphing along beside Harry, leaping from one snow tuft to the next, while Claws clung grimly to the toboggan, refusing to budge until the house came in sight. Then Claws was off like a streak to the kitchen door, meowrling piteously until Victoria let her in.

With the first snowfall came an introduction to their farming neighbours, the Carruthers, who owned the tract of land, including the bush behind their house. Mr. Carruthers was a large, well padded gentleman, perennially garbed in overalls and shod in rubber boots, in spring and summer a stem of hay between his teeth, replaced in the fall and the winter by a pipe, often empty. Mrs. Carruthers was as small as her husband was big. She was not a finger over five feet in any direction, a round, bustling, merry body, full of goodness and warmth. They appeared at Victoria's back door, "just in passing," they said, bringing into Victoria's kitchen the tangy smell of apple pie with cinnamon, straight from the oven and still warm in its paper bag covering. They all sat around the kitchen table in woolly sock feet, relaxed over tea and warm apple pie, and exchanged yarns, Mr. Carruthers filled in the details of the history of their new home and environs, and shook with a great booming, chair-rattling laugh at his own jokes. Harry, awed and silent, listened to the stories, enraptured. And when Mr. Carruthers, "Jephson, call me Jeff," announced that the farm chores waited, Harry surprised himself and his parents by offering to help. It was the beginning of an odd friendship between the elderly farmer and his young admirer.

Christmas loomed on the horizon, casting its magic spell over all the Flapper clan. Bull decreed that this year the whole family would trudge back to the bush to find a tree. He thought the living room, with its exceptional twelve foot ceiling would be just the spot for a twelve foot tree. So they all set out, Jo-Jo on the toboggan with a very reluctant Claws, Bull pulling them while Harry carried the axe. With Dog leaping around them they made their way, singing Christmas carols at full throat, Claws singing the minor chords with a piteous meowrl when she thought she might be heard. A half mile up the valley they came to a ridge of spruce trees. Father Flapper eyed them up and down, measuring them against his thumb, to select one of the right height, while Victoria anxiously enquired about ownership. Bull laughed off the question about rights to a virgin forest, while Harry snuck off to square things with Mr. Carruthers. Bull made several arduous computations on wind velocity, the relative straightness of the tree, the angle of the sun, and so forth, to figure which way the tree should be felled so as not to get caught up with its neighbours. Then with everyone safely at a distance, Bull attacked the trunk of the tree with his axe, narrowly missing his foot in the process. More by good luck than good measure he felled the tree, although it was entirely in the opposite direction planned.

Harry returned just in time to help his father with the swearing needed to get the tree out from among its relatives planted behind. Then they started back towards home with half the tree hanging off the end of the toboggan, everyone except Victoria and Claws called into service to pull. It probably would have been better for Bull's peace of mind if Victoria pulled too. As she was walking behind, it gave her time to think and to make a few calculations of her own. Four feet of tree hung past the front of the twelve foot toboggan, she calculated, and another eight feet behind, inhibiting their progress. She didn't say much until they had lugged the tree up the hill to their front door. Then Victoria casually mentioned the possibility that the tree mightn't fit. Bull, his mental capacity called into question by his wife, was outraged. "Of course it'll fit," he promised. "It just needs trimming at the base."

Victoria surveyed the tree, Bull, the house and the tree again. Then arms crossed and a beaming smile on her face, she left, refusing anything further to do with the tree until it might be fully erected.

With much effort, pushing, pulling and some indiscreet language from Bull, the tree was finally brought into the house, extending from the living room clear through into the dining room and half onto the dining room table, obviously too long. Getting it backwards out through the front door proved impossible, owing not only to its bulk, but also to the fact that the branches were now all facing the wrong way. So Bull supervised the removal of the dining room table, taking it apart to store in the basement. Then, removing the picture window in the rear of the dining room, he directed operations to remove the tree for some further cutting. Victoria retreated to her sewing nook to look after some urgent business, remarking as she went that Bull might measure the thing first before trying again.

Bull figured it was probably a good idea to bring the tree back through the space where the picture window should have been after a further four feet had been cut off. The snow-laden tree made its way back through the house in the opposite direction this time to have another trimming. On the next trip Bull, exasperated, lopped a further six feet off the once magnificent tree. When finally Victoria ventured back downstairs again, it was to see the tree mounted on a table so that it stretched up about three feet from the ceiling. The tree had become bedraggled while being dragged back and forth, with branches missing here and there, and a foot of snow covered the once shiny dining room floor.

Victoria followed the noise of thrashing about to see Bull, his foot firmly planted through the remains of the glass in the picture window, now flat on the ground. He was muttering beneath his breath things too awful to say out loud. There were spruce branches scattered all around the house, along with bits of trunk. The children had long since remembered chores that had to be done, preferably at least a mile away. Victoria put in an emergency call to the glaziers to come and restore her picture window. She firmly extricated Bull from the remains of the window and set him to shovelling the snow out of the dining room and restoring the house to its former pristine state. She ran water through the pipes to help prevent them from freezing until the glazier could arrive to restore the window in its moorings.

Eventually the window was replaced, the mess cleaned out, the branches removed, the floors polished, the rugs vacuumed and, as the house warmed up again, Bull settled in an easy chair with a glass of malt scotch, to admire his tree. He hadn't been there too long before a befuddled bee dropped down to share his scotch. Bull wasn't in the mood for sharing, so flicked the creature off, returning to his chair only to find it surrounded by bees, not all of them befuddled. Some seemed to be downright enraged. Harry arrived just in time to see his father heading for the great outdoors with a swarm of bees on his trail. Bull didn't stop to put on his boots nor his coat nor mitts. In fact he didn't even linger long enough to drink his scotch. Scotch, Bull and all headed off down the road. Fortunately for Bull it wasn't long before the bees realized they had made a tactical error and headed back for the warmth of the house. Harry shut them and his father out and called Mr. Carruthers to enquire on the proper procedure for despatching a swarm of bees.

By the time Mr Carruthers arrived with a hive to reclaim his missing bees, Bull was well past the frigid stage and had started working up to a good bout of pneumonia. Inside the house, Harry had discovered that not all the bees were outside. Judging by the noise coming from the trunk of the tree, he figured it might be judicious to shut himself into his room until arrangements could be made. Mr. Carruthers coaxed his bees out of the tree, and took them off. He paused only long enough to remark that Bull should have chosen a somewhat larger tree for himself as there were plenty of them.

Somewhere during the move from down East, the Christmas tree lights, carefully hoarded from year to year had disappeared. Harry set off with his father to downtown Cootesville to find some. The choice lay between a very large general store, crowded, hyped up with gaudy decorations for the Christmas sales, sporting a turnstile Santa, or the great old fashioned hardware store that stocked everything imaginable, including Christmas decorations, some from a bygone era. Bull wanted a long string of lights. He wondered aloud whether there might be a string with a hundred tiny lights so he wouldn't need to join strings end for end, never knowing where he might wind up or having to calculate how many strings could be joined safely, and whether twenty-five lights in one string had the same power requirements as ten lights in the other kind of string. The store owner, Mr. Finchley, portly, sedate, moving around his store with quiet grace in spite of his size, heard him. And Mr. Finchley took an interest in all his customers, especially Bull.

Mr. Finchley's first introduction to Bull the previous summer was every bit as traumatic as Bull's first sight of Mr. Finchley. Bull had come into the store and felt straight away at home, reminded of another era in the halcyon days of his youth when he was courting Victoria around the piled tins of her father's store. Bull gazed around, completely forgetting his mission, walking through the entire store to the dark recesses at the back.

Mr. Finchley, spotting him heading for the back where the safe stood in a dark corner, hurried after him. Bull, oblivious to the safe, Mr. Finchley and all, just wanted to inhale the faint pungent aroma of wax and paint and admire the implements on the wall and hung from the ceiling. When suddenly Mr. Finchley in his waist coat, tie plumed out over his great girth, held with a gold tie pin inset with a diamond, loomed before him. Bull, steeped in the past, thought it was a ghost come to claim him and stood transmogrified by fear, while the apparition inquired in sepulchrous tones whether it might be of some assistance. Bull fled for the relative safety of the front of the store, pursued by Mr. Finchley. Even with Bull's stuttered explanation, Mr. Finchley had regarded Bull with great suspicion ever since, and always insisted upon seeing to his wants personally whenever Bull put in an appearance. Bull thought it was because the store owner recognized an important person when he saw one.

And Mr. Finchley, always gravely polite, never let him know any different, but kept a surreptitious eye on the safe in the dark corner the whole time Bull was in the store.

So when Bull came looking for Christmas lights, and to reminisce a bit about the past, Mr. Finchley was waiting. Appearing behind Bull, the sepulchrous tones rang out, as always giving Bull a heart-stopping scare and causing him to juggle the glass bowl he had inadvertently picked up to admire. Fortunately Harry caught the bowl. Mr. Finchley led them to the Christmas lights and produced the hundred light string for Bull's inspection. "A hundred tiny lights, to sparkle and wink on your Christmas tree," proclaimed the advertisement on the box. Mr. Finchley carefully explained that the lights must all be lit. "If even one of the little lights blows out, the whole string will go out," he said. "They're in series, you know." he added, as if that explained everything.

Home they went with their new string of lights. As they found out when they got home, the wire and the lights had been packed separately. So Bull stretched the string around the living room and set about plugging in each tiny little light. Then, hauling in the ladder from the garage, Bull started at the top of the tree to string the lights carefully around it. Finally, with Harry's help, the job was completed. At this juncture, Bull discovered that the plug was at the top of the tree. A frantic scramble around the house unearthed an extension cord connecting the freezer to the wall plug. With the bright yellow extension cord stretched from the top of the tree to the wall, barely reaching, the light string was finally connected to the wall plug. Nothing happened.

Bull and Harry returned to the hardware store, where, under the eagle eye of Mr. Finchley, they bought some spare bulbs. Back home they went, Bull to climb up the ladder, Harry to hold it. Bull tried changing every little light, proceeding from one to the next, all around the tree, all the way down the tree until finally, on his knees on the floor, at the last light, he had success. The lights came on.

There was a brief halt during the decorating, for supper. Victoria went off to rummage in the freezer for the wherewithal, returning to inform Bull that turning on the lights must have affected the electrical system as the freezer was not working. Bull went down to attend to the matter, completely forgetting that the extension cord that used to connect the freezer to an outlet now performed that function for the Christmas tree lights. He took a flashlight to survey the ancient fuse box, hidden away in a dimly lit corner of the basement. He slammed the door of the box open, causing the box to come loose from its moorings. The supply wires fused together in a shower of sparks, causing the main fuse to blow out. The house went dark. The sounds of motors slowing down could be heard briefly, then quiet descended over the house. Quiet that is if you ignored Victoria's screams of wrath. She was in the middle of a delicate cooking operation, up to her elbows in pastry.

With the loss of the electrical supply the water pump quit too. Victoria was doomed to an evening coated in pastry. Order was not restored until an electrical contractor could be coaxed to come to the house the following day. Harry, observing proceedings, wondered aloud what his father was doing when the electrical supply had collapsed. His father talked at great length about the electrical supply and how it had collapsed by parts, starting with the freezer. Harry listened in awe to the learned discourse. Then he wondered aloud why his father had unplugged the freezer after the event. His father, remembering, didn't care to discuss the problem any further. Harry was left to conjecture.

Order restored, the tree was decorated by the entire family, gathered around in an evening of fun and festivity. Most of the decorations had been made by Victoria, including stockings for everyone. The stockings, enormous red plush stockings with fake fur tops, were normally filled after the children went to bed. In this instance Harry insisted that his mother and father should surrender their stockings to the children. Mother agreed, providing some material for father's stocking. Father reciprocated with some goodies for mother's stocking. Harry carted them off to plan and connive with Jo-Jo and Charlotte.

Very early Christmas morning, Bull woke up, whether aroused by Dog whimpering in sleep, or by Claws prowling barefoot over the bed, he didn't know. The longer Bull lay there, the more intrigued he became at the prospect of his children filling his stocking. Eventually, he could stand it no longer. As he said later, he only got up to let the dog out and perhaps feed the cat, though it was only six o'clock in the morning. On the way back upstairs to Victoria, he collected their stockings. Giggling like a schoolboy, he whooped into the bedroom, waking a decidedly grumpy Victoria out of a sound sleep. He also woke the children, two squirrels that had decided to winter over in the attic, and an old black bear half a mile further up the valley, hibernating in a cave. The squirrels pitterpatted back and forth overhead, the children hollered "no fair" to their father, who was bent on examining his stocking, and the cat came up to investigate the disturbance. While Harry and his gang berated their parents for prematurely anticipating Christmas, Claws went up into the attic to investigate scratching noises. Down below, Harry, Jo-Jo and Charlotte were tumbled onto their parents' bed, Jo-Jo squealing, while Charlotte smiled benignly and Harry thumped his father on the back. Victoria tried valiantly to keep her eyes open.

Upstairs in the attic, Claws had tracked down her quarry, not realizing that squirrels, even half asleep, were dangerous adversaries. The squirrels screamed, Claws howled and all of them thumped around in the attic until the party down below came to a halt. Upstairs flew Bull, with Harry behind him, into the attic, launching themselves into the fray. It soon became apparent that Claws was winning, the squirrels came second and Bull came last. Harry stepped onto the sidelines to watch the event. Claws chased the squirrels up Bull, Bull tried to fight them off. Eventually he fell off the midfloor onto the beams, then off the beams to the plaster. The plaster didn't hold up long. Bull fell through onto his bed below, accompanied by the squirrels. Claws, sensing that she was missing the fun, leaped down onto the bed too. Victoria, though not fully awake before, now leapt up with a surge of adrenalin and started screaming. Harry looked down from above with some interest to see what might happen.

Bull leapt for the window, taking the squirrels with him. He did open the window first before leaping through. Claws, disappointed at losing her quarry, leapt out after them. Dog, waiting below to be let in, joined the fray. But the frigid air cooled the squirrel's fighting spirit. By the time Bull made it to the bush behind the house, they figured that they really had better get back to their beds, and left their transport to fend for himself. Claws, not yet dug out of the snowdrift into which she had fallen, didn't see them go. Dog did, but decided that squirrels were not on his menu that day. Bull, still barefoot and in pyjamas, finally made his way stiffly back to the house.

Bull, accompanied by a frolicking dog and a disgruntled cat, came in by the front door. He stood surveying the scene, Victoria, demure in her woolly housecoat, seated by the fireplace attended by her coterie of children. Harry, as chief present dispenser in his father's absence, stood by the tree, while the gleeful girls, more intent on Christmas than smashed ceilings and unfriendly squirrels, squealed with delight. They all turned to look at the trio entering, Bull, with squirrel lacerations all over him, hidden in places by thick layers of snow, in his wet pyjamas. Then came Dog, his tongue hanging out in an anticipation of joy, and finally Claws, a sopping wet cat, a cat not at peace with the world. Coffee liberally dispensed, dry clothes, and a jovial air of mirth from the other inhabitants soon restored Bull's good humour if not his health. Claws sulked for the rest of the day. Her only bright spot came when she caught Dog napping in front of the fire and decided to awaken him in a rather painful manner. Otherwise Christmas proceeded as usual. Bull took to his bed afterwards for three days, refusing to budge, in spite of the draft from the hole in the ceiling over his bed.

CHAPTER 35

Gronk

The move had one happy advantage for the Flapper children, they discovered their aunts, uncles and various cousins. Harry's reintroduction to Aunt Clarissa was less than propitious. Victoria decided one fine day the following summer that the Civic Holiday long weekend in midsummer should be spent at the family home in Newnham. She had apparently forgotten the great Canadian pastime for long weekends, sitting in parked cars on highways. The family set out early Friday afternoon for Ontario's great northland. They got as far as Toronto before the traffic caught up with them. All of Toronto's two million inhabitants set out at the same time, going in the same direction, resulting in the most alarming traffic snarl since the Canada Day tie-up on the first weekend in July. Cars overheated and stalled. Tempers flared. Drivers, trying to avoid overheating their cars, shut off their air conditioners so that the entrapped occupants soon started snarling at each other as the discomfort level grew. Then the drivers shut off their cars, sitting in the fumes of the millions of faulty exhaust systems, waiting for the traffic to start moving again. Eventually the cars in front would start moving again, the drivers starting their vehicles with a roar to vent some of their temper. Some people, impatient, cut into adjacent lanes if they thought those lanes threatened to move a little quicker. Most people suffered in silence. Some had brought a picnic supper and proceeded to dine in their cars, while they waited. Everybody suffered, including the Flappers. It was very early Saturday morning before they finally arrived at their destination.

Grandma Flapper had waited up for them in an agony of suspense, coming over queer several times during the evening, but attending to it with admirable restraint. As the Flapper girls tumbled from the car, still sleepy, but radiating cheer, Grandma gathered them up in her arms to hug them, then shepherded them into their beds. Harry followed, lugging his duffel bag along. His place was on the floor of the family room in a sleeping bag, where he sacked out a few moments later with relief.

The following day Harry met his cousins. First in line were Uncle Gronk's kids. Uncle Gronk had left it late to get married, eventually choosing a very beautiful widow who already had two children, both girls. Uncle Gronk had then managed to increase the female population by a further two.

Before he was even out of his sleeping bag the next morning, Harry was inundated by little female children, ranging in age from ten to somewhat less than two. He turned over, still more or less asleep, allowed his eyes to blink slowly open, only to close them again quickly. He was not ready for the sight. Three little girls sat on the floor watching him, a fourth with her face upside down appeared directly in front of his nose. It was too much for Harry's addled brain at that hour. He tried to wish himself back into somnambulance, but without success. Besides, the girls had started to whisper things about him.

"He's not so big." whispered a very junior female voice.

"No," said another, "and Daddy said he was the handsomest boy in the family. He doesn't look very handsome to me."

"Well," whispered a third, obviously speaking with the wisdom of the eldest, "but you have to remember, he's the only boy in the family."

Responded number two, "You mean besides Daddy and Uncle Crawford and Uncle Henry and Uncle George."

"Uncle George doesn't count." said number one, the eldest voice. "He's only an uncle by marriage."

"Oh!" said Two again, then with all the candour of youth, "I thought you meant he doesn't count because he's a wimp."

Number three, anxious to vent her opinion, proclaimed "Maybe Cousin Harry's a wimp, too."

Harry opened his eyes to protest but was met by a malevolent smile, upside down, directly in front of his face. He closed his eyes again quickly.

"Naw," said One, the oldest, "from what Daddy said he's more likely to be a Nerd."

At this Harry opened his eyes again. He was confronted by the littlest, still upside down, smiling in front of his face. He realized that she was bent over, grasping her tiny little ankles, her face tucked in between her legs. She hadn't said a word to this point. But now she said "Oops!" and sitting down on Harry's left ear, proceeded to do her business into it.

"Mom!" screamed One, Two and Three simultaneously, "Cathy's done it again." No action seemed to be forthcoming, and Harry was afraid to move lest it get even more unpleasant. "Mom!" they screamed again, "Cathy just pooped all over Cousin Harry."

Whether it was because they had said the dreaded "p" word or the action so described, it brought their mother on the run. Taking in the scene at a glance, she scooped up little Cathy, told Harry not to move until she could get back, and trundled off, leaving Harry to his misery. The three little girls stayed to watch Harry. They surveyed him rather critically.

"I guess Cathy doesn't like him very much." said number three.

"Oh! I don't know," said One, "she only sits on people she likes."

"Yes, I know," said Two, cocking her head to one side to get a view from another angle, "but she only poops on people she doesn't like."

"I wonder if he can talk." said Three. Harry closed his eyes, hoping the girls would take the hint and disappear. He was afraid to open his mouth. He could feel the mass on his left ear beginning to shift ominously. He hoped Aunt Ellen reappeared soon. He was becoming somewhat nauseous.

"I think he's gone back to sleep again." said One. "Maybe we should go and see whether our other cousins are more fun." she continued.

The three watched Harry for a few more minutes before leaving him to his own devices. Harry kept perfectly still, eyes closed, waiting for rescue. But rescue didn't seem to be forthcoming. A few minutes later he heard some new arrivals. Then the patter of little footsteps interspersed with adult footsteps claimed his attention. "At last!" he thought, "They've come to rescue me."

"There," said One, "we told you Cathy had pooped in his ear."

"My goodness!" said a strange voice from a great height. Then the voice pealed with laughter. Eventually, when she had got her mirth under control, she called "Mom, come and see this."

The melodic voice almost had Harry opening his eyes. "It's a girl," he thought frantically.

Another, deeper female voice joined the first, and said in an awed whisper, "My Heavens! Right in his ear. Do you suppose he's awake?"

Three responded, "He opened his eyes a little while ago but then he closed them. I think he went back to sleep again."

More footsteps joined them, Jo-Jo and Charlotte, who broke up laughing and went off to get their parents and grandparents to come and see Harry. Harry was beginning to develop a crick in his neck. He could feel the mess beginning to dry a little, but the smell was overpowering. His mother's voice penetrated. "Don't wake him," she whispered. "I'll try to clean it up without disturbing him."

It was beyond Harry's comprehension how she was going to accomplish this. He already felt disturbed. That female with the lovely voice, obviously near his own age, had seen him at a great disadvantage. He didn't see how he could live it down. He thought frantically. Maybe if he pretended he was asleep, it wouldn't be so bad. Or maybe if he pretended he didn't know anything about it when he woke up, it wouldn't be so bad. His mother returned and proceeded with the clean-up operation. The pressure was removed from his ear, but then his mother began a campaign to tear his left ear from its roots. He grimaced and scowled and finally began to protest vehemently against the treatment.

Three said, "See, I thought he was asleep. He just woke up now."

Harry reluctantly opened his eyes. They were all there, all gazing at him, his father, his sisters, all four little girls, several adults he thought must be his aunts and uncles, and a very tall, extraordinarily beautiful girl he had never seen before. Harry closed his eyes again and wished for instantaneous death. When it didn't happen, he entreated them hopefully, "Would the last person out mind shutting the door?"

Harry got up, dressed quickly, and went into the washroom to work over his left ear again. He repeated the exercise several times that weekend. He delayed as long as he could but hunger finally drove him to the kitchen. There he met the Amazon. Alice had been adopted at birth by Clarissa and her husband George. Sixteen year old Alice towered over her mother and her father as well. She was not quite as tall as her grandfather, but at least six foot as near as Harry could judge. He looked up at her, to find her grinning at him.

"Well, look at it this way," she said, "Cathy must have a powerful attraction for you. She never managed to get anyone else in quite such a delicate way."

"You mean," said Harry in awe, "she does that to everybody?"

After breakfast, Alice took Harry out to reacquaint him with his grandparents' farm. She took him to the barn for awhile to leap about in the hay. In the process, all Harry's worst fears were confirmed. She could jump farther than could he, she could out wrestle him, she was smart as a whip, and she could outrun him. He decided that this was one female he was going to have as a friend. He certainly didn't want her as an enemy. After the wrestling bout in the hay, Alice decided she liked Harry. He might be short, she thought, but he was a good sport. He let her win in everything they did. When Harry finally cried uncle as she pinned him to the floor, she told him she had a forfeit coming and proceeded to kiss him. It was no cousinly kiss. It practically devastated Harry. It convinced Alice that she ought to practice some more with Harry to improve her technique.

When they came up for air, Harry figured for the sake of propriety and an unexpected ache that seemed to have developed in his loins, among other things, that he should get Alice out of the barn to somewhere more public. So he asked her if she would like to come with him to the swamp for a little excitement. Alice couldn't see how the swamp could provide any more excitement than they already had. She was prepared to argue the point until she noticed that Harry seemed to be in pain and didn't know where to put his hands. She reluctantly agreed to go along to the swamp. When they got there, Harry gazed out over the swamp with longing. Alice interpreted for him and told him that there was a boat somewhere. Harry went off to solicit his father's assistance to get the boat operational. Bull was only too pleased to oblige. While Harry and Alice helped Bull to refloat the boat, Victoria reacquainted herself with the bullfrog population in the swamp. She went around fondling the frogs and petting them and making little cooing noises over them as she enquired about their families. Although the old colony had long since given way to newer generations, the legend of Bull and Victoria lived on in the annals of swamp history. The bullfrogs were soon swarming around Victoria, each trying to claim her attention. Harry treated the frogs with the utmost caution, while trying to wrestle the boat into the water.

Finally the boat was launched with Harry and Alice aboard and ready for their excursion, Alice generously allowing Harry to take over the controls. Harry sat in the driver's seat on the left, while Alice sat beside him. She was a year older than he, four inches taller, and she outweighed him by a good twenty pounds. She was a sturdy farm lassy, used to hard work, with well shaped, muscular arms and thighs. In fact all her curves were in the right places. And Harry, was becoming increasingly aware of it. He felt morally depraved to want to kiss his own cousin, but despite his firm intentions not to let it happen again, he realized that he actually wanted to kiss her. Alice wasn't so inhibited. She had lived on a farm all her life and knew a thing or two about the birds and the bees. She also knew that Harry's thigh was next to hers and she proceeded to rub against him in the most alarming way.

Alice let Harry start the engine, and they shot out from shore. The boat, weighed down to the right under Alice's sturdy weight, careened in that direction and would have overturned if Alice hadn't taken control of the steering wheel to right the craft. Then she dropped her hand carelessly to Harry's knee and left it laying there. The boat took on an erratic course and Alice leaned over Harry to put it right again. Harry thought he had better get back to shore before either the gas gave out or his libido.

⸺∘∘❧❦❧∘∘⸺

In the afternoon Uncle Gronk rescued Harry from Alice. Somehow Uncle Tony didn't sound right, and it certainly didn't match his personality. Like his cousins, Harry called him Uncle Gronk. They went out fishing together in the swamp, using Bull's favourite bait, leeches. It clouded over when they were well out in the swamp, so Uncle Gronk headed underneath the sheltering branches of a great old maple tree, heaving the anchor out into relatively deep water. Then he unfurled the tarpaulin over the frame so they could sit in dry comfort and continue to fish. The sun came out after awhile.

Uncle Gronk rolled the tarp back up and stood up with his body through the frame, slightly off centre. It was a tight fit, Uncle Gronk's stomach resting on one strut, while the centre strut kept him wedged from behind. To balance the boat, Harry sat well over on the right side. When he got his first bite he became very excited, snatching his line up and losing the fish as a result. He was so excited that he scrambled over to Uncle Gronk's side of the boat to get some more bait. The boat leaned ominously to the left. Uncle Gronk, caught between the struts, overbalanced the boat, doing a neat swan dive over the side to escape from the overturning craft. The boat righted itself. Harry looked around for his uncle but couldn't see him.

When Gronk surfaced a few moments later, Harry was amazed. "What are you doing in the water?" he asked, "and with all your clothes on?"

Uncle Gronk was stoical about the adventure. He hauled himself out of the water, stripped to his shorts, and hung his clothes out on the frame to dry. The boat had taken on some water during the activities so required bailing. Harry was delegated to bail. Then Uncle Gronk announced that since they had made so much noise they may as well move to a quieter part of the swamp. He went to pull up the anchor. It wouldn't come. They manoeuvred the boat around with the motor and tried again. Nothing happened. Uncle Gronk thought for a bit, then decided that the anchor rope must have caught around a deadhead on the bottom of the swamp. He said as he was already wet he would dive down to retrieve the anchor. The best way, he said, was to cut the rope near the anchor to free both rope and anchor. He enjoined Harry to keep the anchor rope taut while he followed the rope down. Harry clambered up to the bow of the boat, then gripping the rope he used all his strength to pull it tight.

When Gronk surfaced from his dive a few moments later, the boat was empty. Harry wasn't anywhere to be seen. Gronk heaved the anchor in then climbed aboard to look around. Just as he did so there was a tremendous crashing of branches as Harry fell out of the tree where he had been flipped, and plunged into the water. Gronk pulled him into the boat. Harry stripped off his clothing, which joined Gronk's sunning on the frame of the boat. Questioned about how he came to be up the tree, Harry replied, "Well, I don't know. One minute I was holding the rope tight, then the rope suddenly went slack, the bow went up, and I found myself up in the tree."

They continued to drift and fish for awhile, until Uncle Gronk hooked onto something so massive, it towed the little craft right out into the middle of the swamp. Harry was enthralled. "Wow," he said, "how are we going to get it into the boat?"

Uncle Gronk was wondering the same thing. By now he had deduced that he had somehow hooked onto a giant muskellunge. Harry had given up fishing to watch the spectacle. He was so excited he was shouting. As the fish towed them into their own bay, the whole family came out to see what the ruckus was all about. And just at that moment, Gronk's line broke and he fell over backwards into the water again. When he noticed the crowd waiting for them at the landing he thought he might stay in the water for a bit. So he told Harry to take the boat into shore.

Harry, in his excitement, completely forgetting his state of dress, or rather undress, rowed the boat the few feet to shore then stepped out to beech the craft. It was at that juncture, his back to the crowd, which had gone very quiet, that Harry realized he was all but nude. There were a few sniggers from behind. Then one little voice piped up with "If Harry can go around without any clothes on, why can't I?" Whereupon, all Harry's relatives collapsed all over the ground with mirth. They lay about laughing for several minutes while Harry tried to regain his composure. He didn't think he could come up with a believable explanation for his state of undress. He also realized that Uncle Gronk was not going to be the slightest help.

When Harry finally turned around to face the music he decided to brazen it out. "Uncle Gronk," he said, "hooked onto a giant muskellunge that towed us all over the lake. It just broke his line when you all came down to watch."

From the peals of laughter and ribald comments, Harry glumly concluded that his nearest and dearest didn't quite believe him. So he stood surrounded by his embarrassment until his relatives tired of the sport and turned back towards the house, leaving Harry to his own devices. All except Alice: she stayed to watch Harry. She hadn't had too many opportunities to see men stripped down to nothing before. Even though he had his briefs on, Alice told Harry, they seemed to be so much more erotic than a bathing suit. Harry wasn't ready to talk about anything erotic, so kept his silence.

Alice wanted to know whether Harry would like to wrestle some more. Harry, red with embarrassment, didn't think he wanted to do that either right at the moment, but forbore from telling Alice. Alice was all set to pounce on Harry when Uncle Gronk appeared at the side of the boat. He sent Alice off on an entirely superfluous errand. With a sigh of regret, Alice departed. Uncle Gronk and Harry pledged with each other never to divulge the full details of their fishing trip, at least not until after they had managed to catch the giant fish they were sure had inhabited the swamp. That condition guaranteed their silence on the matter for life.

Harry thought his reintroduction to the family had been less than propitious. He hadn't yet met his Uncle Henry and his wife Lorraine, but he didn't think that branch of the family could top the set he had already met.

Claws and Dog enjoyed the trip as well. Claws soon discovered the barn and set about to investigate its dark recesses. She became so intrigued that she didn't notice the day slipping towards night, and in any case was not dismayed at the prospect of taking time to fully enjoy the visit. She decided to have a quiet evening snooze before setting out on her midnight rounds. The excitement tired her out more than she expected, so she didn't surface until well past midnight. By then all was quiet in the Flapper clan homestead.

Claws came down from her perch in the loft, leaping lightly to the floor of the barn. From there she headed out to scout around the house. There was a large dark shape hovering over the garbage bin, and a tantalizing odour coming from the remains of the family meal. Claws thought she might go and investigate the smell. If she were not prepared to meet the old black bear under those circumstances, the bear was equally put off at meeting her. He dropped the tin with a loud clang and roared his displeasure. Claws had never within living memory seen a bear. She thought at first it might be a very large, woolly dog so prepared to practice nose-biting. But the bear stood up on its hind legs and roared again.

Grandpa was up by now and rummaging about for his shotgun. He poked it through the window and, hardly taking time to aim, fired. Claws had just stood up to have a go at the bear's nose again, when the buckshot found its mark on the bear's bottom. Down it crashed with a great roar and went straight off through the bush at an incredible pace. Claws was astounded. She had hardly touched the great coward before it had given up the fight. Grandpa was chortling with glee. "That'll larn that derned ol' b'ar to come snooping about in my garbage!" he whooped. For the rest of the weekend, Dog found Claws very difficult to live with.

A romp in the wilderness with Grandpa and the farm dogs soon restored Dog to high good spirits. Claws disdained from accompanying them. She was perfectly happy to take on any dog alive, even great shaggy woolly ones that stood up on their hind feet. But when the dogs came in multiples, she retreated to high places and flicked her tail with annoyance.

CHAPTER 36

Collecting Money

For the next few years Harry's education took a new twist. He gave his life up to Mr. Carruthers' farm. Specifically, to the money Mr. Carruthers paid him to take up farming. But Harry was not mercenary. He went to enjoy learn about farming. . So Mr. Carruthers paid Harry to ride in the tractor with him, or to ride shotgun in the truck as he made his deliveries. As far as Harry was concerned, the money was a bonus. Mr. Carruthers had got along without Harry for nigh on forty years. Now he couldn't manage without Harry's assistance for more than a day. Harry thrived on the treatment. After school or on Saturdays, Harry would bicycle over to the farm in summer, or ski over in winter.

It became a common picture to see Harry wielding a pitchfork as he followed along behind the harvester, deftly catching what was missed in the operation and pitching it into the gaping maw of the baler. Mr. Carruthers had a few cows, a couple of hogs, and a free range chicken operation. But mostly his business was agriculture. He grew things: hay, beans, tomatoes, squash, cabbage, cauliflower and broccoli. So Harry learned about fertilizing and furrowing and harrowing. He learned about pests and weeds and "agricultural assistants," those people attached to the ministry who, without a shred of practical experience, offered advice freely to farmers. And because they were attached to the ministry, the farmers would listen politely and wait for them to leave before ignoring the good advice and carrying on after their own devices.

Unlike most farming operations, that of Mr. Carruthers was free of debt. Mr. Carruthers had inherited the farm from his father and from his father's father. And yea, his father, his father's father, his father's father's father and generations before had farmed upon the land. Mr. Carruthers felt the burden of responsibility. But having fathered five daughters, none of whom showed any inclination to follow in his footsteps, he knew that the Carruthers dynasty was about to end. So he tried, in his own way, to inspire as many of the younger generation as possible to respect and revere the land. And in Harry, he had an apt pupil. But there was still the question of money. And Harry discovered not only the land and the joy of companionship with the old man, but he discovered another value in money besides the strictly monetary. Each week as Mr. Carruthers paid him his wages, Harry would look over the coins, noting differences in the designs, setting some aside for further examination at some later time. Gradually he began to put together a great pile of coins. And he soon started sorting them by year, denomination and subtle differences in design.

Money, Harry decided, should be enjoyed as much for its intrinsic value as for its monetary power. Soon he had amassed a substantial collection of Canadian coins. All his pocket money went into purchasing coins to fill in the missing spots in his collection. He read everything he could on the subject of Canadian coins. He read catalogues, memorizing prices. He drew graphs of trends. He encased his coins in plastic and labelled them. He organized the coins into books and would discourse on them at great length, given the opportunity. Few of his family gave him more than one chance, for Harry could drone on for hours about coins in general, and his own collection in particular.

Flea markets proved to be a good source of coins. Harry would approach a prospect who had a coin he wanted. "How much?" Harry would ask.

"Hey, you're nothin' but a kid!" the dealer would say.

"Almost an adult," Harry would say.

"Teenager" the dealer would respond.

Harry practically bit his tongue off trying to contain himself. "How much?" he would ask, gritting his teeth.

"Five bucks" would be the response.

"I'll give you fifty cents," Harry would say.

"No, no, you've got it all wrong," the dealer would patiently explain to Harry. "The way it's supposed to work is, I say five bucks, you say three. We compromise on four bucks."

"Well," Harry would say, "according to <u>Charlton's Catalogue</u>, the current value for that coin in brilliant, uncirculated, or MS-63 condition, is five bucks. Your coin grades about fine, considerably less than MS-63. In addition, according to <u>Coin Trends</u>, the expected three-month trend for the coin is downwards. At most, it might be worth a buck. You can sell it to me for fifty cents, or keep it. But at a guess, there is no one else around here who will buy it or you would have sold it by now. Why not cut your losses and get rid of it to me."

The bemused dealer would agree. Home the dealer would go that night to tell his wife about this crazy kid who practically stole a coin out from under his nose.

Occasionally Harry would become fascinated by some ancient coin, a few thousand years old. He would add it to his collection on a whim. This was to become important a few years later as historical curiosities of a sort.

CHAPTER 37

Wasps and other Natural Calamities

Victoria's home was her domain. She had it fixed up exactly to her liking, except that her liking changed daily. Bull, just home from work, and looking to relax, would be given the task of rearranging the furniture according to Victoria's new plan. This usually meant rotating stuff in the basement to the first floor, some to the second and from the second back down to the basement or into the attic, whichever was least convenient.

Victoria had one constant failing, she adored her husband implicitly and believed him capable of anything to which he might set his hand. There was no justification for this belief whatever. In his finer moments, Bull had a few minor successes: he had graduated from university, more towards the bottom of the class than the top, but he had never actually recorded a failure. In spite of his father's prognostications about his possible lack of success in the world, Bull had exceeded all expectations and managed to remain gainfully employed over the years. His father, taxed on the subject of his earlier pronouncements, attributed all Bull's successes to Victoria. In a way, it was true. Since

Victoria believed in him, Bull found it within himself to succeed, thereby justifying Victoria's good opinion of him.

Grandpa Flapper never did understand Bull. He felt that Bull's mental capacity was only slightly greater than that of a water buffalo, his taste in music was nothing short of heretical, and his appreciation of his culture and heritage nonexistent. In spite of that, Grandpa Flapper loved Bull as deeply as any father could love a son. He would move mountains, or even small molehills, for his son, given the opportunity.

On this occasion, it turned out to be a family of wasps that had taken up residence in the wooden walls of the garage and threatened any living creature that came within ten yards of their domicile. After everyone in the family, including Claws and Dog, had been stung at least once, Bull sent out for reinforcements. This was not entirely an altruistic move on his part. Left to his own devices, Bull might have gone on for years letting the wasps take over the neighbourhood, except that when Victoria became agitated, she started moving furniture. More precisely, she had Bull and Harry move furniture. She was greatly agitated by the wasps, resulting in a lot of furniture moving. So Bull called his father to come and assist with the wasp-removal. Grandpa Flapper called Grandpa Sharp. Together the two of them drove down from Newnham in Grandpa Sharp's pride and joy, an ancient Volkswagon Beetle..

Whereas, either Mr. Sharp or Mr. Flapper might have been considered a menace on the roads, the two of them together were akin to a national disaster. No matter who was driving, each fought the other for control of the steering wheel. When the brakes were applied, usually accompanied by screeching noises, tire squealing, and the drifting of the car into oncoming traffic, it was difficult to tell who had actually applied the brakes. Amazingly, they were the best of friends and took no rancour, one for the others' interference.

As they made their way along the freeway, bypassing the great metropolis of Toronto, they heard on the car radio about a rash of accidents on the freeway. Neither could understand this because they saw no accidents. If they heard the odd almighty crash behind them, they attributed it to the usual noises of the city, not to their own erratic driving. "Sounds like here are a bunch of crazy drivers on the road today," opined Mr. Sharp as he wrestled the steering wheel away from Grandpa Flapper.

"Thank God we missed 'em," said Grandpa Flapper," slapping Sharp's hands away. "Seems to be a lot of dangerous drivers out there lately," he went on.

When they had almost made it past the city, the Volkswagen Beetle, tailed by a van whose driver harboured a death wish, switched lanes in the space of a car length. A tractor trailer laden with spirits intended for the great southern market, happened to be in the process of passing the van at that moment and was confronted by the beetle at the last possible instant. The truck's driver threw on his brakes, causing the trailer to jackknife, sweeping before it the van and its driver. It appeared for several moments as if the truck driver would regain control as the trailer hovered at a critical angle, before finally giving way altogether and stretching itself on its side the width of the highway.

It turned out to be one of Toronto's greatest calamities - not because anyone was injured in the accident, but because the temptation to abscond with the spilled spirits was beyond human endurance. All the car drivers behind rushed to help clean up the unbroken bottles. Since the traffic snarled for miles behind, there were lots of drivers and passengers, all of whom felt the need to relax over a small snort or two. The drivers, it appeared afterwards, had abandoned their vehicles where they sat. It seemed that they were all overcome with an urge to help in the cleanup of the spilled bottles. They were so anxious to help that they fought for the opportunity to do so, bashing in the side of the overturned truck to get at the liquor and so clean it up. After collecting an unbroken bottle or two, each one would wander off the highway to taste the delights of nature, and the illicitly obtained booze, in a nearby park. Drivers in the other direction, witnessing this, not wanting to be left out, joined in the crusade to clean up the bottles, thereby snarling traffic in both directions.

It became impossible for the police to approach the accident site or even establish what had gone wrong, except that the truck driver, trapped in his cab, radioed an unintelligible message for help. "Help," he screamed, "there are spirits all over the place and people are screaming all around me to get at them. If I don't get out of here soon, I'll be overcome by the fumes." At this juncture his radio went dead, either because someone broke off the aerial to use as a weapon to fight a way through to the booze, or because the battery was mortally wounded.

The message was received by the trucking company and immediately passed along to Toronto's police force, the Ontario Provincial Police and the RCMP, without interpretation. The authorities immediately assumed that the truck must have been carrying nuclear weapons or some hazardous chemicals or at the very least, used transformer oil.

Police and fire crews tried to make their way to the scene. Encountering people staggering down the on ramp, they naturally assumed the worst, that it must be poisonous gas that had escaped the truck. Either that or there was a great uprising aimed at sabotaging the main arteries to the city and taking the city by storm. This latter theory gained sway for several hours until the Prime Minister could be consulted. Local authorities hoped he would authorize the army detachment at Borden to be brought in to quell the uprising.

The members of the press converged upon the Prime Minister as the latter made his way from his chambers towards the floor of the House. The gentlemen of the press demanded to know what he was going to do about the Uprising in Toronto. The Prime Minister, in his wildest imagination, couldn't believe there were enough dissidents in Toronto to uprise. But he thought perhaps he had better hold his counsel until he knew more about it.

"We have the gravest concern for the population of that great city," he said, "and will move with all speed as soon as our intelligence reports have been compiled." With these words he managed to convey to the world that he not only knew what was going on but had a plan to do something about it.

The Prime Minister's message was immediately broadcast on TV. It was a great surprise to the residents of Toronto to discover that they were under siege. Word spread quickly, though, and soon half the population of the city were barricaded inside their homes. The phone wires were humming as the populace all tried to find out more information. This great demand on Ma Bell's enterprise caused its immediate and total collapse, thereby creating near panic.

Meanwhile, in Ottawa, the Prime Minister quickly returned to his chambers to summon all his advisors, none of whom had the slightest idea what was going on, but all of whom had been beleaguered by their constituents to do something about it. The Prime Minister turned to the RCMP who were now convinced that the city must be under attack by chemical weapons. The Chief Fuzz reported the message received from the doomed truck driver, without elaboration, leaving the Prime Minister to make what he could of it. The Chief Fuzz then went on to tell the Prime Minister that further communications in or out of Toronto were not possible because the phone system was no longer operable. The Prime Minister wanted good news to report to the House, not this continuous litany of disaster.

At this juncture, the red phone on the Prime Minister's desk rang. The members of his cabinet, gathered in his office fell silent while he picked up the receiver and cooly responded, "Oui?" "Dear" said Mrs. Prime Minister, could you pick up some bread, milk and butterfly shrimp for supper, on your way home?" AS an afterthought she asked, "What on earth is going on in Toronto as there seemed to be some kind of war on there? I never did understand why the fuss over that city! Anyway, it's all over the news. Oh! And don't be late for supper, the frazer's are coming to dine with us."

Mr. Prime Minister immediately dashed to his TV set. Turning it on he was astounded to see pictures of people lying comatose all over the place, or just staggering around. The site had been cordoned off by police for a distance of half a mile, with no one allowed inside the disaster zone. Consequently, long range lenses were used to pick up the pictures, focussing in on the truck lying on its side, now deserted, except for the trapped driver. The booze was all gone, except for the fumes from the spilled spirits, which were overpowering.

The announcer, in an awful, excited whisper, conjectured on the size of the disaster. As he spoke, he kept switching to the accidents which were blocking traffic all across highway 401, starting in the East and moving West, each one snarling more traffic as half the residents all tried to make it to the highway and escape the conflagration in the besieged city. By this time, the rest of the country had been apprised of the scale of operations in Toronto. Dissidents decided to take advantage of the situation resulting in their spokespeople across the country decrying the carnage in Toronto. They then went on to state that it was bound to happen since the Government continued to ignore their plight.

In the House, matters were completely out of hand. Members of the Government lost faith in their leader. Members of the Loyal Opposition, had never had any faith in the Prime Minister. The bells started to ring, summoning all parliamentarians to their seats as a vote of none-confidence in the government's handling of the crisis made it to the floor of the House. An obviously shaken Prime Minister came into the House to take his seat and quell the rising mutiny from within his party ranks. He couldn't: the Government fell. Loyal members of the Senate Opposition woke up for long enough to cackle "Hoorah, Hoorah," before lapsing into their semicomatose state. The

Senators of the Government persuasion didn't bother to wake up.

—∘∘❏❦❐∘∘—

Back in Toronto, the truck driver, deciding to take matters into his own hands, smashed his way out of the truck. Then, reeking in Seagram's best, he made his way towards the police lines. The police were less than enthusiastic to receive him. They were convinced that he was contaminated with deadly gas. In any case, his version of events didn't tally with the official version. So the authorities decided that the poor fellow had gone completely around the bend and carted him off for psychiatric evaluation. At this, he became the first casualty of this "psychological war," as it was later labelled by the press.

It took three days for the city to return to normal. It took several months and an election for the rest of the country to approach normalcy, and then only when public pressure forced the Government to reconsider the Native Land Claims. Not to be outdone, the Italians, Greeks and Scottish immigrants, even from seven generations back, decided to make their own demands. So the country sank into a turmoil, even worse than usual.

The Messrs. Sharp and Flapper heard detailed reports on the crisis unfolding behind them and congratulated themselves on having escaped the great conflagration. Since they had got rid of the unruly van driver, they found they had the road to themselves, except for the masses of cars which kept appearing and disappearing behind them, and about which they were mostly oblivious. It was just as well.

There was no telling what might have befallen, had they been given further opportunity.

Arriving at the junior Flapper household, they were greeted like heros who had braved the uprising just to attend to Victoria's cry for help. They quickly set about their work. Their first idea was to smoke the little beggars out. Mr. Sharp got a good fire going in an old black pot, while Mr. Flapper cut the grass to get the makings for a smudge pot. When the grass cuttings were added, great puffs of thick black smoke emerged, somewhat darkened by the addition of a few old bicycle tires Grandpa Flapper thought to include with the cuttings. The wasps retired to the woodwork to wait out the turn in the weather. Mr. Carruthers and the other neighbours, not being privy to the battle secrets, in fact, entirely ignorant of the battle being waged, came hotfoot down to the Flapper household in case their help might be needed to help put out the fire, and if not, to enjoy the blaze. The deFleurs from down the hill came too. Mrs. deFleur had never learned to speak English, but through her very presentable younger daughter, Lisette, managed to convey her concern very charmingly for the well-being of the Flapper menage.

Harry arrived home from school just as the fire engines arrived. However, the firemen left after only a few moments, not staying for the party, although invited to do so by the cheerful Victoria. The neighbours all stayed to watch the proceedings, from a safe distance. Harry stayed to watch Lisette. Except for his cousin Alice, it was the first time he had ever actually noticed a girl up close, and he was not about to let the chance slip by without making at least some attempt to communicate.

The grandfathers retired to the back stoop for a cold lemonade and to plot their next stratagem, ably advised by various members of the assembled throng. Swearing at the wasps didn't appear to have any desired effect so Grandpa Sharp, armed with a tin of insecticide, tried to outshoot the wasps. They retired inside again, where they could be heard buzzing faintly, angrily, from deep within the walls of the garage.

Harry and Lisette, by now comparing notes on the world in general, began to discuss the possibility of solving the problem by other means. Lisette noticed that the wasps seemed to come out from a crack in the boards. Harry thought out loud that if one simply nailed a board over the crack it might take care of the wasps. Grandpa Flapper, eavesdropping on the pair, adopted the idea for his own. With Grandpa Sharp holding off the wasps under cover of a mist of insecticide, the two wasp fighters descended on the nest once more, armed with board and hammer. The wasps surrendered. So did Harry. He wasn't too sure what to do with Lisette, but he somehow knew that his pocket money from that point on wouldn't be spent on ancient coins.

CHAPTER 38

Ghosts, Apparitions and Spirits

The tree-studded road past the Flapper menage wound down the hill. There was a cedar rail fence along it, and the fields behind, once farmed, now stood idle. There were creeks swiftly flowing down the jumbled rocks of the hill side, sloping gently to the valley below. There were deep swampy ponds cut into the fields, alive with ducks and geese in summer, and polliwogs to delight the heart of every small boy. Halfway between the two neighbours, the deFleurs' and the Flappers', out in the middle of the field was a once grand farmhouse, now deserted. A family squabble over ownership after the war had left the place neglected and unclaimed.

Vandals and small boys with big stones had smashed the windows long since. The door was permanently fastened ajar, held by the warped frame. The once gleaming hardwood floors now showed the ravages of winter snows and summer rains, curling at the sides and edges. In the late afternoon sun, with the valley hidden by the trees and bushes behind, the house seemed benign and friendly, and Harry often paused on his way home from school to look over at it and dream about restoring it to its former glory.

One afternoon when the Flappers' doorbell rang. Victoria answered to find Lisette, schoolbooks in hand, looking faintly embarrassed. Victoria recognized the look straight off. "I was just passing by on my way home from school and wondered whether Harry might be home Mrs. Flapper," she intoned her carefully rehearsed speech. Then she remembered that the school was in the opposite direction, she had to pass her own home to get there. She started again, "I mean, well, what I mean to say is, I thought Harry could help me with some homework," she got out in a rush.

Victoria decided to ease Lisette's embarrassment. "He'll be home in a moment. Why don't you come in and wait?" Smiling compassionately, Victoria led Lisette into the family room, chatting to her in a friendly fashion, putting the young girl at ease. Harry came in a few moments later to find the two of them discussing a sewing pattern, deeply absorbed, hardly noticing him, except Lisette's eyes followed him as he came and went from the room. Eventually, Victoria reluctantly decided it was time to get supper on the go and invited the younger girl to join her in the kitchen. Lisette kept a watchful eye out for Harry. Harry, self- consciously peeped in on them from time to time until finally Victoria took pity on them and suggested to Harry that Lisette had a tricky homework problem and would he mind giving her some help with it.

Harry led Lisette to the dining room table where they sat down to gaze soulfully into each other's eyes. Harry didn't know what the next move was in this game, so he cleared his throat a few times to give Lisette room to make up her mind about what to do next. Lisette hadn't any idea at all about what came next. She was perfectly happy to sit with Harry and do nothing except look at him. Finally, Harry blurted out that he could help her with her homework if she wished. Lisette, who had never needed help with her homework in her life, and in any case hadn't any to do, desperately cast about in her mind for some work which she might pass off to Harry. She opened her book at random and pointed to a problem she had solved two weeks or so before. Harry grasped onto it with a feeling of relief. He carefully explained the problem, then suggested that Lisette try it. Lisette, her brain entirely befuddled by Harry's nearness, completely forgot everything she had ever known about the subject, and quietly sat while Harry went through the entire procedure again. Then, with some desperation, only wanting to hear Harry's voice, she whipped through the problem again, then timidly enquired whether that was right, knowing it was, but wanting Harry's praise.

Harry couldn't believe how quickly Lisette had caught on. He looked at her with some respect for a moment, then decided that he must be a natural born teacher. They happily passed an hour in discussion of the finer points of mathematics, Harry surreptitiously looking at Lisette when her head was bent, Lisette adoring Harry, thinking that she could die of ecstasy on the moment and never want anything further from life.

To prolong the contact, Harry offered to walk Lisette home. They dallied along the road, hanging over the rail fence to admire the scenery every few feet, not really seeing it, but instead basking in the company of each other. At the old farm house they stopped to talk. The sun setting over the house cast a golden glow, rendering the scene idyllic.

Lisette told Harry it was haunted. Harry scoffed. So Lisette told him the local tale about the murder committed within the walls of the house, about the enraged George Ryckards who returned early from the fields to find his unfaithful wife enjoying the amours of a stranger. The husband shot them both then turned the gun on himself. Harry made light of the matter. It was difficult, looking towards the house to even imagine anything so awful. If anything, the house looked warm and friendly in the late afternoon sun.

Together they went in through the gate and walked up to the house. Harry dared Lisette to go in with him. She allowed herself to be persuaded because Harry was with her, and she didn't want to stay by herself outside. Together they walked up the stairs and pushed the door open enough to gain entry. The sun shone through the back windows endowing a warmth to the house that was at odds with its condition. The sunlight filtered through the cobwebs onto the stone fireplace, flickering against the stones, creating a mosaic of spider's webs that moved and transformed the homely setting into one of fascination.

There were a few remnants of furniture, beyond repair or even use. Other than that, there was nothing. The boards creaked under their feet. Harry suggested going upstairs. Lisette, shuddering, declined. But when Harry started slowly up the stairs, Lisette was close behind him. Near the top, Harry unadvisedly leaned against the bannister. Over it went, crashing down on the floor below, leaving the two trespassers gasping for breath. Lisette was all for leaving, but Harry prevailed. Upstairs they went into the first bedroom. Remembering the renovations of his own home, Harry proclaimed that it could all be done up quite nicely. The last rays of the setting sun bouncing off the ceiling reminded them that they should be getting on. They didn't investigate the rear rooms, already dark, so missed the obvious signs of occupation. A few pots and pans, cooking ingredients, some blankets, and a few dishes might have given them pause for thought. Instead they left quietly the way they had come.

Outside, Harry exhibited all the usual signs of adolescent male behaviour, ridiculing Lisette's fears, while glancing occasionally over his shoulder to make sure no ghosts were following. It took them another hour to go the few hundred yards to Lisette's house, where, at Lisette's insistence, Harry went in to meet the family. Mrs. deFleur took one look at the glow on her daughter's face, then promptly invited Harry to stay for supper. A quick phone call home to secure permission, and Harry stayed. He didn't understand all that Mrs. deFleur said to him, relying on Lisette and her father and sister to translate. But it was a jolly meal, and Harry, being Harry, offered to help Lisette clean up afterwards. By the time he left for the short hike home, it was dark, his way lit only by the moon.   Approaching the deserted Ryckard house, Harry was horrified to see figures moving inside, noiselessly. Harry's heart leapt into his throat. He didn't know whether to chance running past, or whether the spirits knew he was there anyway. So he halted in the moonshadow of a big old oak tree to contemplate his next move. Nothing happened in the ten minutes or so that he stood there, so Harry decided to risk sneaking past the house, under the window, rather than along the road. He was able to approach the house on tip toe, making no noise. But once under the window, he knocked into a board leaning against the house. The board scraped its way down the side of the house, smashing into the discarded tin garbage containers, which then proceeded to bounce down the hill, banging and bumping over rocks and debris.

From inside the house came a scream and footsteps, as the transients within raced to the window, dislodging their tin of flour from the windowsill. They managed to rescue the tin, but not its contents, which cascaded all over Harry below. Harry, thinking his time had come emitted a piercing scream, then raced into the house as a shortcut towards home. The two knights of the road were caught racing down the stairs. Those hardened gentlemen, already unnerved by the unexplained noises, were confronted by an apparition, backlit by the moon so that it glowed white with an eerie intensity. They immediately grabbed for the bannister for support, but Harry had already taken care of the bannister earlier in the afternoon. Missing their steps, they fell off the side of the stairs onto the floor below, where they lay momentarily stunned, all in a heap.

Harry, still in full flight, meant to escape by the front door. The tramps saw him coming and found their feet in a hurry, limping with all speed out the front door ahead of Harry. With them in the front, screaming prayers out loud and promising their maker an immediate reform if only He would spare them, and Harry screaming behind them, they all three ran out through the front door and across the field. At that precise moment, the eleven-thirty bus from town happened along the road, returning some of the town's merry-makers to their homes. They were treated to the sight of the three ghostly characters racing across the fields, barely touching the ground, emitting weird piercing noises. The bus driver, terrified, pushed his foot to the floor and the bus careened up the hill, the passengers all instantly sober, praying for redemption, as they rounded a corner and out of sight of the unearthly spirits.

Harry and his two friends ran headlong into the pond, where Harry traded his coat of flour for a coat of green slime. The two tramps, neither of whom could swim, wound up in the centre of the pond screaming for help. Harry pulled first one from the pond, then the other, laying them on the grass beside the pond. The two turned to thank Harry, but Harry had melted into the trees, intent on getting home to wash off the slime before his mother found out. Harry didn't want to chance another trip to the hospital to explain the slime. Behind him the two tramps were convinced they had had a visitation, and that the spook had ultimately saved their lives. They made for the road and safety. By the time they got there, alerted by the passengers on the bus, the press was on its way. The bus passengers had phoned in a report to the paper alleging that they had seen a ghost chasing two others out of the old Ryckard farm house. The one in the rear was flying, with its ghostly arms outstretched, screaming epithets as it chased the other spooks.

The press arrived with television cameras rolling just in time to film the two tramps, streaming water, and screaming "Hallelujah! We're saved." The two were immediately interviewed on nation wide TV on their unique and unusual experiences with the spirit world. The Ryckard Homestead was famous even before Harry snuck in the house and made for the shower before his mother could see him. He wasn't entirely sure what had happened, but he was in no hurry to repeat the experience or try to explain it either.

The following day Lisette was all agog to hear from Harry whether he had seen the spooks at the Ryckard house on his way home. But Harry was not to be drawn. Much to Lisette's disappointment, he disclaimed all knowledge of the events, insisting that he must have passed by the old farmhouse prior to the events recorded on TV and splayed all over the newspapers the following day. There were now few disbelievers in the ghost theory, and the house was shunned, by all but Harry. Harry still dreamed of restoring the old place to its former glory, ghosts or no ghosts.

C H A P T E R 3 9

Learning to Drive

Mr. Carruthers thought Harry should learn how to drive. He wasn't too anxious to teach him, but he was willing to put an old car at Harry's disposal to learn.

"I've got an old Ford, leastways, it's mostly a Ford, you could use to practice driving on. I think it's more or less a 51 Ford coup, but maybe it's a 57 Chevy. Anyway, the transmission's still good, and the body should pass inspection. I'll put some tires on it and you could try driving it around the farm until you get the hang of it."

The following day after school found Harry chatting with Mr. Carruthers about the car. "Can I sit in it?" He asked.

"You might find it a might difficult to drive 'less you're actually in it" was the response. Harry stepped into the car to admire it, but was incapable of taking the car in hand. He did not have a clear idea about the workings of the gear shift for a start. The gear shift, for its part, did not operate quite within manufacturer's specifications. The car appeared to be without synchromesh and had more gears than the manufacturer had installed. It seemed to require that the

273

car be brought to a complete halt before first gear could be engaged. Harry was beyond his depth. He needed help.

Mr. Carruthers' mother was called to action. She was a tiny bit of a person, barely five feet tall and as skinny as a knitting needle. When Harry first met her he thought she must be about a hundred and ten years old because she was all wrinkly and wizened. After talking to her for awhile, he revised his estimate downward drastically. He didn't think she was a teenager, but thought there were times when she acted like one. When she got behind the wheel of the car to show Harry how everything worked, she all but disappeared behind the cowl, sinking into the seat to such a degree that the only thing she could make out with certainty out of the windshield were the clouds in the sky and the odd bird that happened to be in the neighbourhood. A few pillows eased the situation so she could at least see the road. It was a trial for anyone watching her driving towards them. There did not appear to be anyone in control of the car, so low on the horizon did she sit.

Harry climbed into the passenger seat to observe first-hand the operations of the car, as Mrs. Carruthers ("Call me Aunt Heather, Dear.") drove it around the farm at an alarming speed. Down into the sugar bush they went, narrowly missing two giant maple trees. Aunt Heather down-shifted into second, double-clutched into first, then shot back out to the farm periphery. She jammed it into second while doing a remarkable slalom around some old fence posts and the piles of rocks in the middle of the field before heading out to the farm road and back to the barn again. Pulling up in front of the barn in a swirl of dust and screeching brakes, she turned to Harry and said, "There now, you see how it's done, Sonny? You just climb into the driver's seat and copy what I did."

Harry traded places with Aunt Heather, moving her pillows over to her seat to make way for his five foot eight inch frame in the driver's seat. With the patient instruction of Aunt Heather, Harry managed to start the car. Then, with the car in neutral, Harry tentatively pushed down on the accelerator. The super-charged engine immediately responded, "vroom-vroom." As the car rocked in time with the engine, Harry's foot went into resonance with it, pushing harder at each stroke until the engine was almost screaming at each shot. Aunt Heather calmly took out her teeth, checked their operation carefully, then slipped them back in. Harry eventually got his foot back under control.

"Now Sonny you jest depress the clutch slide the gear shift into first, pull off the handbrake, then while letting the clutch out give it some gas."

The rest of the afternoon was spent stalling the car and restarting it.

The following day Harry managed to get the car moving, bucking back and forth with head-shaking movements. In first gear he set off towards the sugar bush. Aunt Heather wasn't too keen on tackling the sugar bush just yet. "I think you better stick to the open fields 'til you get used to it." She said comfortably. Harry was more than happy to comply. He was hoping that he might eventually get the car into second gear!

Over the next several weeks Harry spent many happy hours with Aunt Heather, roaring around the farm. Gradually he developed some facility with the car. Finally, Aunt Heather pronounced

"I think you're about ready to try the open road! What do you think? Ready to give it a try?"

Harry happily agreed.

"But first we better get you a beginner's license," she said. Aunt Heather at the wheel, they set off for the examination centre. She drove into the lot, downshifting as she made the turn in, then accelerating out with a roar as she sped off to the unit housing the driver examination centre. One of the examiners was on the road in front of the centre when he was confronted by the apparently driverless car. He leapt for the sidewalk to hide himself behind a pillar and await the crash. Aunt Heather brought the car to a smooth stop and Harry jumped out to enter the centre. He encountered the examiner cowering behind the pillar. Harry looked him up and down curiously. The examiner straightened up, glowered at Harry, and asked him if that had been him driving in a moment ago. Harry, quite truthfully remarked that he hadn't driven. He had just come for a license to learn. The official glared at Harry then whirled around to look at the apparently unoccupied car.

Harry proceeded into the centre, procured his beginner's permit with a minimum of fuss, then returned to the car again, under the watchful eye of the suspicious examiner. Harry climbed into the passenger's side. As soon as he was in, the apparently driverless car started up again with a great roar, shot around the side of the lot within a few inches of the gaping examiner, then sped out of the lot and on its way. Harry was now licensed to learn. Some way from the centre, Aunt Heather pulled to the side of a deserted road and invited Harry to take over. Harry took over with great excitement, he jammed the gear shift into first gear, screeching out onto the road without a thought for oncoming traffic, when a driver behind, sweeping around beside Harry, honked. Startled, Harry jerked the wheel, upending the car into the ditch.

Harry was still glued to the wheel. Aunt Heather pried his fingers loose, then extricated him from the car. She walked around the car, checking underneath at intervals, all the while muttering to herself. At last she straightened up and came over to the chastened Harry to deliver her verdict. "Good!" she said, "There ain't too much damage. But we gotta go get the tractor to haul 'er out." With that she set off up the road with Harry trailing behind. At this juncture, Aunt Heather thought she had better tell Harry some of the rules of the road. During the two mile walk back to the farm she drilled Harry on appropriate procedures when driving in traffic.

Arriving at the barn, Aunt Heather climbed up onto the tractor. Harry became agitated. "Aren't you going to call Mr. Carruthers?" asked Harry.

"Land sakes alive!" responded Aunt Heather, "Why would ya want ta bother him fer? C'mon up here, Sonny and let's get rollin'." she continued.

Harry complied and they set off. Aunt Heather drove the tractor with as much abandon as she drove the car. In no time they arrived at the accident site. Aunt Heather directed Harry in the placement of the tow chain, then instructed him to get in the car and steer it while she pulled the car out of the ditch with the tractor. The car was soon back on the road. Aunt Heather, climbing down from the cab of the tractor, told the shaken Harry to climb up into the cab and drive it back to the farm. She got into the car and roared away, leaving a stuttering Harry in the middle of the road ineffectually protesting that he had never driven the tractor before.

Harry reluctantly climbed up into the cab of the tractor. He discovered to his amazement that the tractor controls were much easier than those for the car. To begin with, the tractor was all automatic. Putting the instructions so recently given him by Aunt Heather to good use, it was no time at all before Harry got back on the road, and keeping to the verge, made it back to the farm without further incident.

With some pride he climbed down out of the cab to find an anxious Aunt Heather waiting. At least she appeared anxious when Harry first spotted her, but he might have been mistaken. She merely grunted when Harry approached. Then the two of them examined the car. "Got some damage to the exhaust system." opined Aunt Heather, wheeling out the welding equipment. She donned the welding apron and helmet, crawled under the car, lit the torch and proceeded to repair the damage. Harry watched, fascinated.

When the job was finally finished, Aunt Heather suggested that it might be wise not to upset anyone else by telling them about the incident. Harry wasn't too anxious to tell anyone about driving the car into the ditch. On the other hand he would have been quite happy to tell everyone about driving the tractor. He couldn't tell one story without the other. It was a tough problem. It was taken out of his hands by Aunt Heather who casually mentioned to Mr. Carruthers that Harry could now drive the tractor, too. So Harry's range of jobs on the farm expanded to cover other things, while his wages went up in proportion.

On the home front things were going exceptionally well. Mr. Carruthers had offered Harry unlimited use of the old Ford if he managed to pass the driving examination, subject, of course, to Harry paying for the insurance out of his wages. Mr. Carruthers thought it a stroke of genius, guaranteed to keep Harry down on the farm for the next half century or so to accumulate enough wages to pay for the insurance. Harry didn't know about the small details and had no idea of the cost of insurance, so he happily agreed. Mr. Carruthers paid the insurance to cover Harry's driving. Lisette, without any justification whatever, figured the use of a car could improve her romance no end.

Aunt Heather took Harry to do his driver's test. When they got there, Harry went into the centre, only to discover that his examiner was the chap who had eyed Harry so suspiciously on his previous visit. They went out to the car and Harry got into the driver's seat. Noting the stick shift, the examiner eyed Harry dubiously, and instructed him to start the car. Harry started it up and the supercharged engine, which started with a roar, subsided into a gentle purr, ticking over with precision. The examiner told Harry to pull out of the centre parking lot and into traffic. Harry complied. Pulling into traffic, Harry shifted up, eventually shifting into overdrive. The number of gears didn't seem to tally with what the examiner thought there should be. It sounded like five when he expected three. He told Harry to turn left at the next intersection, and Harry downshifted, putting Aunt Heather's skilled instruction to good use as he double-clutched into first gear, almost coming to a complete halt. By now the examiner had completely lost sight of all his objectives. The clutch manoeuvre had disoriented him long enough that he found himself in unfamiliar territory. Giving some random instructions, he watched Harry making the shift changes, instead of watching where they were going.

Harry found himself on the Queen's Highway 403, hurtling towards Toronto at 100 kilometres an hour. The examiner came to with a start to realize they were picking up speed at an alarming rate. Harry, who had often taken this route with Aunt Heather knew very well that an incoming lane of traffic often brought out the maniacs who would cut him off at a moment. But what he hadn't expected was a huge tractor trailer breathing down his neck, its driver pounding on the horn behind. At the same time, the maniac entering from the right side on-ramp lost control of his car and went into a spin. Harry saw it coming. There was only one way out and it was closing fast, a spot in front and to the left between two transports. Harry floored it, braked, went into a controlled skid, eased through the gap, then floored it again, skidding into position between the trucks, while the tractor trailer slammed its brakes on and the maniac entering the highway struggled to regain control. Harry looked over at the examiner who had automatically assumed the crash position, arms over his head, well braced.

"It's okay now." Harry said kindly, "would you like me to exit left here?"

The examiner, still shaking from reaction, looked about to see the speeding tractor trailer in the distance and the miscreant who had caused the problem nowhere to be found. He agreed that they should exit. Harry downshifted smoothly, eased onto the exit ramp, then picked up speed onto the next highway and proceeded back, at the examiner's suggestion, by back roads. The examiner insisted that Harry parallel park on the main street in town. Harry had been well trained, though, and he executed the manoeuvre flawlessly. Arrived back, the examiner played for time before he had to actually face the prospect of walking on legs that felt and acted like rubber. Gripping the side of the car as he tried to stand, the examiner feigned interest in what might be under the hood, so Harry showed him. Harry went into a long technical description about overhead cams and dual-barrel carbs, with a minor digression to discuss exhaust systems, radial tires, transmissions, and some discussion about the difficulty of transplanting engines from one manufacturer to another followed. He was just getting wound up, when the examiner, still a little green, allowed as how he had another pressing engagement elsewhere, preferably a long way away. Harry was still puzzling over that remark when the examiner, on shaky legs, began to walk away.

Harry called after him, "Did I pass?"

The examiner turned back, breathing heavily for a moment, remembering the expected life span of automobile licensing examiners and reflecting on the probability that he might be called upon to judge Harry's driving again, snarled, "Just!" then walking on, still watching Harry warily, until he clunked his head on the pillar.

CHAPTER 40

History and Harry

Harry's high school catered to older students who had decided to return after dropping out previously, some of whom subscribed to the motorcycle culture, while others dedicated themselves to completing their diplomas. For no apparent reason the former had acquired the nickname of scuzzies, while the latter were clearly nerds.

Nerds didn't trust Scuzzies and Scuzzies didn't trust Nerds. On balance, Scuzzies generally reckoned that anyone who dressed the way Nerds did couldn't possibly be worth knowing. This attitude was due to the entirely varying philosophy of living they each held. The Scuzzies lived for pleasure. They took the biblical injunction to "take no thought for the morrow" to extremes. The Nerds, on the other hand thought only about the morrow. They studied continuously, avoided the Scuzzies and planned their lives meticulously. The Scuzzies drove motorcycles in summer and half ton trucks in winter. The Nerds were mostly driven to school by their mummies and daddies. Harry tried to run a thin line between the two groups, with the inevitable result that neither of the groups trusted him. Harry had another problem: his transportation didn't come up to scratch. He rode the city bus.

To add to his difficulties, he soon discovered that history was not the sinecure he thought. The teacher expected things Harry wasn't enthusiastic to do, like writing essays. Harry struggled with the essays but it soon became apparent as the year progressed that he was falling behind. He was desperate to achieve a decent mark but couldn't see how he might do it. Added to that, relations between Harry and the Scuzzies began to deteriorate. They thought he was an RCMP spy sent to infiltrate their ranks and determined to get revenge on him for his defection. Harry was aware that there were problems in his relationships with the Scuzzies, but had no idea of the scale of resentment harboured against him.

Harry's performance in History did not match that of his driving. As the year progressed, Harry didn't: he was failing, and getting desperate. As Easter approached, he realized that he was coming up for his last chance, a project, worth forty percent. He could redeem his dismal marks with a superb project. Finding such a project proved to be elusive. As the Easter holidays loomed closer and closer, Harry became increasingly despondent. His plan was to use the holidays to map out his project, but still he had not found an acceptable idea for a project. Worse news was yet to come: he was informed by his mother that Cousin Alice was planning to spend some time visiting at the Flapper household. Alice had finished her high school program and thought it might be nice to disturb Harry's equilibrium for awhile. Harry wasn't in total agreement. It was alright having both Lissette and Cousin Alice to dote on him, but only so long as they were separated by a lot of miles. Harry didn't think that Lisette would be overjoyed to find Alice keeping company with him.

Cousin Alice arrived a few days later. She insisted she keep company with Harry, in school and out of it. The first day in school, the day before the holidays, was a revelation to both Harry and his school mates. Alice didn't meet the dress code for either the Nerds or the Scuzzies. She wore a demure frock with long sleeves to hide her biceps, and a high neck to emphasize her height. She confounded everyone by wearing four inch spike heels. She dwarfed Harry, who didn't mind, and every other male in the school, all of whom did. There was no doubt, with her easy grace and maturity, she represented the ultimate challenge to every male in the school. All attempts to pry her loose from Harry's side were gently but firmly rebuffed. It was one more strike against Harry, and a few unfitting remarks were said in his presence, ignored by both Harry and Alice. The day seemed interminable to Harry, but at last it was over and he could collect Lisette so the three of them could dash off home again, ready for the holiday.

It was Alice who saved Harry's bacon, really. She was intensely curious about Harry and his way of life. Even Harry's coin collection merited a good deal of unwarranted attention. Alice, plainly enthralled with Harry, wanted an explanation for every coin in his collection. When Harry got around to his few ancient coins, Alice was enraptured. "Don't you think these old coins suggest a lot about that era?" she asked.

"Yeah, but they aren't Canadian," responded Harry.

"So what?" She smiled. "Your course is supposed to be ancient history."

"You think that would work?" asked Harry dubiously.
"Absolutely!"

Harry spent much of the holiday planning his project around the coins. He constructed a display board which ingeniously held the coins in pop out holders so they could be removed for transportation. Alice lent support at every stage of the operation, helping Harry to glue the various bits and pieces on the board, suggesting the wording to start his essay, and most of what followed. Alice also provided some distraction when the going got tough. She rubbed her thigh against Harry's leg whenever possible, and leaned over to display her remarkable assets at other times, totally destroying Harry's train of thought. She smiled, showing her dimple, and her perfect teeth, taking Harry's breath away, leaving him confused. But Alice was never confused.

Harry had desperate times at night, trying frantically not to repeat certain dreams which seemed to plague him after a session with Alice in the late evening. He was worried that he might have to rinse his sheets out in the pond again, and wasn't looking forward to the consequences. Eventually it did happen again. Cousin Alice's magic proved entirely too potent for Harry. He woke up very early one morning to discover his sheets were drenched. Switching on the lights, Harry surveyed the damage with a heavy heart. He figured there was no way he was about to cart his sheets off to the pond again. Certainly not with Cousin Alice in residence. So he snuck into the bathroom to steal his mother's hair dryer. Closing his door to block out the noise, in a fever of anxiety, he switched on the hair dryer at high to play over the sheets, trying to dry them before the rest of the household awoke.

The noise seemed to Harry quite deafening, and sure to be heard by everyone around, including Lisette, several yards down the road. Harry didn't relish trying to explain his problem to anyone, least of all Lisette. So he held the offending portion of sheet closer to the dryer. When nothing seemed to be happening, in desperation, he jammed the dryer against the sheet and waited for results. They weren't long in coming. The sheet caught fire. Harry dropped the dryer and tried frantically to beat the now flaming sheet out with his hands. When that didn't appear to be working he tried smothering it with his blanket. That had far more effect, but resulted in great clouds of smoke, which immediately set off the fire alarms.

Harry ran downstairs, grabbed a pail, filled it with water and dashed back upstairs to his room, pitching the water at his bed. Back to the bathroom he went to refill the pail, returning to pitch it at his bed. His father, still groggy in pyjamas, had come to investigate. Bull took the full brunt of the charge in the frontal position, leaving him drenched from breastbone to crotch. It quite took Bull's breath away. It certainly woke him up. Bull's "Whoosh," combined with the strident tones of the fire alarm had everyone running to see what was going on, including Cousin Alice, bewitching in flimsy gown. Harry's worst fears realized. He reckoned without the hair dryer. It took some time for the water to reach the electrical parts in the dryer. When it did, the fireworks were spectacular, until the lights went out, plunging the room into darkness, leaving only the wail of the battery-operated fire alarm for comfort.

Bull struggled off to find his flashlight, stuck away in a closet. When he had finally turned the closet inside out,

Victoria reminded him that he had removed the flashlight to the bedside table for quick access. Then, flashlight in hand, Bull made his way down to the basement to check the master fuses. Switching off the power, Bull pried the two big fuses out of their holders then looked around for some means to check them. There wasn't any. He finally decided to use his flashlight, connected by wires to the ends of a fuse. If the light still lit, he reasoned, the fuse would still be good. But he didn't have enough hands for the exercise. He yelled to Harry to come and help. Obediently Harry descended into the basement. The two of them grappled with wires and flashlight batteries and the light bulb from the flashlight, finally succeeding in getting the bulb to light. Then in the dark, Bull tried to reassemble the flashlight, without success. He didn't much feel like mucking around inside the fuse box unless he could see. So he sent Harry off on a quest for candles. Several stubbed toes later Harry reappeared with a candle already lit.

With the fuses back in place Harry started up the stairs again, figuring that he didn't want to be around when his father was finished the job. On the way, he turned on the lights. They blinked on. Bull, in the act of investigating deeper into the box was astonished. "How did you do that?" he wanted to know.

"It was simple, Dad, I just flicked the light switch."

Peering into the box again, Bull was chagrined to find that only one small fuse had blown. Harry escaped while he could. Back up in his bedroom he found his mother, sisters and Alice, rocking with laughter. It was almost more than his tormented soul could take. He removed the dismembered dryer from his bed, stripped off the soaking, burnt sheets, then remade his bed in silence, crawling into the damp nest with dignity and determination. "Turn out the light when you're finished." he said, and rolled over onto the dry part of the bed with his face to the wall.

If Alice was a torment to Harry, Lisette, dainty and gentle Lisette, dark haired, blue-eyed, exotic Lisette, was even more so. One girl haunted his dreams, the other captured his heart. Harry was in love. With whom he wasn't sure. But he was in love. Victoria, who had great difficulty picturing Harry in anything other than diapers, could not imagine that Harry harboured an all-consuming lust for Cousin Alice. Victoria thought they made excellent playmates and sent them off on walks or to the store or to the movies or wherever, whether it was in Harry's mind to go or not. Harry co-opted Lisette's company whenever possible, under the mistaken theory that there was safety in numbers. There wasn't. The girls were in competition with each other and they knew it. Where before, Harry was a simple diversion for Cousin Alice, now he became a challenge. She brought all her considerable womanly talents into the fray. Older, with no illusions about the act of coupling, having witnessed it often on the farm, Alice was intrigued with the thought of trying it out for herself, with Harry. Harry was trying to avoid that fate. He wasn't too sure why it was necessary to avoid it. But his resolution began to harden, as he realized that if he wanted any of the good things in life, emotional entanglement with any woman right now might prevent him from achieving some of his goals. And one of his goals was to hie himself off to the university to follow in his father's footsteps.

The holidays dragged to a conclusion. Cousin Alice decided to stay on to continue her campaign to seduce Harry.

She wasn't operating under the same illusions as Victoria. Alice had long ago figured out why Harry was "drying his hair in the middle of the night under the sheets." She didn't share her findings with Victoria who still remained somewhat puzzled over that episode. And Victoria didn't want to raise the matter again with Bull as it appeared to bring on an attack of apoplexy every time she mentioned it. Bull wasn't sharing his knowledge of the episode with anyone either.

On the first day back at school, the Scuzzies began open warfare with Harry. Harry set up avoidance manoeuvres, with Alice unwittingly running interference. Skirmishes in the hall between classes taxed Harry's patience, but with Alice strategically placed between Harry and the miscreants, clashes were kept to a minimum. To add to Harry's woes, his project came due with frightening speed. On the fateful day of his presentation, Harry decided to use Mr. Carruthers' souped-up car to transport the project. Carting the display into the school very early in the morning, Harry managed to avoid conflict.

As Harry set up the display, a few teachers wandered in to examine it. One asked Harry whether he collected coins, whereupon Harry talked at great length about his collection of Canadian coins. To shut Harry up the teacher offered her entire collection of confiscated pennies, pennies she had taken from the knees-up penny flippers as they flipped coins at the wall in the dark recesses underneath the stairs. Harry, too polite to point out the coins were worth only pennies, took the bag and stuffed it into his knapsack.

Zero hour was two o'clock in the afternoon. Harry was brilliant. He went into great detail about the various

Roman emperors depicted on the coins, and their eras. He was so genuinely enthusiastic about his project that it carried over into the classroom. Everybody was awed at Harry's strength of purpose. Everybody was interested. The Scuzzies were especially interested in the worth of the coins. Harry intimated that the coins were only worth a minimal amount, and that only to collectors. By this it was taken to mean that Harry was giving house room to a very large fortune in coins. The Nerds quizzed Harry on the exact details of scholarship surrounding the coins. But if they thought to shake his confidence, they were doomed to disappointment. The more questions they asked, the more Harry waxed enthusiasm all over the subject, until growing tired of baiting him, their questions dried up. Totally misreading the situation, the teacher was amazed at the interest apparently being given to the subject. His opinion of Harry's net knowledge of the subject of history was revised upward drastically. Proceedings were finally brought to an end as the bell sounded.

A happy Harry collected his display board, carefully removing his precious coins from it for storage in his knapsack. The other bag of coins he took out to make room. Juggling the entire lot he set off with Alice for the parking lot. The Scuzzies were waiting in ambush. They wanted Harry's "Fortune in Coins." Harry wasn't prepared to turn it over. Alice and Harry made a break for the car with the Scuzzies quick behind them. Twenty feet from the car, one grabbed Harry. Harry's reaction was to bop the fellow with the bag of pennies. Down went Harry's assailant, while the pennies scattered all over the parking lot. Alice grabbed the nearest Scuzz by the neck and the crotch of his already tight jeans, and hoisted the fellow on high to his great discomfort in lower regions. Alice ignored his screams of anguish as she launched him into the crowd of Scuzzies chasing close behind. They went over like nine pins. Alice and Harry hopped into the car.

While some of the Scuzzies were distracted by the fortune in coins rolling all over the parking lot, for others the matter had become one of personal revenge. They ran for their motorcycles. Harry, thinking he was clear of the lot, started sedately out onto the road, heading for home. When he saw the great crowd of Scuzzies closing in on him on their motorcycles, he momentarily panicked. Harry's first instinct was to outrun them. Even with the supercharged engine it rapidly became clear that tactic wouldn't work. The motorcycles were too fast and too manoeuvrable for Harry to lose. He made it to Mr. Carruthers' back forty before the Scuzzies caught up and drove him off the road. But this was Harry's home turf. He knew every rock and groundhog hole on the farm. So Harry began evasive manoeuvres. As a motorcycle came alongside to drive him off into the bush, Harry would peel the fellow off against a tree, or run him into a hole. He successfully dumped three of them into the hog's watering hole. Then he got rid of another couple along the stone fence which was well concealed with weeds and brush. Harry squeezed between two trees in the sugar bush just as two more tried to turn him away. They never made it past the trees, leaving one chap seated on a limb ten feet off the ground, while the other found the only thistle patch for several miles around.

Back out on the farm track again, Harry noticed there was only one motorcycle left behind him. He slowed to a stop by the bend in the stream, just where it widened into the daintiest little trout pond. Harry and Alice got out of the car and waited, while the one remaining Scuzz roared up, apparently under the mistaken impression that there were several hundred more of his friends behind. Within a few feet of Harry he got off his bike to stride threateningly over to where the pair stood. He told Harry graphically what he was going to do to him. But the tension got too much for Alice. She used the same tactic she had used earlier, picking the fellow up by neck and crotch to dump him into the trout pond. He screamed that he couldn't swim, whereupon Harry invited him to stand up then if he didn't want to swim. Alice politely asked him whether he wanted his motorcycle. The chap tried to scramble up the bank yelling all kinds of obscene things. Alice took that to mean that he did indeed want his motorcycle. She got on, started it, and rode it towards the pond. The bike's owner was just making his way up the slippery bank when he saw his bike coming towards him full tilt. He dove back into the water just as Alice stepped off the bike, allowing it to careen down the bank to join him. As the motorcycle came to a glugging halt underwater, Harry was heard to enquire why it was that for a fellow who couldn't swim, he had developed such a magnificent diving style.

The target of his barb wasn't listening. He was crying. Huge tears rolled down his face as he looked at the spot where his bike had last been seen. He turned around to make some more ragged remarks to Alice and Harry. Then as he looked at the two, not a hair out of place on either of them, and realized the fact that all the rest of his friends had been singularly dispatched, he thought better of it. Harry and Alice climbed back into the car and set off for home, waving jauntily to the remnants of the biker clan as they went, and enquiring solicitously whether anyone would like a tow truck sent out. They decided they wouldn't enlighten Mr. Carruthers about the afternoon's work, but drove home virtuously within the speed limit.

For his part, Mr. Carruthers was not in an entirely benevolent mood by the time the evening was over. He spent most of the rest of the day towing smashed motorcycles out to the edge of the road and muttering mild epithets about people who would run a motorcycle tournament all over his property without permission. It took several months for the Scuzzies to get their machines back on the roads. The residents of Cootesville talked about the following summer for years afterwards. They couldn't think what might have happened to all the motorcycles in town to keep them so quiet. As it turned out, whenever Harry came down the hallway towards classes during the rest of the school year, the Scuzzies took avoidance manoeuvres. No one could understand why, and Harry never enlightened them. But he passed history. With quite a good mark, too, all things considered.

CHAPTER 41

University, the Aftermath of Education

Harry received his first shock towards the end of term regarding the possibility of attending Cootesville U. They didn't want him. Certainly not in engineering at any rate. A very polite letter suggested he might try social sciences or music or anything else. Harry thought about it for awhile then decided he would do the only decent thing he could. He decided all by himself to apply pressure. He wrote a very nice letter to the Dean in charge of admissions, remarking on his father's status and his father's great record as an important personage in the hierarchy of affairs.

The Dean invited Harry in for an interview, which Harry was only too pleased to attend. The Dean informed Harry that the Chairman of the department had inexplicably changed his mind about allowing Harry to enter the program. It was the strangest thing, the Dean went on. When Harry's application had first arrived, the Chairman had stated clearly that there were no further vacancies. Ten students was all they could handle this year and they had already been accepted. In a department known for admitting upwards of a hundred students every year, this news was not met with favour anywhere. The Chairman eventually capitulated and agreed to accept another ninety, with Harry's name included on the list. The Dean said Harry could expect his letter of admission shortly. Harry was overjoyed. He shouldn't have been.

Through the long summer months, Harry slaved away on the farm, adding to his already sizable bank account. Mr. Carruthers was in a state of shock. He had expected to keep Harry down on the farm forever, paying for car insurance. He didn't know about Harry's sizable stock and bond collection. In fact no one except Harry and his stock broker knew about that, and neither were willing to divulge the information. Harry's finances were well in order. But he loved working on the farm, even if he didn't view it as a lifelong occupation.

Harry's life had returned almost to normal, since Cousin Alice had reluctantly returned home to help in the family general store for the summer. Lisette, back in control of Harry's emotional well-being again, made good her opportunities, initiating Harry into the world of passionate kissing and other things that embarrassed Harry no end. Harry's education on that arena moved forward with shocking speed during the summer. As fall approached, and a return to studying loomed imminent, Lisette kept Harry on the fine edge of frustration, allowing a certain freedom to him that she would never dream of telling her mother about, and especially not her straight-laced father. That was her last resort. If all else failed, Lisette planned to lure Harry into a totally compromising situation, with her father's entry timed to the crucial moment.

She figured that her father would delay shooting Harry long enough for her to suggest marriage as an option. But it never came to that. Harry was entirely besotted with Lisette as it was. He didn't need any assistance in the matter, only time. He wanted to make a life for themselves, hoping and dreaming of the means to do it. So, as he told Lisette, it was absolutely necessary for her to finish high school and join him in university. By now Harry had concluded that Lisette was at least a genius and certainly smarter than he was. He didn't expect she would have any trouble gaining admission to engineering. In fact, he could hardly wait for her to join him.

At various times during the summer, Harry's family made the long trek back to the homestead, where Harry was once again treated to Alice's charms. After these forays Harry would return to Cootesville totally disoriented. How, he wondered, could a woman, for woman Alice certainly was, how could a woman that tall want anything to do with someone as short as him? For that matter, how could Harry, in her presence, be so awestruck. He couldn't quite sort it out, so in the end, gave it up in favour of enjoying her attentions at the homestead, and Lisette's attentions when he got back to Cootesville.

On the Wednesday following Labour Day, Harry registered to attend classes. He soon discovered that university was not going to be a lot of fun, at least not if he wanted to stay in engineering. Harry had fun anyway. He discussed the matter with his father. Bull was only too happy to share his own stories of university life with his son. He even told Harry about Grommet and the dog, Harry. Although Bull didn't come right out and tell Harry about how he happened to get his name, he left it wide open for speculation.

"It's a funny thing," said Bull, "Grommet left good ol' City U. shortly after I graduated. There was some rumour that the president took an intense dislike to Grommet. He even threatened to shoot his dog if it set any of its four feet on the campus again. It seems that Grommet left in a fit of pique." Bull then went on to show Harry through his graduation yearbook, reminiscing as he did on the way life had turned out. Harry was the willing recipient of Bull's confidences, eagerly encouraging his father to tell more, until Harry at last had a picture of the way things were and of the various personalities that had gone to shape his father's life.

Harry struggled, but made it through to midterm examinations before disaster struck. His marks were pathetic. Shortly thereafter he was invited to an interview with the Chairman of the department to explain himself. Harry went. Not willingly, but he went anyway. Harry figured it was a necessary evil. Just how much so, he had no conception. He approached the Chairman's office with some trepidation. The Chairman's secretary, Harry discovered, was a sour faced personage of sharp disposition and in a mean temper. She told Harry that undergraduates simply were not welcome in the office. Harry agreed with her and told her that he didn't want to be there either, but the Chairman had sent for him. Clearly suspicious about this breach in procedure, the secretary grimly led Harry to the Chairman's inner sanctum door. Opening the door only wide enough to let Harry pass, she stuffed him into the dim confines beyond and slammed the door shut.

Harry's eyes became accustomed to the low light at the same time that he heard an ominous rumbling nearby. Looking down he saw a snarling Schnauzer, straining at its lead some three or four inches from his left ankle and slathering in its efforts to reach it. Harry followed the dog's lead with his eyes back to the desk to which it was attached, then looked up with trepidation to see Grommet, relaxed in the chair behind the desk. Harry recognized him from his father's photos. It was an older Grommet, to be sure, but it was Grommet all the same. And he was smiling. Not a nice smile, but a nasty sort of smile. "Flapper," mused Grommet, "Flapper, no relative of Crawford, I trust." Harry was backed up against the door to escape the immediate attentions of the dog.

"Yes, Sir." said Harry. "He's my father."

"Well, well!" remarked Grommet, his eyes narrowing to evil slits. "Come in and sit down. We have a few matters to discuss."

Harry looked at the dog, looked at Grommet, then switched his attention back to the dog. "That's alright, Sir," he said, not moving from his place by the door. "I'm perfectly happy here." But Harry wasn't alright. His pulse went into overdrive as Grommet growled and the dog snarled. They were like a tag team!

Harry felt doom settle around him nlike a black cloud. He thought about what lay befrore him with the revelation that he had placed himself in Grommet's clutches. He thought of how this would affect his life with Lissette. He thought of the years he had yet to go. He was thinking of another time and another place. He was thinking of his mother's reaction at the mere mention of Grommet. In that instant Harry reasoned that his life, his dreams and everything that mattered were over.

The dog took matters into its own control, suddenly lunging at Harry's pant leg, and having achieved its objective started to drag Harry further into the office. Harry held onto the doorknob like grim death, enquiring meekly, "Are we through now, sir?"

At a command from Grommet, the dog let loose Harry's shredded pant leg, allowing Harry this freedom. Harry gratefully escaped. Immediately on the other side of the door, Harry encountered the secretary who was now smiling. "I told you he didn't see undergraduates!"